SIDESWIPE

Other Books by Charles Willeford

Proletarian Laughter
High Priest of California
Pick-Up
The Black Mass of Brother Springer
No Experience Necessary
The Director
The Burnt Orange Heresy
Cockfighter
The Machine in Ward Eleven
Off the Wall
Miami Blues
New Hope for the Dead
Something About a Soldier

SIDESWIPE

A NOVEL BY

CHARLES WILLEFORD

St. Martin's Press
New York

This novel is a work of fiction. The events depicted herein have never occurred. Names, characters, places, and incidents either are the product of the author's imagination or are used fictitiously.

Design by Amy R. Bernstein

Library of Congress Cataloging in Publication Data

Willeford, Charles Ray, 1919–
Sideswipe.

I. Title.
PS3545.I464S5 1987 813'.54 86-26216
ISBN 0-312-00188-6

First Edition

10 9 8 7 6 5 4 3 2 1

For Jim, Liz, and Jared

Life is an effort that deserves a better cause.

—KARL KRAUS

There's a lot of bastards out there!

—WILLIAM CARLOS WILLIAMS

SIDESWIPE

Storeowners Gunned Down in Daring Daytime Holdup

Los Angeles (UPI)—In a daring daylight holdup, Samuel Stuka, 53, and his wife, Myra, 47, owners of Golden Liquors, 4126 South Figueroa Street, were shotgunned and wounded fatally by a tall man wearing a gray cowboy hat at ten this morning, according to Detective Hans Waggoner, University Station, investigator of the case.

"There was an eyewitness," Waggoner told reporters, "and we are tracking some leads now. The man was alone and drove away in a red vehicle that was either a Camaro or a Nissan two-door with a horizontal fin across the trunk."

The eyewitness, who was not named, heard the two shots, the detective said, and dived behind a hedge next to the store. He looked up when the killer got into the vehicle and drove away, but did not get the license number.

"The M.O. is familiar," Waggoner said, "and we

have some good leads." He did not elaborate, because the investigation was continuing.

Mrs. Robert L. Prentiss, the couple's daughter, who resides in Covina with her husband and two children, Bobby, 4, and Jocelyn, 2, said that her father had bought the store three months ago, after moving to Los Angeles from Glen Ellyn, Ill., to be closer to his grandchildren.

"He was semi-retired, but needed a place to go every day," she said, "and that's why he bought the store. My mother was only helping him out temporarily—" Mrs. Prentiss broke down then, and could not continue.

The robbery of Golden Liquors was the third liquor store robbery this week in southwest L.A., but the Stukas were the only proprietors killed, Waggoner said. A shotgun was employed in the other two holdups as well.

"Mr. Stuka probably put up some kind of resistance," Detective Waggoner said, "which is a mistake if the robber has a sawed-off."

CHAPTER

1

Detective-Sergeant Hoke Moseley, Miami Police Department, opened the front door of his house in Green Lakes, looked to the left and to the right. Then, barechested and barefooted, and wearing droopy white boxer shorts, he dashed out to pick up the *Miami Herald* from the front lawn. At six A.M. there was little need for this modesty. His neighbors were not up, and the eastern sky was barely turning a nacreous gray.

The paper was usually delivered by five-thirty each morning by an angry Puerto Rican in a white Toyota, whose erratic throw from his speeding car never found the same spot on the lawn. The driver was still angry, Hoke thought on those mornings when he stood behind the screen door waiting for the paper, because Hoke had returned the delivery man's stamped, self-addressed Christmas card without including a check or a five-dollar bill as a tip.

In the kitchen, Hoke pulled the slippery transparent cover from the paper, wadded it into a ball, and tossed it into the overflowing grocery bag that served as a garbage receptacle. He read the first paragraph in all of the front-page stories. Another American hostage had been killed by a Shiite skyjacker in Lebanon. The new fare for Metrorail would (perhaps) be a quarter, a half-dollar, or a dollar, but the newest fare system would probably depend on which station the rider used to board the train. An eighteen-year-old Haitian, a recent graduate of Miami-Norland High School, had miraculously managed to obtain an appointment to the U.S. Air Force Academy, and the congressman who had appointed him had just discovered that the boy was an illegal alien and was awaiting deportation at the Krome Detention Center. This item reminded Hoke of the tasteless joke Commander Bill Henderson had told him yesterday in the department's cafeteria.

"How can you tell when a Haitian's been in your back yard?"

"How?"

"Your mango tree's been stripped and your dog's got AIDS."

Hoke hadn't laughed. "That won't work, Bill."

"Why not? I think it's funny."

"No, it doesn't work, because everyone doesn't have a mango tree in his back yard, and not every Haitian has AIDS."

"Most of them have."

"No. I don't have a mango tree and neither do you."

"I mean AIDS. Most Haitians have AIDS."

"Not so. I think the figure's less than one-half of one percent."

"Go fuck yourself, Hoke." Henderson got up from the table and left the cafeteria without finishing his coffee.

Hoke's reaction to Henderson's crummy humor had been another sign, but Hoke hadn't spotted it and neither had Bill Henderson. Ordinarily, when Bill told one of his jokes, Hoke at least grinned and said, "That's a good one," even when it was an out-of-context gag Bill had written down from the Johnny Carson monologue.

But Hoke hadn't smiled for more than a week, and he hadn't laughed at anything for almost a month.

Hoke sprinkled a liberal helping of Grape-Nuts into a plastic sieve and ran hot water from the tap over the cereal to make it soft enough that he could eat it without putting in his false teeth. When the cereal had softened sufficiently, he dumped it into a bowl and covered it with half-and-half. He then sliced a banana into the cereal, upended a pink packet of Sweet 'n Low over the mixture, and took the bowl and the newspaper out into the Florida room.

The sun porch had open, jalousied windows on three sides, and a hot, damp breeze blew through them from the lake. The Florida room faced a square lake of green milk that had once been a gravel quarry. The backs of all of the houses were toward the lake in this Miami subdivision called Green Lakes. Not all of the homeowners, or renters, had glassed-in porches like Hoke. Some of them had redwood decks in back; others had settled for do-it-yourself concrete patios and barbecue pits; yet all of the houses in Green Lakes had been constructed originally from the same set of blueprints. Except for the different colors they had been painted, and repainted, and the addition of a few carports, there was little discernible difference among them.

Hoke sat at a glass-topped wrought-iron table in a webbed patio chair and then realized that he didn't have a spoon. He returned to the kitchen, got a spoon, sat at the table again, and slowly gummed his Grape-Nuts and chopped bananas as he read the sports section. Ron Fraser, the Miami Hurricanes' baseball coach, who had coached the team to its second win in the college World Series in Omaha, said he might retire in three, maybe four more years, or he might even renegotiate a new contract. It must be hard, Hoke thought, for a sports writer to turn in something every day when there was nothing worthwhile to report.

Hoke then turned to Doonesbury, which was poking fun at Palm Beach for requiring mandatory ID cards for nonresident blue-collar workers on the island. Hoke was overwhelmed instantly with a formless feeling of nostalgia. Palm Beach was right across the inlet from Singer Island, and Singer Island, at the moment, was where Hoke wanted to be. Not in his father's huge four-bedroom house up there, on the Lake Worth intracoastal waterway, but in a hotel or motel room facing the sea where no one could find him and force him to read the fifteen new Incident Reports, with their fifteen attached Supplementary Reports, or "supps" as they were called in the department.

Hoke shook his head to clear it, glanced at the box scores, and noticed that the Cubs had dropped another game to the Mets—three so far in a three-game series. He threw the paper down in disgust. The Cubs, he thought, should be able to beat the Mets every game. What in hell was the matter with them? Every season it happened this way. The Cubs would be three or four games ahead of everybody, and then drop into a mid-season slump, and then down and down they would plummet into the supps, the supps, the supps . . .

The drapes were pulled back suddenly inside the master bedroom by Ellita Sanchez. Hoke turned slightly and waved languidly with his right hand. Ellita, still in her pink shorty nightgown and wearing a purple satin peignoir, smiled broadly and waved back. Then she waddled away from the sliding glass doors toward the bathroom, the one she shared with Hoke's daughters, Sue Ellen and Aileen—and with Hoke when he could find it unoccupied.

The morning had begun, another broiling, typically humid June day in Miami. It was Thursday, but it could just as easily have been a Tuesday or a Friday. The summer days were all alike, hot and blazing, with late-afternoon thundershowers that did nothing to relieve the heat and only added to the humidity. Ellita Sanchez, eight months pregnant and now on indefinite maternity leave from the department, would make a pot of Cuban coffee and bring it out in a Thermos to Hoke. She would have one quick cup with Hoke before returning to the kitchen to fry two eggs, sunny side up, and to toast four slices of Cuban bread that she would slather with margarine. Ellita's doctor had told her not to drink any more coffee until after the baby was born, but she drank the thick black Cuban brew anyway, at least one cup, and more often two.

"My baby," she explained to Hoke, "will be half Cuban, so I don't see how one or two little one-ounce cups of coffee can hurt him before he's born."

Ellita didn't know the father's last name. His first name was Bruce; she had picked him up for a one-night stand (her first, she had told Hoke) and gotten pregnant as a result. Bruce, whoever he was, did not know that he was going to be a father, and he had probably never thought of Ellita again after the two hours he spent with her in his Coral Gables apartment. A blond, blue-eyed insurance salesman twenty-five years old—that was almost all Ellita knew about Bruce. That much, and that he had two black tufted moles one inch below his left nipple. Ellita was thirty-two years old, and she was not only reconciled to having the unplanned baby, she was looking forward to it. If it was a boy, she was going to name him Pepé, after her uncle who had died in one of Castro's prisons; and if it was a girl, she was going to name her Merita, after her aunt, Pepé's wife, who still lived in Cuba. Ellita didn't care whether it was a boy or a girl, just as long as she had a healthy baby. She had prayed that her child would not have any tufted moles beneath its left nipple—in either case—but she was prepared to accept them if that was the will of God.

When her eggs and toast were ready, Ellita would bring her plate out to the glass table and rejoin Hoke. With her knife and fork she would fastidiously cut away the white part surrounding the barely cooked yellow yolks and eat the white part first. Then she would eat the yolks, scooping them up one at a time and shoveling them into her mouth without breaking them. This was the part Hoke could barely stand to watch, the runny yellow yolk oozing through Ellita's strong white teeth. But he couldn't say anything to Ellita about this practice, this disgusting habit, because she paid half the rent and half the utilities on the Green Lakes house. Ellita was Hoke's partner in the Homicide Division, and she would be his active partner again when her maternity leave was over and she came back to work, so Hoke could only give her criticism or suggestions as a police officer. His supervisory status did not extend to the home, to her eating habits, to her sleeping with earrings on, or to her wearing a layer of sprayed musk on top of her overdose of Shalimar perfume.

Hoke did not sleep with Ellita; he never had, and he never would. She was an investigator assigned to him as a junior partner in the Homicide Division, and that was that. But Hoke needed her in the house, and not just because he wouldn't have been able to swing all of the expenses by himself. Ellita had also helped him considerably with his two teenage daughters.

The girls had been living with Hoke for six months now, after being sent back to Hoke by their mother, who had moved from Vero Beach, Florida, to Glendale, California, to marry Curly Peterson, a black pinch hitter for the Dodgers. Sue Ellen, sixteen, had a job at the Green Lakes Car Wash and planned to drop out of school permanently when high school started again in September, so she could keep making monthly payments on her new Puch moped. Aileen, fourteen, had been helping around the house and had found a few baby-sitting jobs in the neighborhood, but she would be required by law to go back to school in the fall. Aileen wanted to quit school, too. Both girls adored Ellita Sanchez, and they ate their fried eggs each morning in imitation of Ellita. Hoke could not prevent the girls from continuing this disgusting habit; anything he said to them would be construed by Ellita as an indirect critique of *her*.

Hoke had discussed this dilemma with Bill Henderson, his previous partner, and Bill had told him that the only thing he could do was to eat his breakfast alone, preferably before Ellita and the girls got up in the morning. If he didn't watch them eating their eggs, and if he tried to put it out of his mind, perhaps, in time, he wouldn't think about it. And as a rule, this was what Hoke did. He would eat his Grape-Nuts out on the porch, and then when Ellita joined him with her plate, he would pour his coffee and take it into the living room, there to sit in his La-Z-Boy recliner in front of the television while he watched the morning news.

Hoke preferred to get up before the females anyway, so he could take his shot at the bathroom for his shower and shave. Once the rest of them were up, the wait for the bathroom could be interminable. One bathroom was not enough for four people, but that was the way the contractor had saved money when he built the Green Lakes subdivision in the mid-fifties, and there were several families much larger than Hoke's in the subdivision making do.

Ellita brought out the Thermos of coffee, an empty regular-sized cup, and a demitasse cup. She poured the coffee—four ounces for Hoke, one ounce for herself—and asked what was new in the paper.

"I'm finished with it." Hoke shrugged. He took his filled cup into the living room and sat in his La-Z-Boy, but he didn't switch on the television.

When Ellita had started her maternity leave, two weeks

before, Major Brownley, the Homicide Division chief, had told Hoke he wouldn't be able to replace her. Hoke had Ellita and a young investigator named Teodoro Gonzalez (immediately nicknamed "Speedy" by the other detectives in the division) working for him on the "cold case" files. In the beginning this was supposed to have been a temporary assignment, but the three of them had so handily solved a half-dozen old murder cases that the major had made it a permanent assignment, with Hoke in charge. Without Ellita, and without any replacement for her, Hoke would have to depend solely on Gonzalez—a bright young investigator, but a man without a sense of direction—for most of the legwork. Gonzalez had a B.A. degree in economics from Florida International University in Miami, and had served only one year as a patrolman in Liberty City before being promoted to plainclothes investigator in the Homicide Division. He hadn't actually earned this promotion, but had been elevated because he was a Latin with a bachelor's degree. His black patrol sergeant in Liberty City had recommended Gonzalez for the promotion, but that was because the sergeant had wanted to get the man the hell out of his section. Despite the map in his patrol car, and the simple system of streets and avenues in Miami (avenues run north and south; streets run east and west), Gonzalez had spent half of his patrol hours lost, unable to locate the addresses he was dispatched to find. Gonzalez was willing and affable, and Hoke liked the kid, but Hoke knew that when he sent him out to do some legwork, an important function on cold cases, Gonzalez would spend most of his time lost somewhere in the city. Once Gonzalez had been unable to get to the Orange Bowl, even though he could see it from the expressway, because he couldn't find an exit that would get him there.

Gonzalez had, however, prepared Hoke's income tax return, and Hoke had received a $380 refund. Gonzalez had also prepared Ellita's Form 1040, and she had received a refund of $180 when she had expected to pay an additional $320, so they thenceforth both admired Gonzalez's ability with figures. Hoke had given Gonzalez responsibility for the time sheets and mileage reports, and they had had no trouble in getting reimbursed. Beyond this, however, Hoke didn't know quite what to do with Gonzalez and the fifteen new supps that had been deposited in his in-box the day before.

These supps all represented new cold cases which, in Hoke's opinion, were still too warm to be considered inactive. What these cases really were were difficult cases that other detectives in the division considered hopeless. But they were also much too recent to be hopeless, as Hoke had discovered by glancing through them yesterday afternoon. Hoke was getting them via interoffice mail because Major Brownley had put a notice on the bulletin board directing detectives in the division to turn over all of the cold cases they were currently working on to Sergeant Moseley. These new cases, added to the ten Hoke had selected already from the back files to work on, because they had possibilities, were not, in Hoke's opinion, beyond hope. Even his cursory reading of the new supps had indicated that the detectives could have done a lot more work on them before putting them on his back burner. What it amounted to, Hoke concluded, was a way for these lazy bastards to clear their desks of tough investigations and shift them over to him and Gonzalez. All fifteen supps had yellow tags affixed to the folders, meaning that there was no statute of limitations on these crimes because they were homicides, rapes, or missing-person cases. Hoke realized that his desk would be the new dumping ground for more and more cases from detectives who had run out of routine leads and gotten down to the gritty part of thinking about fresh angles that were *not* routine. The chances were, he thought gloomily as he finished his coffee and put the cup on the magazine table next to the La-Z-Boy, that there would be a few more of them in his in-box when he got down to his cubbyhole office on the third floor of the Miami Police Station.

Hoke stopped thinking about this new idea. Then he stopped thinking altogether, closed his eyes, and sat back in the chair.

The girls got up. (They shared a bedroom, Ellita had the master bedroom, and Hoke had the tiny eight-by-six-foot bedroom that was originally supposed to be either a den or a sewing room at the back of the house next to the Florida room.) They used the bathroom, took their showers, and fixed their breakfasts. They jabbered with Ellita out in the Florida room but didn't disturb Hoke when they saw him with his eyes closed, sitting in his chair. At 7:45, Sue Ellen kissed Hoke on the forehead (he apparently didn't feel it) before getting on her moped and riding off to work at the Green Lakes Car Wash. Ellita and Aileen washed and dried the dishes in the kitchen, and then, at eight o'clock, Ellita touched Hoke's bare shoulder gingerly, told him the time, and said that the bathroom, if he wanted it, was clear again. But Hoke did not reply.

At eight-thirty Ellita said to Aileen:

"I think your father's gone back to sleep in his chair. Why don't you wake him and tell him it's eight-thirty? I know he has to work because he told me last night he had fifteen new supps to read through today."

"It's eight-thirty, Daddy," Aileen said, her right hand ruffling the stiff black hairs on Hoke's back and shoulders. Aileen, every time she got an opportunity, liked to feel the hair on Hoke's back and shoulders with the tips of her fingers.

Hoke didn't reply, and she kissed him wetly on the

cheek. "Are you awake, Daddy? Hey! *You* in there, old sleepyhead, it's after eight-thirty!"

Hoke didn't open his eyes, but she could tell from the way he was breathing that he wasn't asleep. Aileen shrugged her skinny shoulders and told Ellita, who was sorting laundry from the hamper into three piles, that she had given up on waking her father. "But he's really awake," she said. "I can tell. He's just pretending to be asleep."

Aileen was wearing a white T-shirt with a "Mr. Appetizer" hot dog on the front; some of the egg yolk from her breakfast had spilled onto the brown frankfurter. Ellita pointed to it, and Aileen stripped off the T-shirt and handed it to her. Aileen did not wear a brassiere, nor did she need one. She was a tall skinny girl, with adolescent chest bumps, and her curly sandy hair was cut short, the way boys used to have theirs trimmed back in the 1950s. From the back, she could have been mistaken for a boy, even though she wore dangling silver earrings, because so many boys her age in Green Lakes wore earrings, too.

Aileen returned to her bedroom to get a clean T-shirt, and Ellita went into the living room. "Hoke," she said, "if you aren't going downtown, d'you want me to call in sick for you?"

Hoke didn't stir in his chair. Ellita shrugged and put the first load of laundry into the washer in the utility room off the kitchen. She then made the bed in her bedroom (the girls were supposed to make their own), hung up a few things in her walk-in closet, and gave Aileen $1.50 for lunch money. Aileen, together with her girl friend Candi Allen, who lived on the next block, were going to be driven to the Venetian Pool in Coral Gables by the girl's mother. They would be there until three P.M., and then Mrs. Allen would pick them up and bring them back to Green Lakes. Aileen left the house, carrying her bathing suit in a plastic Burdine's shopping bag, after kissing her father again and running the tips of her fingers through the hair on his back and shoulders.

By eleven A.M., when Hoke had not stirred from his chair —he had urinated in his shorts, and there was a large damp spot on the brown corduroy cushion—Ellita was concerned enough to telephone Commander Bill Henderson at the Homicide Division. Bill Henderson, who had been promoted to commander a few months back, was now the Administrative Executive Officer for the division, and all of the paperwork in the division—going and coming—crossed his desk before he did something about it or routed it to someone else. Bill did not enjoy this newly created position, nor did he like the responsibility that went with it, but he liked the idea of being a commander, and the extra money.

Ellita told Bill that Hoke had been sitting in the chair since breakfast, that he had pissed his underpants, and that although he was awake, she could not get him to acknowledge her presence.

"Put him on the phone," Bill said. "Let me talk to him."

"You don't understand, Bill. He's just sitting there. His eyes are open now, and he's staring at the wall, but he isn't really looking at the wall."

"What's the matter with him?"

"I don't know, Bill. That's why I called you. I know he's supposed to go to work today, because he got fifteen new supps yesterday and he has to read through them this morning."

"Tell him," Bill said, "that I just gave him five supps on top of that. I handed them to Speedy Gonzalez about fifteen minutes ago."

"I don't think that will make an impression."

"Tell him anyway."

Ellita went into the living room and told Hoke that Bill Henderson just told her to tell him that he now had five more supps to look at, in addition to the fifteen Bill had sent him yesterday.

Hoke did not respond.

Ellita returned to the phone in the kitchen. "He didn't react, Bill. I think you'd better tell Major Brownley that something's wrong. I think I should call a doctor, but I didn't want to do that without talking to you or Major Brownley first."

"Don't call a doctor, Ellita. I'll drive out and talk to Hoke myself. If there's nothing radically wrong with him, and I don't think there is, I can cover for him and Major Brownley'll never know anything about it."

"Have you had lunch yet, Bill?"

"No, not yet."

"Then don't stop for anything on your way over, and I'll fix you something here. Please. Come right away."

Ellita went back into the living room to tell Hoke that Bill was coming to the house, but Hoke was no longer sitting in his chair. He wasn't in the bathroom, either. She opened the door to his bedroom and found him supine on his narrow army cot. He had pulled the sheet over his head.

"I told Bill you weren't feeling well, Hoke, and he's coming right over. If you go back to sleep with the sheet over your face, you won't get enough air and you'll wake up with a headache."

The room air conditioner was running, but Ellita turned it to High-Cool before closing the door. Low-Cool was comfortable enough for nighttime, but with the sun on this side of the house, it would be too warm in the afternoon.

Bill arrived, and after pulling the sheet away from Hoke's face, talked to him for about ten minutes. Hoke stared at the ceiling and didn't respond to any of Bill's questions. Bill was a large man with big feet and a huge paunch, and he had a brutal, metal-studded smile. When he came out of Hoke's room, he carried his brown-and-white seersucker jacket over his left arm, and he had taken off his necktie.

Ellita had fixed two tuna salad sandwiches and heated a can of Campbell's tomato soup. When Bill came into the kitchen, she put his lunch on a tray and asked him if he wanted to eat in the dining room or out in the Florida room.

"In here." Bill pulled out an Eames chair at the white pedestal dining table and sat down. "It's too hot out there without any air conditioning. The announcer on the radio coming over said it would be ninety-two today, but it seems hotter than that already."

Bill bit into a tuna salad sandwich, sweet with chopped Vidalia onions, and Ellita put two heaping tablespoons of Le Creme into his steaming tomato soup.

"What's that?" Bill said, frowning.

"Le Creme. It turns ordinary tomato soup into a gourmet treat. I read about it in *Vanidades.*"

"When you called me, Ellita, I thought maybe Hoke was just kidding around, and I was half ready to kick him in the ass for scaring you. But there is something definitely wrong with him."

"That's what I was trying to tell you."

"I know. But I still don't think we should tell Major Brownley. Was Hoke sick to his stomach, or anything like that?"

"No. He was all right when I fixed his coffee this morning, and he'd already read the paper."

Bill stirred the soup in his bowl; the creamy globs of Le Creme dissolved in a pinkish marble pattern. "I don't want to scare you any more than you are already, Ellita—but—how's the baby coming, by the way? All right?"

"I'm fine, Bill, don't worry about me. I've put on ten pounds more than the doctor wanted me to, but he doesn't know everything. He told me I'd have morning sickness, too, but I haven't been sick once. What about Hoke?"

"What it looks like to me, and I've seen it more than once in Vietnam, is 'combat fatigue.' That's what we used to call it. A man's mind gets overwhelmed with everything in combat, you see, and then his mind blanks it all out. But it isn't serious. They used to send these guys back to the hospital, wrap them in a wet sheet for three days, put 'em to sleep, and they'd wake up okay again. Then they'd be back on the line as if nothing had happened."

"It's all psychological, you mean?"

"Something like that—and temporary. That wasn't a big problem in the Army. In the department, though, it could be. If Major Brownley calls in the department shrink to look at Hoke, I'm pretty sure that's what he'd call this. I mean, not 'combat fatigue,' but 'burnout' or 'mid-life crisis,' and then it would go on Hoke's record. That's not the kind of thing a cop needs on his permanent medical record."

"Hoke's only forty-three, Bill. That isn't middle-aged."

"It can happen at thirty-three, Ellita. You don't have to be middle-aged to go through a mid-life crisis. Instead of telling Brownley, it might be best if we keep this to ourselves. I'll fill in the papers, and we can put Hoke on a thirty-day leave without pay. I can forge his name easily enough. I did it plenty of times when we were partners. Then I'll call his father up in Riviera Beach and get him to take Hoke in for a few weeks. If Hoke's up there on Singer Island, instead of here with you, Brownley won't be able to come and check on him."

"I don't think Mr. Moseley'll like that, Bill. And I know his wife won't. I met her once, when the two of them were going on a cruise, and she's one of those society types. The sundress she had on when she came to the ship must've cost at least four hundred dollars."

"There's not even any back to a sundress."

"Make it three-fifty then. But she looked down her nose at me. She doesn't approve of lady cops, I think."

"Hoke's old man's got all of the money in the world. I'll talk to Mr. Moseley, and he can get his own doctor to look at Hoke. A visit to the department shrink is supposed to be confidential, but it always gets out sooner or later. This thing with Hoke'll blow over soon, I know it will, and if we can get him out of town for a few days no one'll ever know the fucking difference."

"What'll I tell the girls?"

"Tell them Hoke's gone on a vacation. I'll call Mr. Moseley on your phone after I finish eating—the soup's good with this stuff, by the way—and you can drive Hoke up there this afternoon. You can still drive, can't you?"

"Sure. I go to the store every day."

"Okay, then. Take Hoke's Pontiac. Your car's too small for him, and you can drive him up there right after I call and explain everything to Mr. Moseley. You'll still be back in plenty of time to fix dinner for the girls. If not, you can always send out for a pizza."

Ellita nibbled her lower lip. "You really think Hoke'll be all right?"

"He'll be fine." Bill looked at his wristwatch. "It's one-fifteen. If anyone ever asks you, Hoke's been on an official thirty-day leave of absence since eight A.M. this morning."

Hoke hadn't planned it that way, but that's how he got back to Singer Island.

CHAPTER 2

Stanley and Maya Sinkiewicz lived in Riviera Beach, Florida, in a subdivision called Ocean Pines Terraces. The subdivision was six miles west of the Atlantic Ocean and the Lake Worth waterway. There were no pines; they had all been bulldozed away during construction. There were no terraces, either. Not only was the land flat, it was barely three feet above sea level, and flood insurance was mandatory on every mortgaged home. Sometimes, during the rainy season, the canals overflowed and the area was inundated for days at a time.

Stanley was seventy-one years old but looked older. Maya was sixty-six, and she looked even older than Stanley. He had retired from the Ford Motor Company six years earlier, after working most of his life as a striper on the assembly line. During his last three years before retiring, he had worked in the paint supply room. Because of his specialized work on the line for so many years, Stanley's right shoulder was three inches lower than his left (he was right-handed), and when he walked, his right step was about three inches longer than his left, which gave his walk a gliding effect. As a striper, Stanley had painted the single line, with a drooping striping brush, around the automobiles moving through the plant as they got to him. These encircling lines were painted by hand instead of by mechanical means because a ruled line is a "dead" line, and a perfect, ruled line lacked the insouciant raciness a hand-drawn line gives to a finished automobile. Stanley's free-hand lines were so straight they looked to the unpracticed eye as if they had been drawn with the help of a straight-edge, but the difference was there. During Henry Ford's lifetime, of course, there were no stripes on the black finished Fords. No one remembered when the practice began, but Stanley got his job as a striper on his first day of work and had kept it until his final three years. He had been transferred to the paint shop when it was decided by someone that a tape could be put around the cars; then, when the tape was ripped off, there was the stripe, like magic. Of course, it was now a dead stripe, but it saved a few seconds on the line.

Stanley and Maya had lived in Hamtramck, and they had paid off their mortgage on a small two-bedroom house in this largely Polish community. On a Florida vacation once they had spent two weeks in a motel in Singer Island. During this time they had enjoyed the sun so much they had decided to retire to Riviera Beach when the time came. The Ocean Pines Terraces development had been in the planning stages, and because pre-phase construction prices were so low, Stanley had made a down payment on a two-bedroom house and hadn't had to close on it for almost two more years. After Stanley retired, he and Maya trucked their old furniture from Hamtramck down to the new house and moved in. The house Stanley had closed on for fifty thousand dollars, six years earlier, was now worth eighty-three thousand. With his U. A. W. pension and Social Security, Stanley had an income of more than twelve thousand a year, plus three ten-thousand-dollar certificates of deposit in savings. Their son, Stanley, Jr., now lived with his wife and two teenage children in the old house in Hamtramck, and Junior paid his father two hundred a month in rent. Maya, who had worked part-time, off and on, at a dry-cleaning shop a block away from their house in Hamtramck, also drew Social Security each month, and both of them were on Medicare.

Despite their attainment of the American Dream, Maya was not happy in Florida. She missed her son, her grandchildren, and her neighbors back in Michigan. She even missed the cold and snow of the slushy Detroit winters. Maya didn't like having Stanley at home all of the time, either, and they had finally reached a compromise. He had to leave the house each morning by eight A.M., and he wasn't allowed to return home until at least noon. His absence gave Maya time to clean the house in the morning, do the laundry, watch TV by herself, or do whatever else she wanted to, while Stanley had the morning use of their Ford Escort.

After eating lunch at home, which Maya made for him, Stanley usually took a nap. Maya then drove the Escort to the International Shopping Mall on U.S. 1, or to the supermarket, or both, and didn't return home until after three. Sometimes, when there was a Disney film or a G-rated film at one of the six multitheaters in the International Mall, she took in the Early Bird matinee for a dollar-fifty and didn't come home until five P.M.

When they first moved to Florida, Maya had telephoned Junior two or three times a week, collect, to see how he and his wife and the grandchildren were getting along, but after a few weeks, when no one ever answered the phone, she had called only once a week, direct dial, on Sunday nights. She then discovered that Junior would be there to talk—for three minutes, or sometimes for five. Her daughter-in-law was never at home on Sunday nights, but sometimes Maya would be able to talk to her grandchildren, Geoffrey and Terri, a sixteen-year-old boy and a fourteen-year-old girl.

Stanley was a clean old man, and very neat in his appearance. He usually wore gray or khaki poplin trousers, gray suede Hush Puppies with white socks, and a white short-sleeved shirt with a black leather pre-tied necktie that had a white plastic hook to hold it in place behind the buttoned collar. The necktie, worn with the white shirt, made Stanley look like a retired foreman (not a striper) from the Ford Motor Company, and he always said that he *was* a retired foreman if someone asked him his occupation. He hadn't been able to make any new friends in Florida, although, at first, he had tried. For a few weeks, Stanley had been friendly with Mr. Agnew, his next-door neighbor, a butcher who worked for Publix, but when Mr. Agnew bought a Datsun, after Stanley had told him that the Escort was a much better car, and an American car to boot, he no longer spoke to Mr. Agnew, even if Maya was still friendly with Agnew's wife.

When Stanley left the house in the mornings, he wore a long-billed khaki fishing cap with a green visor. He always carried a cane, even though he didn't need one. He wore the cap because he was bald and didn't want to get the top of his head sunburned, but he carried the cane to fend off dogs. The gnarled wooden cane had a rubber tip and a brass dog's head handle. The handle could be unscrewed, and Stanley had a dozen cyanide tablets concealed in a glass tube inside the hollowed-out shaft of the wooden cane. Stanley had appropriated these cyanide tablets from the paint shop at Ford because he found them useful for poisoning vicious dogs in Hamtramck, and later in Florida. Stanley was afraid of dogs. As a boy, he had been badly mauled by a red Chow Chow in Detroit, and he didn't intend to be bitten again. During the last three years, he had used three pills to poison neighborhood dogs in Ocean Pines Terraces, and he was ready to poison another one when the opportunity arrived. Stanley had a foolproof method. He would make a hamburger ball approximately an inch and a half in diameter, with the cyanide pill in the center. Then he rolled the ball in salt and put the ball in a Baggie. When he took a walk and passed the house where the targeted dog lived, he would toss the ball underhand onto the lawn, or drop it beside a hedge or a tree as he continued down the sidewalk. When the dog was let loose in its yard, it would invariably find the hamburger by smell, lick the salt once or twice, and then gulp down the fatal meatball. Thanks to Stanley's skill, the neighborhood was shy one boxer, one Doberman, and one Pekinese.

Stanley's cane had also helped to make him a fringe member of the "Wise Old Men," a small group of retirees that congregated each weekday morning in Julia Tuttle Park. This small two-acre park had been constructed by the developer as a part of his deal to get the zoning variance that he needed for Ocean Pines Terraces. There was a thatched shed in the park, where a half-dozen retirees played pinochle in the mornings, and there was a group of rusting metal chairs under a shady strangler-fig tree, where another, smaller group of elderly men sat and talked. The group that met under the tree was called the "Wise Old Men" by the pinochle players, but they meant this sarcastically. The two groups didn't mingle, and if a man went to the park every day he would eventually have to decide which one to join. Stanley didn't play pinochle, and he didn't talk much either, having little to say and a limited education, but for the first few weeks, after silently watching the boring pinochle games, he had joined the group under the tree, to listen to the philosophers. The dean of this group was a retired judge, who always wore a starched seersucker suit with a bow tie. The other Wise Old Men wore wash pants and sport shirts, or sometimes T-shirts, and comfortable running shoes. Except for the judge, Stanley was the only one who wore a necktie. The group had changed personnel a few times since Stanley's retirement —some of the older men had died—but the judge was still there, looking about the same as he had in the beginning. Stanley, when he looked in the mirror to shave each morning, didn't think that he had changed much either. He realized deep down that he must have aged somewhat, because the others had, but he felt better in Florida than he had ever felt back in Michigan when he had had to go to work every day.

One morning the topic under discussion was the "dirtiest thing in the world." Theories and suggestions had been tendered, but they had all been shot down by the judge. Finally, toward noon, Stanley had looked at his cane, cleared his throat, and said: "The tip of a cane is the dirtiest thing in the world."

"That's it," the judge said, nodding sagely. "There's nothing dirtier than the tip of a cane. It taps the ground indiscriminately, touching spittle, dog droppings, any and everything in its blind groping. By the end of a short walk, the septic tip of a cane probably collects enough germs to destroy a small city. I believe you've hit upon it, Mr. Sinkiewicz, and we can safely say that this is now a closed topic."

The others nodded, and they all looked at Stanley's cane, marveling at the filthy things the rubber tip had touched as Stanley had carried it through the years. After that triumph, Stanley had contributed nothing more to the morning discussions, but he was definitely considered a fringe member and was greeted by name when he sat down to listen.

But Stanley didn't go to Julia Tuttle Park every single day like the others. He was too restless. He sometimes drove to Palm Beach instead, parked, and walked along Worth Avenue, window shopping, marveling at the high prices of things. Like Maya, he visited the International Mall on U.S. 1, or parked in the visitors' lot of the West Palm Beach Public Library. He would browse through the obituaries in the Detroit *Free Press,* looking for the names of old acquaintances. The fact was, Stanley didn't quite know what to do with his long free mornings, yet although he was frequently bored, searching for something to do to pass the morning hours, he was unaware of his boredom. He was retired, and he knew that a man who was retired didn't have to do anything. So this was what he did: Nothing much, except for wandering around.

Once a week he cut the lawn, whether it needed it or not. In the rainy season, lawns had to have a weekly cutting; in the winter, when the weather was dry, the lawn could have gone for three weeks or more. But by mowing one day every seven, on Tuesday afternoons, he broke up the week. Maya did all the shopping and paid all the monthly bills from their joint checking account. Stanley cashed a check for thirty-five dollars every Monday at the Riviera Beach bank, allowing himself five dollars a day for spending money, but almost always had something left over at the end of the week.

In the evenings, Stanley and Maya watched television. They were hooked up to the cable, with Showtime and thirty-five other channels, but they rarely changed the channel once they were sitting down. Sometimes they watched the same movie on Showtime four or five times in a single month. Maya went to bed at ten, but Stanley always stayed up and watched the eleven o'clock news. Because of his afternoon nap, he could rarely fall asleep before midnight. He rose at six A.M., though, got the *Post-Times* from the lawn, drank some coffee, and read the paper until Maya got up to fix his breakfast.

* * *

On a Wednesday afternoon in June, Stanley was asleep on the screened porch behind the house at three-thirty when Pammi Sneider, the nine-year-old daughter of a retired U.S. Army master sergeant who leased a Union gas station out on Military Trail, came through the unlocked screen door. Pammi was a frequent visitor when Maya was home, because Maya would give the girl cookies and a glass of red Kool-Aid, or sometimes, when she had been baking, a slice of pie or cake. The Sneiders lived four doors down from the Sinkiewiczes, and once Mrs. Sneider had told Maya that if Pammi ever pestered her to just send her home. Maya had said she liked to have the little girl drop by, and that Pammi reminded her of her granddaughter back in Michigan, whose name was Terri, a name ending with an *i*, just like Pammi's. Despite that conversation, the two women were not friends. There was too much difference in their ages, and in just about everything else. Mrs. Sneider was only thirty-six, and she belonged to Greenpeace, the La Leche League, Mothers Against Drunk Drivers, and the West Palm Beach chapter of N.O.W. Mrs. Sneider was away from home a good deal, but this was a safe neighborhood, and Pammi was allowed to play with other children and was also authorized to go to Julia Tuttle Park in the afternoons, by herself. In the afternoons, very few of the older men went to the park. It was too hot to sit there, for one thing, and when school was out, the older men did not like to hear the small children squealing on the playground equipment and chasing each other around. There were almost always a few mothers there with smaller children, so the park was considered a safe place to send children to get them out of the house.

Pammi was barefooted, and she wore a blue-and-white striped T-shirt and a pair of red cotton shorts with an elastic waistband. She carried a leather sack in her left hand, a sack that had once contained marbles. She tiptoed over to the webbed lounger, where Stanley was sleeping on his back, and gave him a French kiss.

Stanley spluttered and sat up suddenly. Pammi giggled and held out her grubby right hand.

"Now," she said, giggling again, "you gotta give me a penny."

Stanley wiped his mouth, blinking slightly. "What did you do?"

"I gave you a kiss. Now you gotta give me a penny."

"My wife's at the store," Stanley said. "But she should be back soon. I don't know if she's got any cookies for you or not, Pammi. I haven't been in the kitchen—"

"I don't want a cookie. I want a penny for my collection." The girl held up her leather bag and shook it. The coins inside rattled.

"I didn't ask you for a kiss, and you shouldn't kiss a man like that anyway. Not at your age. Who taught you to stick out your tongue when you kissed?"

Pammi shrugged. "I don't know his name. But he comes to the park every day when it begins to get dark, and he gives me a penny for a wet kiss, and five pennies for a look. You owe me a penny now, and if you want a look you'll have to give me five more." Pammi put her sack on the terrazzo floor and stripped off her red shorts. Stanley looked, and shook his head. Pammi's hairless pudenda, which resembled a slightly dented balloon, did nothing to excite the old man.

"Put your shorts back on. What's the matter with you, anyway?"

As Stanley got off the lounger, Pammi laughed and danced away. He picked up her shorts from the floor and stalked the little girl, trying to drive her into a corner so he could put her shorts on again. Maya drove into the carport in the black Escort and parked, then came into the kitchen with a bag of groceries and looked through the sliding glass doors to the porch. By this time, Stanley had Pammi by one leg and was trying to insert it into the shorts, while Pammi giggled and tried to get away from him.

"You owe me six cents first!" Pammi said. "You looked, you looked!" Then, when Pammi saw Maya's face through the glass doors, she stopped giggling and began to cry. Maya hurried through the living room and went out the front door, slamming it behind her. When Pammi began to cry and ceased struggling, and the front door slammed, Stanley let go of the little girl's leg. He was still holding her shorts in his right hand when Pammi ran out the back screen door and into the yard. She cut through the unfenced back yards and, bare-butted, raced home, four doors away.

Still holding Pammi's shorts, Stanley went into the kitchen. He looked into the bag of groceries on the sideboard by the sink. There was a quart of milk and a dozen eggs in the bag, as well as some canned things. He put the eggs and the milk into the refrigerator. He wondered where Maya had gone; she had, apparently, taken her handbag when she'd gone back out the front door. Maya's car keys were still on the counter beside the bag of groceries.

It did not occur to Stanley that he was in an awkward position. Instead, he was irritated because Maya had left the house without telling him where she was going. He was also a little concerned about Pammi. A girl that young shouldn't be French-kissing a man old enough to be her grandfather—or great-grandfather, for that matter—and showing off her dimpled private parts for pennies. He wondered who had taught her those games, but he couldn't think of any of the old men in the park who would do any such thing. Later on that evening, he decided, he would go down to Mr. Sneider's house and talk to him about it.

Stanley picked up the leather bag of coins and looked

inside. He dumped the pennies on the kitchen table and counted them. There were ninety-four. He guessed that Pammi had needed six more pennies to make a hundred, so that was why she had kissed him and showed him her private parts. If she had a hundred pennies, she could change them for a dollar bill.

Stanley put the rest of the groceries away and sat in the living room waiting for Maya to come back. Twenty minutes later, Maya came briskly up the walk, accompanied by Mr. Sneider. Stanley, still holding Pammi's red shorts in his lap, got out of his chair as Maya unlatched the front door. When it swung open and he saw the expression on Mr. Sneider's face, Stanley started to run out toward the back porch. Sneider, rushing past Maya, moved uncommonly fast for a man his size and he hit Stanley in the mouth before Stanley could say anything to either of them.

An hour later, Stanley was in the Palm Beach County Jail.

CHAPTER 3

Hoke Moseley spent the next three days in the back guest bedroom in his father's house. Hoke's father, Frank Moseley, had been upset when Ellita Sanchez arrived at his Singer Island home with his son, even though Bill Henderson had telephoned and explained things before Ellita drove the seventy miles up from Miami. Frank, a spry seventy-five-year-old, had rarely been sick in his life and had never missed a day of work in his hardware store and chandlery in Riviera Beach. He had been a widower for many years after Hoke's mother had died of cancer, and had then married a wealthy widow in her early forties named Helen Canlas.

Frank had called his doctor, as Bill Henderson had suggested, a physician he had known for thirty some odd years in West Palm Beach, and Dr. Ray Fairbairn, who had a dwindling practice, had driven over immediately. Dr. Fairbairn, whose breath always smelled like oil of cloves, examined Hoke privately in the guest bedroom. He then told Frank and Ellita that Hoke was all right but needed rest. Lots of rest.

"I've given him a tranquilizer, and I've written out a prescription for Equavil," Dr. Fairbairn said, handing the slip of paper to Frank. "I think he'll be okay in a few days."

"What did he say?" Frank asked.

"He didn't say anything." Dr. Fairbairn shrugged. "He's in good shape physically, but the fact that he won't talk to me indicates that he's probably decided to avoid everyday life for a while."

"I don't understand," Frank said, running his fingers through his thick white hair. "How in the hell can a man avoid everyday life? Hoke's a homicide detective in Miami, and every time I've talked to him on the phone—about once a month—he tells me how busy he is."

Ellita, who had been listening, cleared her throat. "Hoke's on a thirty-day leave without pay, Dr. Fairbairn. Will that be enough time for him to rest? I mean, if he needs additional time, Commander Henderson can probably get his leave extended."

"I haven't kept up too well with all of these new psychological theories, madame," Dr. Fairbairn said, addressing Ellita thusly because he had already forgotten her name and could see that she was pregnant. "But Hoke has what they now call 'burnout.' I've known Hoke since he was a little boy. He's always been an over-achiever, in my opinion, and these types frequently have attitude problems when they mature. Hoke's heart is fine, however, and he's as strong as a mule. So when someone like Hoke turns away from everyday life, as he's apparently decided to do, it's nature's way of telling him to slow down before something physically debilitating does happen to him. And the buzzword, according to pop psychology, is 'burnout.' I read an interesting article about it last year in *Psychology Today.*"

"Then this could be partly my fault," Ellita said. "I'm his partner, and I started my maternity leave two weeks ago, so I'm not around to help him on the job anymore."

"You're a police officer?" Dr. Fairbairn raised gray eyebrows. "You don't look like a police officer."

"That's because I'm eight months pregnant. A pregnant woman, even in uniform, doesn't look like a police officer."

"Are you going to stay here with him?"

"No, I've got to get back to Miami. I share a house with Hoke and his two daughters, and I have to look after them. But I won't drive back right away if I'm needed here and can help Hoke in any way."

"Will my son need a nurse?" Frank asked. "Or should I send him to the hospital?"

"No hospital, Mr. Moseley," Ellita said, shaking her head. "If this is just a temporary condition, like Dr. Fairbairn says, it wouldn't look good on Hoke's record to have a hospital stay. Rather than do that, I'll take Hoke back to Miami with me and look after him myself."

"He doesn't need a nurse," Dr. Fairbairn said, "or hospitalization either. Just let him rest tonight, Frank, and I'll come by tomorrow and take another look at him." The doctor consulted his watch. "It's too late to go back to my office now, so I could do with a drink."

"What'll you have?" Frank asked. "Bourbon? Gin?"

"I could use a martini, but no vermouth, please. And before I leave, Frank, I'd better give you a prostate massage. You haven't been into the office for more than two months."

Frank flushed slightly and glanced sideways at Ellita. "Helen gives them to me now, Roy. That's why I haven't been in."

"In that case, I'll just settle for the martini."

"Would you like something, Miss Sanchez?"

Ellita shook her head. "Not till after the baby. I'll just go in for a second and say good-bye to Hoke. Then I'd better head back to Miami."

"Why not stay for dinner first? Helen'll be back from her Book Review Club soon, and Inocencia's cooking a roast."

"Thanks, but I'll have to fix something for the girls. And

they'll want to know that their father's all right. What book are they reviewing?"

"I don't know the title, but it's something by Jackie Collins. She's Joan's sister, you know. Jackie's the writer, and Joan's the actress. We saw Joan in *The Stud* on cable the other night, and Helen said their new book reviewer is so good at explaining the good parts she no longer has to read the books."

"I'll just look in on Hoke."

Hoke was lying on his back on the king-sized bed, still wearing his stained boxer shorts, but he wasn't under the covers. The room was cool, and there was a whispering hiss from the central air conditioning duct above the door. The sliding glass doors to the back yard were closed, but the draperies were pulled back partially, giving Hoke a view, if he wanted to raise his head and look at it, of the swimming pool, the gently sloping back lawn, a short concrete dock, and Frank's Boston Whaler tied to the pilings. Across the narrow blue-green waterway there were mangroves, and high above the mangroves black thunderclouds were billowing toward the island from the Everglades.

Ellita tapped Hoke on the arm. He flinched slightly, but didn't look at her. "The doctor said you were going to be all right, Hoke. You're going to stay here with your father for a while. I'm going back to Miami, and I'll look after the girls. If you want your car, call me, and I'll have someone drive it up. Don't worry about me or the girls. We'll be all right. Okay?"

Hoke turned on his side and looked out the window.

"Your robe's over on the chair. I put your toilet articles in the bathroom. Your teeth are in a glass in the bathroom, and there's plenty of Polident. There are slacks, sport shirts, underwear, and socks in the suitcase. I forgot to pack your shoes, but your gun and buzzer are in the bag with your wallet. Tell your father to get you some sneakers or something from his store, and I'll send up your shoes when you want your car. I guess that's it, then. I'll be in touch with your dad if you need anything." No response. "Well, good-bye, then."

Ellita closed the door behind her, said good-bye to Frank Moseley and Dr. Fairbairn, and drove back to Miami.

Later that evening, when Inocencia, the Moseleys' Cuban cook, brought Hoke's dinner in to him on a tray, Hoke was sitting in a chair by the sliding glass doors. He had taken a shower and was wearing his white terrycloth shaving robe. Inocencia put the tray on the table beside the chair and left the bedroom without trying to talk with him.

The rain was coming down hard on the patio tiles outside the sliding doors, and it was difficult to make out the mangroves across the waterway in the driving rain. Hoke put in his teeth in the bathroom, then made a roast beef sandwich with one of the rolls Inocencia had brought. He didn't touch the Waldorf salad, the broccoli, the baked potato, or the wedge of blueberry cobbler. He drank a glass of iced tea, took another Equavil, and went to sleep on top of the covers.

Later that evening, when Frank and Helen looked in to see him, Hoke was asleep on his back, breathing through his mouth and snoring.

Frank and Helen had a long talk about what to do with Hoke when they went into their bedroom that night after watching TV. Helen didn't want Hoke to stay with them, even though they had a large house with two spare bedrooms. Frank told her that Hoke would stay as long as it was necessary. Helen patted off her makeup with cold cream, stared at her handsome face in the mirror for a moment, and then hunched her plump shoulders combatively.

"I want to know that he'll be leaving," she said.

"We can't decide anything now, Helen. We'll see what the doctor says tomorrow or the next day, and if it turns out that the police department's too much for Hoke to handle any longer, I can always let him clerk in the store. He worked in the store summers and Saturdays when he was in high school, and he was one of the best clerks I ever had."

"He's forty-three years old now, Frank, and he's been a cop for fourteen years. He can't go back to being a clerk in the store."

"Why not? Mrs. Grimes has been in the store for thirty-two years, and she's sixty years old. I still go to the store every day, and I'm seventy-five. What makes you think forty-three's too old to be a hardware clerk?"

"That isn't what I meant."

"What did you mean?"

"I just meant that he's too old to be coming back home to live. Especially after being a police detective. It wouldn't work out for Hoke, and it wouldn't work out for us."

"We'll talk about that tomorrow. By the way, Dr. Fairbairn said I was overdue for my prostate massage."

Helen sighed, and then she smiled. "I'll get the Crisco." She got up from her vanity table and padded lightly down the hall toward the kitchen.

Later on, when Hoke recalled this dormant three-day period, he remembered every detail of this long first day: Ellita's frequent reminders of the time, his daughter's kisses, the drive up the Sunshine Parkway from Miami, and Steely Dan playing "Rikki Don't Lose That Number" on the car radio. Hoke had huddled on the back seat of the old Le Mans with his terrycloth robe pulled over him. He had tried, for a while, to count the kingfishers poised above the hyacinth-choked canal, clinging to telephone wires. The kingfishers, loners to a bird, had been spaced out along the wire about five miles apart, with their heads pulled in as if they had no necks. But he soon lost count, and wondered if it could be the same kingfisher he was counting each time, the same old bird flying ahead endlessly to fool him.

He didn't know why he couldn't bring himself to answer Ellita, his daughters, Bill Henderson, or old Doc Fairbairn, who had set Hoke's broken arm when he was eleven, but he had known somehow, cunningly, that if he didn't say anything to anyone, eventually they would all let him alone and he would never have to go down to the Homicide Division and work on those cold fucking cases again.

It was funny-peculiar too, in a way, because he had been thinking about Singer Island while he was reading the newspaper, wishing he were back on the island, and now, without any conscious effort, here he was, all alone in his father's house, lying on a firm but comfortable mattress in a cool and darkened room. And no one was bothering him, or trying to force him to read all of those new Incident Reports and supps that were piled up on his desk.

Hoke did not, after his first night's troubled sleep, take any more of the tiny black Equavils. They hadn't made him feel funny while he was awake (although they must have been responsible for his weird and frightening dreams), but while he *was* awake, they had robbed him of any feelings, and his mind became numb. If he took four of them a day, as the doctor ordered, he would soon become a zombie. Besides, Hoke didn't need any chemicals to maintain the wonderful peace of mind he now enjoyed. The bedroom was cool, and although he wasn't hungry, the little he did eat when Inocencia brought in his trays was delicious. He told himself that he would never have to go back to the police department. All he had to do was lie quietly on the bed, or sit by the glass doors and look out at the blue-green pool or at the occasional boats that passed on the inland waterway ignoring the NO WAKE signs, and everything would be all right. There was no need to think about anything, to worry about anything, because, as long as he kept his mouth closed and refused to react to anybody, he would be let alone. When a man didn't talk back or answer questions, people couldn't stand it for very long.

When Hoke looked back later, those three days had been the happiest he had ever known, and he often wondered if he would ever have such peace again. But he had also known, or suspected—even at the time—that it was too wonderful to last.

On the fourth morning, Hoke awoke at six, his regular time, opened the sliding doors, and dived bare-assed into the swimming pool. He swam ten slow laps in the tepid water, showered, dressed, put in his teeth, shaved, and then, because he had no shoes, walked barefooted into the kitchen and made a pot of coffee. When Inocencia arrived at seven, driving her whale-colored VW Beetle, Hoke asked her to make him a big breakfast.

"You want to eat now, Mr. Hoke, or wait and eat with Mr. Frank?"

"I'll wait for Mr. Frank."

Hoke took his coffee into the living room to get out of Inocencia's way, and sat on one of the tapestried chairs that were spaced evenly around the polished black mahogany table. There were twelve of them, and room at the table for two more. These other two chairs flanked the arched entrance that led down a step to the sunken living room. Inocencia, when she had let herself into the house with her key that morning, had brought the newspaper in from the lawn and dropped it on the table. Hoke didn't open it. He just waited for his father, sipped his coffee, stared at the bowl of daisies in the centerpiece, and wondered what he should say to the old man.

* * *

Anyone who saw the two together would notice a family likeness. It would be difficult to explain where it was, however, because the two Moseley men, except for their chocolate eyes, did not resemble one another. They were both a quarter-inch over five-ten, but Frank's shoulders slumped and he was stooped slightly, making him look much shorter than his son. He was also thin and wiry, and not more than 150 pounds, whereas Hoke weighed 190. When he had lived alone, Hoke had maintained an off-and-on diet and had once got down to 180 pounds, but after his ex-wife returned his daughters to him and Ellita had moved into the house in Green Lakes, Ellita had done all of the cooking. The starchy foods she liked—rice and black beans, fried plantains, baked yucca, chicken and yellow rice, pork roasts and pork chunks—had soon restored his lost poundage, and then some.

Frank Moseley had a full head of white hair. When a few people had told him that he resembled the ex–auto maker John DeLorean, the old man had let his hair grow and had fluffed it out on the sides, which made his resemblance to the automobile designer almost uncanny. But Frank, oddly enough, looked much younger than DeLorean. Perhaps it was because he had led such an untroubled life.

Hoke's face was as long as his father's, but it looked longer because he was balding in front, and his high brown dome and sunken, striated cheeks made his face seem a good deal narrower as well. Hoke had sandy hair, with no gray in it as yet, but he wore it roached back and without a part. His barber had suggested once that he comb it straight forward and let it grow a bit, which would give him a fringe effect. That style would minimize his baldness, he said. But Hoke thought that men who wore bangs looked like fruits, and he rejected the suggestion. A suspect would not, in Hoke's opinion, take a cop seriously if he looked the least bit gay.

Hoke's face was almost as dark as iodine from his lifetime exposure to the Florida sun, and his hairy forearms were deep mahogany because he always wore short-sleeved shirts. When he took off his shirt, his upper arms were ivory-colored; the rat's nest of black chest hair, and the long black hairs on his shoulders and back, looked like tangled nylon thread against the whiteness of his skin. As a teenager, when Hoke had worked on a live-bait ballyhoo boat out of Riviera Beach during the summers, he had been tan from the waist up as well, but he no longer went out in the sun without a shirt, and, like most Miamians, he rarely went to the beach. Because of his cheap blue-gray dentures, Hoke looked older than forty-three; but then, when one looked into his eyes, he seemed younger than that. Hoke's eyes, so dark it was difficult to see where the iris left off and the pupil began, were beautiful. Here, then, in the eyes, was where the family resemblance had concentrated itself. To see one man with eyes like that was remarkable; to see two men with eyes like theirs together was astonishing.

"Morning, son," Frank said, picking up the paper and turning to the business section. "How d'you feel?"

"Okay."

The old man put on his glasses and checked the stock market reports with a forefinger. He grunted, shook his head, and removed the glasses. "You going back to Miami, or what? You've been mighty quiet the last few days."

"I've been thinking, Frank. I've decided to resign from the department, and I'm never leaving the island again."

"You mean you're moving back here to Riviera Beach?"

"No, not exactly. I'm not going to leave the island, or cross the bridge to the mainland. I'm going to get a room here on the island, and find a job as a fry cook, maybe, or something like that."

"You can come back to work at the store."

Hoke shook his head. "Then I'd have to drive across the Blue Heron bridge to Riviera every day. I don't want to leave the island. I intend to simplify my life."

"That ain't the way to do it, Hoke. You've got the two girls to look after—"

"They can go back to Patsy. That ballplayer she married makes three hundred and twenty-five thousand bucks a year. He can take care of them, or put them in a boarding school. I'm concerned with my survival."

"If it was just me, Hoke, you could stay here, I think you know that. But Helen wouldn't want you to live with us on a permanent basis. Now, I've got a little place near the Ocean Mall you can have. I own the apartment house—eight units in all, all efficiencies—and you can have one of 'em. You can live in the apartment rent-free, and I'll give you a hundred dollars a week to manage them for me. They rent for a thousand a month during the season, and six hundred a month the rest of the year. There's a two-week minimum on rentals, and it's three-fifty for just two weeks. Paulson Realtors has been managing the place, but he hasn't been doing what I'd call a bang-up job. I had me some trouble over there last month. A single man rented an apartment for two weeks, and then moved in six of his buddies from Venezuela. It was an entire professional soccer team, and they almost ruined the apartment before Paulson even found out about them. I need someone on the premises, you see, not sitting in an office in Riviera Beach. If you're there all the time, you can rent out the units, take care of problems like that, and sort things out for me."

"Are you talking about the El Pelicano Hotel?"

"It was a hotel, but I had it converted a couple of years back to efficiency apartments. I thought maybe at first I'd make it a time-shared condo, but it works out better as rentals. Those time-share apartments are more trouble than they're worth. Three of the units are rented out already on annual leases to people working here on the island, and they get a special rate. I'll drive you over there right after breakfast, and you can move right in."

"I need to stop at Island Sundries first and buy some sneakers."

Frank nodded. "This'll be a better deal for you than working as a fry cook."

Hoke shrugged. "I really don't care what I do, Frank. I'm not leaving the island again. I'll be glad to run the hotel for you."

"It's not a hotel now, Hoke. I had the sign changed and call it the El Pelicano Arms. I had the boy paint a brown pelican on the sign, too. It looks nice."

Hoke had a substantial breakfast of fried eggs, bacon, grits, and biscuits, but the old man ate a single piece of dry toast and a small dish of stewed prunes. In January, the single cool month of the year, Frank sometimes had oatmeal as well; otherwise this was his standard breakfast throughout the year. This was a frugal meal, but Hoke knew that the old man would leave his office in the hardware store at ten-thirty and go next door to Matilda's Café, eat two jelly doughnuts, and drink a cup of chocolate. Frank did this every working day, and he went to the hardware store six days a week.

On the drive to the El Pelicano Arms, Frank stopped at Island Sundries, and Hoke bought a pair of sneakers, paying for them with his Visa card. Frank drove a new Chrysler New Yorker, and told Hoke it handled a little on the stiff side. For a few months he had driven a Bentley, just because Helen had wanted one, but business had dropped off at the store because the townspeople had thought he was doing too well. So he had sold the Bentley and bought the New Yorker, and business was back up to normal again.

The sign was new, but long strips of ochre paint hung from the rest of the building like the shredding skin of a snake. There was an empty apartment on the second floor facing the ocean. Hoke put his suitcase on one of the Bahama beds, opened the window, and took a long look at the sea, two hundred yards away across the wide public beach. A one-legged man in a skimpy bikini was hopping across the sand toward the water. Three teenage girls in bikinis played a listless game of volleyball, two of them on one side, one on the other of a sagging net. By noon the beach would be crowded with bathers, and all of the parking spaces on Ocean Drive would be full.

"This is perfect, Frank. It's only a block away from the Giant Supermarket, and I won't even need my car."

"You might feel different in a few days, Hoke. But I'll get a 'Manager' sign from the store and bring it back tonight. You can tack it to your door. There's a bulletin board downstairs with the rates posted and all, and you can put up a note saying the manager's living in 201."

"Anything you say, Frank."

"Here's your first hundred in advance." Frank handed Hoke five twenties. "If you need more now, just holler, and I'll give you a second advance."

"No, that's plenty. Thanks."

"I've got to get over to the store. But I'll call Paulson and have him come over here with the books and explain things to you."

"I could walk to his office—"

"You'd better rest easy for a while. I'll send him over. There's a black-and-white TV over there, but no phone. I better order a phone for—"

"I don't want a phone, Frank."

"You'll need one in case you want to call someone, or if someone wants to call about a rental."

"I don't want a phone. I want to simplify my life, like I told you. If someone wants to rent a unit, and one's available, they can come over here and look at it. I'll be here."

"You might like to call the girls, or Ellita."

"I don't think so, but if I do, there's a pay phone over at the mall. If Ellita calls you, tell her to send someone back up with my car. She can get one of the kids in the neighborhood to drive it up. I'll give him twenty bucks and he can take the bus back to Miami."

"I'll call her. Anything else?"

"I guess not. Mr. Paulson'll fill me in on what I need to know. And thanks, Frank. I think everything's going to be all right. I don't want you and Helen to worry about me."

"I'm sure it will, son."

The old man left, and Hoke closed the door.

Frank Moseley wasn't so sure that everything was going to be all right. Hoke had seemed to be his old self again, but he was still a little preoccupied. Perhaps the pills Dr. Fairbairn had ordered made him like that. At any rate, Frank had gotten his son out of the house, and Helen would be pleased about that. This afternoon she had her bridge group coming to the house, and she had been worried last night that Hoke might lurch out into the living room in his urine-stained boxer shorts.

CHAPTER

4

Instead of throwing Stanley into the twenty-man tank with the assorted drunks and coke-heads, the jailer put him in a two-man cell with an alleged holdup man named Robert Smith. One of the tank drunks looked hostile, and the jailer thought he might pick on the old man if he found out that he was accused of a short-eyes offense. Stanley had had to take off his belt and remove his shoelaces. He held his pants up with both hands, and he scuffled, dragging his feet as he came down the corridor, to keep from stepping out of his shoes.

Robert Smith, *né* Troy Louden, was lying on his back in the lower bunk with his hands clasped behind his head. Troy was wearing scuffed cowboy boots, a blue-denim cowboy shirt with pearl snap buttons, and a pair of gray moleskin ranch trousers with empty belt loops. His tooled leather belt and silver buckle were with his other effects in the property room. Troy's blond hair was cropped short, but he had retained thick sideburns, and they were down to the level of his earlobes. His deep blue eyes were slightly hooded. Sometimes a woman would tell him, "Your eyes are the same blue as Paul Newman's." When a woman said this, Troy would always smile and say, "Yeah, but he puts drops in his." In other respects he bore no resemblance to

Paul Newman. Troy was tall and rangy, an inch or two over six feet, with long ropy arms and bulging biceps. His nose had been broken and poorly reset, and the lines that ran from the wings of his nose to the corners of his slightly crooked mouth looked as though they had been filled with coal dust. His wide lips were about the thickness of two dimes. When he grimaced occasionally—he had a slight tic —he reminded Stanley of a lizard. Stanley didn't mention this, and neither did anyone else, but Stanley was not the first man to notice the reptilian look that appeared on Troy's face whenever he pulled his lips back hard for a split second, then relaxed them.

The cell was four feet by eight, with a two-tiered bunk bed, and there was a stainless-steel toilet without a seat at the back of the cell. There was a steel sink in the back corner, but it only had one tap, and that drizzled cold water. There were no towels or soap. The bars were painted white and were flaked away here and there, indicating that they had been repainted many times. There was no window, and a single forty-watt bulb in the ceiling, covered with heavy wire, lighted the cell dimly. With Troy stretched out on the bottom bunk, there was no place for Stanley to sit, unless he climbed into the upper bunk or sat on the rim of the toilet.

"I've got to use the toilet," Stanley said, after clearing his throat.

"Go ahead. It's right in front of you."

"I can't go with you looking at me."

Troy closed his eyes; then he put his fingers into his ears. "Okay. I won't look and I won't listen."

Stanley urinated, and then washed his hands and face at the sink. There was a deep cut on his upper lip, and he wished that there were a mirror so he could see how badly it was split. There was a lot of blood on the front of his shirt, but his lip had stopped bleeding.

"Let me take a look at that lip." Troy didn't sit up, so Stanley had to bend over the bunk for Troy to examine it.

"If it was me," Troy said, "I'd have a couple of stitches put in. Otherwise, you're gonna have a nice little scar. Seems to me you're too old to be brawling anyway. A man your age'll lose more fights than he'll win, Pop."

"I wasn't fighting. My neighbor hit me, and he didn't have no call to do it. I was going to explain, but he hit me and then twisted my arm up behind my back while my wife called the police."

"Did you hit your wife?"

Stanley shook his head. "I been married forty-one years, and I never hit her a single time. Not once." He said it as though he'd had ample reason to.

"Then why'd your neighbor bust you in the mouth?"

"My wife told him I molested his little girl, and I didn't do a darned thing to her, nothing at all, but he wouldn't listen to me."

"How old was the girl you showed your weenie?"

"I didn't show her nothing. She showed *me*, and she's nine, going on ten."

"You're lucky there, old man. If she was eight or under you'd be looking at twenty-five years. But once they hit nine they're old enough to take instructions in the Catholic church. So eight's the magic number in most states. But when they hit nine or ten, sometimes you can make a deal with the state attorney. Unless you hurt her. Did you hurt her?"

"I didn't touch the girl. I was taking a nap out on my back porch, and she came in the screen door and woke me up by putting her tongue in my mouth."

Troy nodded and made the lightning grimace. "You must've seemed irresistible to her, laying there with your mouth open. I had a girl friend once in San Berdoo who used to wake me up by sticking her tongue up my asshole.

But she was thirty-five and didn't have very much else going for her. What did she do then, Pop, pull your pants down?"

"No, she took off *her* pants, her shorts, red shorts. I was still half asleep, or half awake, and didn't quite catch on to what she was doing at first. She had a bag of pennies, you see, and she wanted one penny for the soul kiss, and then asked for another five pennies after she took off her shorts."

"That's cheap enough, God knows."

"She said some old man in the park—Julia Tuttle Park—was giving her pennies for doing this, and I guess she thought that because I was old I'd do the same thing."

"But you didn't start anything?"

"No, I was asleep, I told you. Then Maya, that's my wife, came into the house while I was trying to catch Pammi and put her shorts back on. She ran down the block and told Mrs. Sneider. She called her husband at the gas station, and he came over and hit me in the mouth. Nobody would listen to me. I don't know what Pammi told her mother."

"Pammi? Short for Pamela?"

"No, just Pammi, with an *i* at the end and no *e*."

"Did you make your phone call? You're entitled to a phone call, you know."

"The deputy said I could make a call, but the only one I could think of to call was Maya, and my wife knows I'm in here already." Stanley began to cry.

Troy got to his feet and told Stanley to sit down on the bunk. He pulled Stanley's shirttail out of his pants and wiped the old man's face. "Crying ain't gonna help you none, old-timer. What you need's a good jailhouse lawyer. You listen to me, and I'll help you. Then you can do something for me. Okay?"

"It's all a big mistake," Stanley said. "I'd never do nothing to that little girl in a million years. I ain't even had a hard-on for more'n three years now. I'm seventy-one years old and retired."

"I believe you, Pop. Just listen a minute. Here's what'll happen to you. This father, Mr. Sneider—"

"He's a retired Army master sergeant, but he leases a Union station now."

"Okay, Sergeant Sneider. What he'll do is file a complaint, and then they'll send you out of here for a psychiatric evaluation. That'll mean three or four days in a locked ward at the hospital. The doctor'll listen to your story, just like I did. Psychiatrists don't say much, they mostly listen, and I have a hunch he'll tell the state attorney to let you go. Meanwhile, this sergeant'll be thinking things over, and he'll realize if this case goes to trial his little girl will have to take the stand. After he and his wife talk about it, they'll decide they don't want to put the kid through the trauma of a courtroom appearance. So whether you're guilty or not, this case won't go to trial. But how you handle yourself when you talk to the psychiatrist is very important. He'll ask some very personal questions. How often do you masturbate?"

Stanley shook his head. "I don't do nothing like that."

"That's the wrong answer, Pop. Tell him once or twice a week. If you tell him you don't do it at all, he'll put it down on his report that you're evasive. And in shrink jargon, 'evasive' means lying. How often do you have relations with your wife?"

"None at all. Not since we came down to Florida, and that's been six years now. I still wanted to at first, but Maya said she wanted to retire, too, just like me, so we just quit doing it. I wasn't all that keen myself, to tell you the truth."

"For Christ's sake, Pop, don't tell the analyst that. Tell him once a week, at least. Otherwise, he'll think you're abnormal and you need little girls for an outlet."

"I don't need any little girls! I never touched Pammi. I told you that already."

"I *know* that, but you've got to tell a shrink what they want to hear. You'll have to persuade him that you have a normal, regular sex life."

"Maya'll tell him different."

"He won't talk to her. She's not accused of anything; you are. Apparently she believes what she thought she saw, so she'll be on Sneider's side. You understand what I'm talking about?"

"I think so. But it seems to me that Pammi, if she tells the truth, could clear all this up in a minute."

"Of course she could. But she'll want to cover her own little ass. Little girls lie, big girls lie, and old women like your wife lie, too. Come to think of it, all women lie, even when the truth would do 'em more good. But you've got an honest face, old man, and the psychiatrist'll believe you when you lie."

"My name is Stanley. Stanley Sinkiewicz. I don't mind being called Pop, because that's what they used to call me on the line at Ford, but I don't much like 'old man.' "

"Okay, Pop, fair enough. My real name's Troy Louden, but I'm signed up in here as Robert Smith. Let me finish telling you what to do, and you'll be out of here in no time. Stick to the same story you told me, but keep it simple. Maybe, when one of the detectives questions Pammi, she'll break down and tell the truth. But whether she does or not, it's still your word against hers. I realize your wife says she saw something, but all she saw was you trying to put the girl's shorts back on. Right? Admit this much, and that'll probably be the end of it. But I can guarantee you that you won't do any time if this is your first offense. This is your first offense, isn't it? You didn't get caught with any little girls before?"

"I never did nothing with a little girl, except when I was

a little boy, and I never got caught then. I worked on the line at Ford all my life, and most of the time I was sick at night from smelling paint and turpentine all day."

"You haven't got a record, then?"

"None. I never been in jail before."

"Then you're in the clear, Pop. Feel better?"

"I think so." Stanley nodded. "My lip still hurts though."

"I can't do anything about that. But when you get out, you should get a doctor to take a couple of stitches in it. Or, if they send you to the psychiatric ward in the morning, ask the nurse to get it sewed up for you. If I had a needle and thread I'd do it for you myself."

"You know how to do things like that?"

"Sure. I'm used to taking care of myself when I get hurt. I'm a professional criminal, a career criminal, and when I get hurt on the job, or someone with me does, we can't go to a doctor—not a regular one, anyway. I've set bones, and I even took a bullet out of a man's back once. If I hadn't, he'd of been paralyzed."

"How come you're in jail, Troy?"

"Call me Robert, Pop, while we're in here. Robert. After we get out, then you can call me Troy. Remember I told you I'm signed in here as Robert Smith."

"Sure, Robert. I'm sorry. I'm still upset, I guess."

"No need to be. You'll get out of this okay, Pop. But to answer your question, I'm a professional criminal, what the shrinks call a criminal psychopath. What it means is, I know the difference between right and wrong and all that, but I don't give a shit. That's the official version. Most men in prison are psychopaths, like me, and there are times—when we don't give a shit—when we act impulsively. Ordinarily though, I'm not impulsive, because I always think a job out very carefully before I get around to doing it. But I misjudged this truck driver this morning. I thought he was a little simple-minded, in fact, just because of the way he talked. But he turned out to be devious. He didn't have much education, but apparently he had more native American intelligence than I gave him credit for— Somebody's coming."

Troy crossed to the bars and watched the black trusty coming down the corridor with an enameled metal plate and a cup of coffee.

"Who was it missed supper?" the trusty asked as he reached the cell.

"Just pass it through. I'll give it to the old man."

"I'm not hungry," Stanley said.

"Never mind," Troy said. "Somebody'll eat it."

The trusty passed the plate and the cup through the slot in the cell door, and Troy sat beside Stanley on the bottom bunk. The plate contained beef stew, mustard greens, lime Jell-O, and a square of corn bread. There was a tablespoon in the cup of black coffee, which had been heavily sugared.

"Sure you don't want some of this, Pop? It'll be a long time till breakfast. Here, eat the corn bread, anyway."

Stanley ate the corn bread, and Troy ate the stew and the lime Jell-O, but not the mustard greens. He sipped the coffee and grimaced. "I don't mind food mixed up on the plate, because it all goes to one place anyway, but I can't eat greens without vinegar. Can you?"

"I'm not hungry. But this is good corn bread."

"I'm not hungry either, but I never pass up a chance to eat when I'm in jail. Ever been in jail in Mexico, Pop?"

"I never been in jail before. I already told you that. I never been in Mexico, either."

"I was in jail in Juarez once, right across the border from El Paso. They only feed twice a day there, at ten and four, and the guys who're doing the most time take half your beans. All you get is tortillas and beans twice a day, and the guys who've been there longest need the extra calories. They presume that a man who just got in's been eating good already, and they need to keep up their strength. There's more of them than there are of you, so you have to give up half your beans."

"What did you do to get thrown in a Mexican jail?"

"That's another story, Pop. Let me finish telling you what went down this morning, 'cause you're gonna help me with my situation. I'm on my way to Miami, and I got stuck just outside of Daytona, hitchhiking. Hitchhiking ain't what it used to be, unless you're a soldier or a sailor in uniform, because there are a lot of criminals on the roads these days, and people aren't picking up strangers the way they used to. I waited on U.S. One for almost three hours before I got a ride. Finally, a guy named Henry Collins gave me a lift. D'you know him, by any chance?"

"No, I don't. But I don't know many people."

"He lives right here in West Palm Beach."

"I don't live in West Palm. I live in Ocean Pines Terraces, over in Riviera Beach, the retirement settlement the other side of the canal."

"Well, Collins lives here, and he told me West Palm was as far as he was going when I first got into his car. He drives a 1984 Prelude."

"That's a Japanese car. You know, it's un-American to drive one of them. The foot pedals in a Honda are too small, and there's more leg room in a Ford. A Ford'll do anything a Honda'll do, too."

"I'm not complaining about the car, Pop. After three hours standing in the sun, I was willing to ride in the back of a pickup with a load of sheep. Anyway, Collins is a truck driver, and works out of Jacksonville. But he had two full days off, and he was coming home to spend it with his wife. I got to thinking about standing on the highway for another three hours or so, and the more I thought about it, the more I hated the idea. So I decided to take Collins's car and drive to Miami myself."

Stanley widened his eyes. "You mean you stole the man's car, after he was good enough to give you a free ride?"

"No, it didn't work out that way. I took my pistol out from under my belt and shoved it into his side, but before I could explain that I was only going to borrow his car, and that I wasn't going to hurt him, Collins jerks the wheel and we pile into a concrete bridge rail. About a mile north of downtown Riviera Beach. I'd already seen the sign marking the city limits. The damned fool could've killed us both."

"That's right. 'Specially in a tinny Japanese car."

Troy laughed. "He was frightened, I suppose. He banged his head against the windshield, and he was stunned for a minute, but I was braced and wearing my seatbelt. I always wear a seatbelt. Seatbelts save lives."

"I don't wear mine. I figure if I'm hanging on to the wheel I'm braced enough."

"It didn't work out that way for Henry Collins, Pop. The swamp was right there, with water going under the bridge, and it looked pretty deep there, so I tossed my gun as far as I could into the water. Collins was only out cold for a few seconds, but then he came to and glared at me."

"You should've run," Stanley said. "If I'd a been you I'd've started running."

"I never run, Pop. What could Collins prove? It was only his word against mine. We didn't wait long anyway, because people stopped right away to see if we were hurt. Within three minutes there was a state trooper there to investigate the accident. It was just inside the city limits, so he called for a Riviera cop. Meanwhile, Collins was filling the trooper in about me pulling a pistol on him."

"What did you say?"

"I told the trooper and the cop both that Collins was either drunk or crazy. They made him walk a straight line and then take a breath test. And he wasn't drunk. They didn't think he was crazy either, so after he said he'd prefer charges, they locked me up. Hell, he's a homeowner here, and I don't have any fixed address. Not at the moment anyway, except for this cell."

"Did they ever find your gun?"

"Not yet, and they won't try very hard, not in all that stinking muck out there. But even if they find a gun they can't prove it's mine. There must be hundreds of guns thrown off bridges here in Florida."

Frowning, Stanley took the plate and cup from Troy and put them down by the door. "You're in a lot of trouble, son. That's an awful thing to do, pulling a gun on a man that way. What ever made you do it?"

"I explained that to you. I'm a criminal psychopath, so I'm not responsible for the things I do."

"Does that mean you're crazy? You don't look crazy, Troy—I mean John."

"Robert."

"Robert. Of course, pulling that pistol on that man—"

"Let me finish, Pop. I don't have time to go into all of the ramifications of my personality, it's too complex. I've been tested again and again, and it always comes out the same. Psychopath. And because I'm a criminal, I'm also a criminal psychopath. You follow me?"

"Yeah, I think so. But if you aren't crazy, what are you?"

"It's what I told you already. I know the difference between good and bad, but it makes no difference to me. If I see the right thing to do and want to do it, I do it, and if I see the wrong thing and want to do it, I do that, too."

"You mean you can't help yourself then?"

"Certainly I can. I'll put it another way. I can help myself, but I don't give a damn."

"And because you don't give a damn, you're a criminal psychopath, is that it?"

"You've got it."

"But why"—Stanley made a sweeping movement with his arm—"don't you give a damn?"

"Because I'm a criminal psychopath. Maybe, when they give you some tests, you might could be one, too."

"No, I'm a responsible person, Robert. I worked hard all my life, took good care of my wife and son, and even put my boy through junior college. I own a home up in Detroit, and I own my own home here in Florida. I never done nothing wrong in my life, except for—well, I won't go into some little things, maybe."

"Even after they test you, Pop, you still won't know how they came out. They never tell you. I had to give a man at Folsom two cartons of Chesterfields to get a Xerox of my medical records. That's how I know. Otherwise I wouldn't know that I was a criminal psychopath, and I would think I was doing strange things instead of acting naturally. I read a lot, you see, even when I'm not in jail."

Stanley pointed to the dish and cup on the floor. "Do I have to wash this plate and cup?"

"Hell, no, just leave it for the trusty. Until a man's been adjudicated and found guilty, he don't have to do anything in jail. They'll try to get you to do things, but you can tell them to go fuck themselves because you're innocent until you're proven guilty. You and me are both innocent, so we don't have to do a damned thing. Sit down over there, Pop, I want to talk to you."

"I don't want to hear no more about those tests."

Stanley sat beside Troy, and Troy put an arm around the old man's shoulders. "Never mind the tests. I want you to do me a little favor, Pop. If you don't want to help me, say so, and I won't ask."

"Sure, I don't mind helping you, Robert, I guess. But in here, I don't know—"

"You won't be in here much longer. If you call a lawyer he can get you out right away on your own recognizance."

"My what?"

"Rec— The fact that you know who you are and that you're a property owner. Just listen to me a minute. I'm not wanted anywhere at present, but the first thing the sheriff'll do is send my fingerprints up to Charleston, South Carolina, to see if there's any criminal record on me, or if I'm wanted by some southern state. Florida's still the South, you know, despite all the snowbirds who moved down here from the North. And in the South, they always send the prints to Charleston first, because it's the southern version of the FBI records center. They won't get a make on my prints in Charleston, because I did all my time in California."

"They didn't take my prints yet. Will they send mine to Charleston, too?"

"I don't think so. As I said, you probably won't even be booked. Let me finish, then I'll answer your questions."

"Sorry, Robert. It's just that this is so darned interesting. How come they don't just send your fingerprints to the FBI in Washington?"

"They will. But later. They're interested first in whether a southern state wants a man or not. In the South, they really don't give a shit about the rest of the United States. If there isn't any make on the prints in Charleston, *then* they send them to Washington. And that's what I'm worried about, you see. It'll take about three days to get a negative report from Charleston, and then they'll forward my prints to Washington, which'll give me another three days. So I only have about six days altogether before they find out who I am. Washington's got a list on me about this long"—Troy spread his arms—"beginning with my yellow discharge from the Army and everything else. Right now, I'm okay. With just the two of us involved, me and Henry Collins, the State Attorney, when he looks at the case, wouldn't be too eager to prosecute. But when he sees my record, I'll be arraigned, and the judge'll be all set to convict me even though I'm innocent, just because of my record."

"But you aren't innocent, Robert. You already said—"

"I'm innocent until they prove otherwise. They can't prove anything, but my record'll make me look bad. That'll put me in a tight spot."

"I'm not seeing how I can help you."

Troy crossed to the bars, looked down the corridor, then sat down again. He pulled off his left boot, extracted a nail from the heel, and slid the lowest layer of the heel to one side. From a hollowed-out recess in the heel he removed three tightly folded newspaper clippings. Troy unfolded the clippings, thumbed through them, and handed one of them to Stanley. He replaced the other two clippings in the heel, twisted it back, and reinserted the nail.

"Go ahead and read it, Pop."

The clipping contained three short paragraphs. Stanley didn't have his reading glasses, so he had to hold it at arm's length to read it. Stanley read it three times before returning it to Troy. "I don't understand, Robert—"

Troy smiled and patted the old man on the knee. "What did you get out of it, Pop? Tell me."

"Maybe I missed something, I don't know. All I got out of it was that a man held up a liquor store in Biloxi, Mississippi, and then beat the owner unconscious because there wasn't enough money in the cash register to suit him."

"What's the dateline? Up at the top?"

"Biloxi, Mississippi."

"Right. That shows that the item was printed somewhere else. If something happens here in West Palm Beach, they don't put the name of the city down, but if something happens up in Jacksonville, and they run an item here, they put Jacksonville in the dateline, you see. Anyway, all you're supposed to get out of it is the story."

"This wasn't you, was it, son?"

"Of course not."

"Then why . . . I mean, what—?"

"You don't have to keep asking me questions, Pop. I'll tell you what I want you to do for me. First, put the clipping away—in your shirt pocket."

Stanley refolded the clipping and put it away. Troy rubbed his nose for a moment, then looked intently at the old man. "It's really simple, Pop. When they turn you loose, later tonight or tomorrow morning, look in the phone book and find out where Henry Collins lives. As a truck driver, he's bound to have a phone, but if he doesn't, check the city register for his address."

Stanley nodded. "I can do that easy enough."

"Fine. Then go to his house and see him for me. Hand him that clipping, and tell him to read it."

"Is that all?"

"Not quite. After he's read the clipping, tell him to drop the charges against me or I'll kill him. But tell him I won't kill him until after I've killed his wife and child first."

"I can't do that!"

"Of course you can, Pop. I wouldn't hurt a fly, any more than you would. But Collins doesn't know that. Just tell him what I said. Then he can tell the desk sergeant he was dazed by the accident and only thought I had a pistol, and now that his memory's come back he wants to rectify his mistake and withdraw the charges."

"But you really did have a pistol—"

"That's right, a thirty-eight Smith and Wesson."

"And Mr. Collins knows you had the pistol."

"That's right."

"I don't think he'd do it."

"I do."

"Well . . ." Stanley thought for a minute. "I don't think I could do nothing like that. You've been mighty nice to me and all, telling me about things and cheering me up, but that's a lot to ask—even if I do get out."

"You'll get out, don't worry."

"You really think so?"

"I know so. And what I asked you to do, a small favor for me, won't take much of your time. You're retired, so what else have you got to do with your time?"

"It ain't the time, son. I'm afraid. If I went to Mr. Collins with a message like that one, he might think I'm in on it and call the police. Then I'd be back in here with you."

"I see what you mean. There's a way around that. Write out the message. Print it on a plain piece of paper, and keep it short. Then put the message and the clipping in an envelope, and print Mr. Collins's address on the outside."

"I don't know his address."

"You can look it up, like I already told you, in the phone book. Then you can take it to Collins, and tell him you found the letter on the street, and it didn't have any stamp on it, so you thought you'd bring it to his house because it might be important. In fact, you might even ask him for a reward, or a tip. That might be even better. And if he or his wife aren't home, just drop it in his mailbox."

"I could put a stamp on it and mail it instead."

"No, that would take too long, and mailing it could get you into trouble with the Post Office—if they found out about it. I haven't got that kind of time."

"I guess I could do that much all right."

"Sure you could. And this way, you'll just be a good Samaritan delivering a letter you found on the street, the way any good citizen returns a lost wallet to someone who's lost it."

"All right. If I get out, I'll do it."

"Thanks, Pop. I really appreciate it. Now you better let me tell you some more questions the shrink'll ask you, in case you get a psychological examination. Suppose you're playing baseball, and you knock your ball into a circular field surrounded by a ten-foot wall. How do you find the ball?"

An hour later, Stanley was out on the street again. They had given him back his wallet, his belt and shoelaces, an unused Kleenex tissue, and eighty-four cents in change. John Sneider, Pammi's father, was waiting outside the jail in his tow truck to drive Stanley back to his empty house in Ocean Pines Terraces.

CHAPTER

5

The El Pelicano Arms apartment house was a hundred yards north of the public tennis courts, about sixty yards south of the Ocean Mall, and on the Atlantic side of Ocean Road. There was direct access to the public beach through a wooden gate to the left of the lobby entrance. There were reserved parking spaces for each apartment, and a special parking place for the manager—a marked slot next to the lobby entrance. There were no visitor spaces, but visitors could usually, except on weekends, find parking in the Ocean Mall lot.

The Singer Island beach, an important asset of the Riviera Beach municipality, was one of the widest beaches in Florida. In most respects, it was the best public beach in the state. The Gulf Stream was closer to shore here than anywhere else, making the water warm enough to swim all year round. During January, the cool month, the ocean was always warmer than the air, which made the water easier to get into than it was to get out. Now, toward the end of June, the water temperature was eighty-five degrees, the same as the humid air.

Across from the El Pelicano, in the older business section of Singer Island, there was a row of one- and two-story office buildings and shops, and a three-story hotel. Several shops sold T-shirts and other resort clothing, and there was a discount drugstore. Back in the 1970s, one of these stores had been the office of *Alfred Hitchcock's Mystery Magazine*, but the magazine had moved to New York, and now there was a realtor occupying the spot. Most of the space between these older buildings and the new Ocean Mall was taken up with a macadam parking lot that had no meters.

The mall had three restaurants, a dozen or more stores, a game room, and several small offices above the stores at the northern end of the mall. The Ocean Mall was "new," as far as Hoke was concerned, because the mall hadn't been there during the 1960s, when he grew up on Singer Island. There had only been one building then beside the municipal beach, a drive-in hamburger restaurant with girls on roller skates who waited on the parked cars that encircled the building. It had been a favorite place for the younger people in Palm Beach County to hang out, day and night. Sometimes the cars had been parked three deep, which meant that there was a constant movement, backing and filling, as people sought to get out or get in, and there was considerable visiting between cars.

The new mall was still a favorite place for young people. In bikinis and trunks they slouched and ran up and down the sidewalks on both sides of the mall, or cut through passageways and through the stores. There were also a great many tourists, and hundreds of middle-aged and elderly condominium residents stumbled and tottered about the mall.

There were a dozen motels and more than thirty high-rise condominiums along the single island highway, with more condos under construction. There was a narrow bridge exit at the northern end of the island, which led into North Palm Beach, as well as the Blue Heron bridge at the southern end, which took people into downtown Riviera Beach. The traffic on Blue Heron Road was always heavy.

In recent years, especially during the summer, Miami's Latins had discovered Singer Island, thanks to the Sunday *Miami Herald* travel section, where motel ads announced cheap weekend rates. It was possible for a couple (with children under twelve free) to get a motel room on the ocean, a free piña colada, two free breakfasts, and a three-day, two-night stay for as low as fifty-eight dollars a room (tax not included). A few motels, anxious for summer business, offered even lower rates if the room was rented during the week and if the couple vacated it before the weekend. Miami's Cubans, who had a long-standing tradition of going to Veradera Beach in Cuba for holidays, now flocked to Singer Island on weekends, bringing their parents, their aunts, and from three to five children per family. There were plenty of trash barrels on the beach, but the weekenders usually disdained them.

When Hoke picked his way among the sunbathers to take his first morning swim, he stepped on a discarded sanitary napkin with his bare left foot. Backing away from that and saying "Shit," he stepped into a pile of the very thing with his bare right foot. No dogs were allowed on the beach (a rule that was strictly enforced), so Hoke was worried that he had stepped in human shit. He scraped it off with an empty beer can and decided, then and there, that he would not rent out any of his El Pelicano apartments to Latins.

Hoke swam beyond the surf for almost an hour, then walked up the beach, staying close to the hard-packed sand of the littoral. By the time he reached the third condo, the beach was almost deserted. The condos, especially the older ones, were sold out completely, but only about thirty percent of the owners lived in their apartments full time. The majority came down at Christmas and at Easter, or spent three or four winter months there; most of the year their apartments were unoccupied. At least, Hoke thought, they aren't all year-round residents, like the condo owners in

Miami and Miami Beach. If all of the apartments and motel rooms on Singer Island were occupied at the same time, there probably wouldn't be enough room on the island to hold all of their cars. The island population would triple overnight. He wondered if the people buying into those condos under construction were aware of the population glut that was coming if they kept putting up these twenty- and thirty-story buildings. The condos all had heated pools on the ocean side of their buildings, explaining why very few condo residents took advantage of the warm Atlantic. Hoke decided that from now on he would walk down here and swim in front of one of these condos instead of swimming at the public beach.

As Hoke started back toward the public beach, he noticed a man seated in a webbed chair beneath a striped beach umbrella behind the Supermare, a twenty-story condo with a penthouse on top. The man had a blanket, an open briefcase, and was talking on a white portable telephone. As Hoke stopped to look at him, the man put the phone on the blanket and made a notation with a gold pen on a yellow legal pad.

Hoke crossed over to the blanket and looked down at the man. He was balding in front, but he wore a thick gray moustache, and there was a thick cluster of curly silver hair at the back of his head. He wore a rose-colored cabaña set with maroon piping on the shirt and on the hems of the swimming shorts.

"Good morning," he said, not unpleasantly, taking off his sunglasses.

"Morning. D'you mind if I use your phone?"

"Local or long distance?"

"Long distance. Miami. But I'll call collect."

"No need to do that." The older man shrugged as he handed Hoke the phone. "I've got a WATS line. Don't worry about it."

Hoke dialed Ellita Sanchez in Green Lakes, and she picked up the phone on the third ring.

"Ellita? Hoke."

"How are you, Hoke? I've called your father a couple of times, and—"

"I'm fine. You won't have to call him again. I'm living in a new place. You got a pencil?"

"Right here."

"It's the El Pelicano Arms. Apartment number 201, upstairs, here on Singer Island."

"What's the phone number?"

"No phone. The address is 506 Mall Road, Singer Island, Riviera Beach. I'm going to need a few things. My checkbook, bankbook, and probably my car. I bought some surfer trunks yesterday, but the legs are too long, so pack my swimming trunks when you send someone up with the car."

"What other clothes will you need?"

"None. I've got a new plan. I've still got my gun, badge, and cuffs, and I won't need them either. Maybe you can turn them in at the department for me?"

"*Espera,* Hoke! Let's wait awhile on that. You've got thirty days of leave, and Bill Henderson's covering for you just fine. Don't rush into any rash decisions. Your dad told me you were going to stay for a while, but you might change your— What's that roaring sound?"

"Roaring sound? Oh. I guess that must be the surf you hear coming in. I've borrowed a portable phone from a guy on the beach."

The owner of the phone laughed. Hoke moved twenty feet away from the blanket to keep him from listening in on their conversation. "I guess that's about it, Ellita."

"There must be a few other things you need."

"I don't want to tie up this man's phone, Ellita. He's working."

"On the beach?"

"Yeah. We're on the beach side of the Supermare condo —or in the back. I thought Frank already told you, I'm going to manage the El Pelicano for him, so I won't be coming back to Miami."

"What? What about the girls—and the house?"

"You can have the house. I'll send you my half of the rent from my savings until you can get someone else to share it with you. The girls will have to go out to California and live with their mother."

"Suppose Patsy won't take them back?"

"I don't want to think about that. I've still got some other things to sort out, but that's my immediate plan."

"Don't you want to talk to Aileen? She's home, but Sue Ellen's out."

"I do, yes, but I don't want to tie up this man's phone. There's no hurry about the car. But I'll need my bankbooks and checkbooks so I can buy a few things and send you the rent money."

"You didn't ask, but the baby's fine. I'll see that you get your car—"

"Thanks, Ellita." Hoke cut her off. "It was nice talking to you." Hoke walked back to the blanket and handed the man the telephone. "I don't mind paying for the call. You can check the amount, and I'll bring you the money later. It should be about a dollar eighty-five, but I don't have any money with me."

"That's okay. It won't matter to my WATS line." The older man balanced the phone on his bare knee. "I didn't mean to eavesdrop on your call, but I had to laugh. She asked about the roaring sound, didn't she?"

Hoke nodded.

"That's one of the reasons I come down to the beach to make my morning calls. I've got the penthouse up there, but they always ask me about the sound. Then I tell them

I'm on the beach under my umbrella, and that's the surf they're hearing twenty feet away. It puts me one up, you know, because then they know I'm wearing swimming trunks and sitting on the beach here in Florida, while they're in an office wearing a three-piece suit in New York." He chuckled. "Or else they're sweating down there in an office in Miami, on Brickell Avenue."

"It's been a long time since I wanted to be one up on anyone—"

"Everybody needs an edge, my friend. You've got an edge with your badge and gun. What are you, a detective?"

"How'd you know?"

"Just a guess. I heard you mention your gun and badge. If you'd just said gun, I might've figured you for a holdup man."

"I'm a detective-sergeant, but I'm retiring from the Miami Police Department."

"To manage the El Pelicano Arms?"

"Yeah. For now, anyway."

"Have you heard about the burglaries here on the island? Pretty soon the island'll be as bad as Miami."

"What burglaries?"

"In the condos. We've had three right here in the Supermare. And whoever it is, he's only taking valuable items. The cops in Riviera Beach aren't doing a damned thing about it, either." He smiled smugly.

"You don't know that. They must be working on it. They don't always tell you everything they're doing."

"I don't know about that, Sergeant. But stuff is disappearing. People are gone for a few weeks, or months, and when they come back paintings and other valuables are missing. We've got a security man on the gate twenty-four hours a day, so who's taking the stuff?"

"There's no guard back here," Hoke pointed out, "on the beach side. I could climb those steps to the pool, walk into the lobby, and take an elevator right up to your apartment. This is a public Florida beach. Anyone can walk or jog all of the way up to Niggerhead Rock and back. In fact, when I get settled, that's what I plan to do every day." Hoke edged away.

"I'd like to talk to you again about these burglaries sometime."

"I'm not a detective any longer. I was in Homicide, not Robbery. Was. Now I'm an apartment manager."

"Take my card anyway. Some evening, if you've got nothing better to do, stop up for a drink. If you're not interested in the burglaries, we can talk about something else. I have two martinis every day at five o'clock."

Hoke read the card he was handed. E. M. SKINNER. CONSULTANT. "What's the E.M. stand for?"

"Emmett Michael, but most people call me E.M. My wife used to call me Emmett, but she's been dead for three years now."

"Hoke Moseley." The two men shook hands.

"Any relation to Frank Moseley?"

"My father. You know him?"

"I know his wife. I only met him once, but Helen has an apartment here in the Supermare. I knew Helen before they got married. She still owns her apartment here."

"I didn't know that. With the big house they have, why would Helen still keep an apartment here?"

"As an investment, a tax write-off, probably. Some owners live here for six months and one day to establish a Florida residency, just because we don't have any inheritance or state income tax. They might make their money in New York or Philly, but legally they're Floridians."

"That's not my family, Mr. Skinner. We go back a long way in Florida. The original Moseleys lived here before the Revolutionary War and then went to the Bahamas during the war because they were Loyalists. Then, after the war was over, they came back to Riviera Beach."

"Not many families in Florida go that far back."

"I know. There are still a few here in Riviera Beach, and even more down in the Keys. That's why we're called 'Conchs,' you know. Originally, we were conch fishermen, both here and in the northern Bahamas. The term's been corrupted now, because they call any asshole born in Key West nowadays a Conch. But the Moseleys are truly Conchs in the original sense."

"What's the difference between a Conch and a Cracker?"

"Crackers are people who moved to Florida from Georgia, from Bacon County, Georgia, mostly. Farmers and stock people. So they're called Florida Crackers instead of Georgia Crackers. I don't know how the word 'Cracker' got started. All I know is there's a helluva difference between a Conch and a Cracker."

The phone rang, and Skinner picked it up. Hoke moved away down the beach, and Skinner waved. Hoke nodded back and headed for his apartment. The guy loved attention, Hoke concluded, and would have talked all morning.

Hoke was mildly curious about E. M. Skinner. The old man had everything, including a penthouse overlooking the Atlantic, but he was obviously lonesome as hell, looking for adventure or something. All the guy needed was a phone and a pencil, apparently, and he could sit under a beach umbrella and make money. Lots of money. Old Frank Moseley was like that, too, but his father's knack for making money hadn't been passed along to Hoke. Frank had once owned the land now occupied by the Supermare condo, and he probably still had a few points in the building as well, though Hoke didn't understand exactly how points worked. Hoke knew the difference between being alone and being lonely, however, and he knew he would never be lonely as long as he stayed on Singer Island.

Hoke showered, slipped into slacks and a sport shirt, and walked to the Tropic Shop in the Ocean Mall to see if his jumpsuits were ready yet. He had ordered two yellow poplin jumpsuits when he bought his surfer trunks, but had asked the shop owner to have the sleeves cut off and hemmed above the elbow. This was Hoke's first positive step toward simplifying his life. He would wear one of the jumpsuits one day, wash it at night, and then wear the other one the next day. That way he wouldn't need any underwear, and he could wear his sneakers without socks. He had selected the jumpsuits because they had several pockets, including zippered pockets in the back. He had wanted the long legs, however, instead of cutoffs, because they could be Velcroed at the ankles. Insects were not a big daytime problem on the island, because of the prevailing breeze from the ocean, but when the direction changed and the winds came from the 'Glades, it usually brought in swarms of tiny black mosquitoes at night.

The woman at the Tropic Shop told Hoke that she hadn't got the jumpsuits back from the tailor yet, but would send them over to the El Pelicano when her daughter came back from the mainland.

"She doesn't have to do that. I don't know where I'll be, so I'll check back later this afternoon or tomorrow morning."

"I could call you when they come back."

"I don't have a phone."

Hoke left the shop and crossed Blue Heron Road to the Giant Supermarket. He picked out potatoes, onions, celery, carrots, summer squash, and two pounds of chuck steak. He bought a dozen eggs and three loaves of white sandwich bread. He added a bottle of Tabasco sauce, and a jar of peppercorns for seasoning, and carried the two bags of groceries back to his apartment. His new plan was to eat two meals a day. He wanted to lose at least ten pounds, so he would eat two boiled eggs and a piece of toast for breakfast each morning, and skip lunch. At night he would eat one bowl of stew, and he had enough ingredients to make a stew that would last for five days. Then, the following week, he planned to make enough chili and beans to last for five evening meals. This would solve his cooking problems, and he could eat two slices of bread with each bowl of stew or chili. On the other two days, when the beef stew or the chili ran out, he would just eat eggs and bread for breakfast, and perhaps go out at night for either a hamburger or a fried fish sandwich. With a plan like this one, he wouldn't get bored with his meals, because when the stew started to bore him, it would be time for two days without stew, and then the following week he could look forward to chili and beans.

Hoke was taken with the simplicity of his plan. He chopped the vegetables for the stew while he browned the cut-up chunks of meat in the cast-iron Dutch oven. Then he dumped in the vegetables, added water, and turned the electric burner to its lowest setting. He threw in a handful of peppercorns, then sat at his dining table to examine the account books Al Paulson had brought him last night.

Three units were rented on one-year leases: to a schoolteacher, to a salad man at the Sheraton Hotel, and to a biology professor from the University of Florida who was on a one-year sabbatical. Hoke, of course, had 201, so there were only four other apartments. Two were already rented to two elderly couples from Birmingham, Alabama, who were vacationing for two months on the island. So two units were still unrented. The sign on the bulletin board in the lobby said that there was a two-week minimum, but the sign hadn't deterred a few people from coming up to Hoke's apartment and asking about weekend rentals. All he could do then was to repeat what the sign said, but that hadn't kept one asshole from Fort Lauderdale from arguing with him about it. There would be more assholes like that, Hoke suspected, from his experience in living at the Eldorado Hotel in Miami Beach for two years. The Eldorado had also been a hotel for permanent or semi-permanent guests, and it didn't take overnighters or weekenders either. Poor old Eddie Cohen, the day and night manager of the Eldorado, must have had a hundred arguments with transients who just wanted an overnight stay. The best thing to do, Hoke decided, was to try and get all permanent residents for one-year leases, if he possibly could. If he could manage that, he could just collect the rent from everyone once a month and hang out a NO VACANCY sign. Perhaps the best way to start was to change the policy from a minimum rental of two weeks to a two-month minimum? Hoke went downstairs, crossed out "weeks" and wrote in "months" above it. His father might not like the new policy, but then he wouldn't have to tell him about it—not until he had the empty units rented, anyway.

Paulson had also given him a list of people to call when things went wrong—a plumber, an electrician, a handyman, and a phone number for Mrs. Delaney, a widow who lived in a private home two blocks away. She cleaned apartments when they were vacated, and was paid a flat rate of thirty-five dollars, no matter how dirty or clean the apartment was when the tenants left. Hoke recalled her name vaguely from when he was a boy, but couldn't remember what she looked like. Perhaps, when the time came to clean the next vacated apartment, he could do it himself and pocket the thirty-five bucks. He could see already, from the cost of the groceries at the Giant Market, that a hundred bucks a week wasn't going to go very far.

When he resigned, he could either take his retirement-fund money in a lump sum, or leave it and wait until he was fifty-seven, and then draw a small monthly retirement check. He didn't know which one was the best course to follow. He didn't like the idea of living on one hundred dollars a week for the next fourteen years. But he didn't want to think about money right now. He didn't want to think about Ellita and her baby, Sue Ellen, or Aileen. He didn't want to think about anything at all.

Hoke stripped down to his shorts and went to sleep on the Bahama bed, with a warm, damp wind blowing over his body from the window facing the sea.

CHAPTER 6

When Stanley saw Mr. Sneider standing beside his tow truck waiting for him, he involuntarily put the fingers of his right hand to his cut lip and considered darting back inside the jail.

"Everything's all right, Mr. Sinkiewicz," Sneider said, holding up a hand. "I'm here to drive you home."

Sneider opened the door to the cab, and Stanley climbed into the passenger seat. After Sneider got into the cab, he sat for a long moment with both hands on the wheel, staring through the windshield. Sneider was a hairy, ursine man, who had grown a bushy black beard after retiring from the service. His fingernails were black with embedded grease, and Stanley could smell beer on Sneider's breath.

"This whole thing's been a damned farce, Mr. Sinkiewicz, and I want to apologize. I had no reason to hit you, even though I thought you were going to run. I just wasn't thinking clearly, that's all, after talking to my wife and Mrs. Sinkiewicz. Besides, I had a bad day. A bastard in a blue Electra stiffed me for twenty bucks' worth of gas. He filled up at self-service and tore out of there at sixty miles an hour. But that's beside the point. I'm still sorry, but that's what happens when you listen to two hysterical women talking at the same time."

"I—I didn't do nothing bad to Pammi."

"I know that now, but I didn't know it at the time, you see.

"After I got back home from here I had a long talk with Pammi in her bedroom and managed to get the truth out of her. I know now you didn't instigate anything, because Pammi has been carrying on with a couple of old geezers in the park in the evening. We've been letting her go out after dinner, because she was supposed to play with her friend Ileana down the street. Instead, she's been meeting one old fart or another in the pinochle shed in the park. Apparently this has been going on for weeks. She's still a virgin, however. I checked that out myself, and her hymen's still in one piece. But she's been doing some other dirty things with these old men that I'd rather not go into just now. I think you know what I mean."

"I was asleep, and she stuck her tongue in my mouth and asked for a penny."

Sneider sighed. "I know. She told me. You're off the hook, Mr. Sinkiewicz, and I'm sorry if I caused you any trouble. But that fucker in the blue Electra had me going to begin with—well, what difference does it make? Did you get any dinner? If not, I'll spring for a Big Mac and a shake before I take you home." Sneider started the engine and put the stick into first gear.

"I'm not hungry. I had a piece of corn bread, and my lip's too sore to eat anyway."

"You could probably use a stitch or two, but if you've got some adhesive tape at home, I can put a butterfly stitch on it for you, and it'll be good as new in a day or so."

"There's some tape in the medicine cabinet. It's old, though."

"That don't make no difference. Adhesive tape, unless it gets wet or dried out in the sun or something, is good for years."

On the drive to Ocean Pines Terraces, Sneider told Stanley about a kid he caught breaking into his Coke machine a couple of weeks back. "He didn't get anything, but when I took the kid home to his father, I told his old man that the kid had stolen about ten dollars' worth of Cokes from me during the last month or so, and the guy came up with ten bucks." Sneider laughed, relishing the story.

When Sneider pulled into Stanley's driveway, Stanley noticed that his Escort wasn't in the carport. "Is Maya still with your wife, Sergeant Sneider?"

"No. My wife went off to one of her meetings, and I made her take Pammi along. I don't know where your wife is. Let's go inside, and I'll fix up your lip."

Stanley found the roll of tape and got a pair of scissors from Maya's sewing basket, and Sneider put a neat butterfly bandage on Stanley's lip. "Just leave it there for two or three days. Shave around it, and the old lip'll be as good as new."

The two men shook hands at the door, and Sneider apologized again before driving off down the street in his tow truck. Stanley looked around the house for a note, but didn't find one. Then he stopped looking, realizing that if Maya knew that he was in jail, she wouldn't leave a note for him because she wouldn't expect him to be coming home to read it. Stanley went next door to the Agnews' and rapped on the front door. The jalousies on the door opened slightly, but not the door.

"Go away!" Mrs. Agnew said.

"Is my wife in there with you, Mrs. Agnew?"

"No, she isn't, and if you don't go away, you pervert, I'll call the police!"

"Do you know where she went?"

The jalousies were cranked closed. Stanley could hear Mrs. Agnew's tapping footsteps as she walked across her terrazzo floor toward the kitchen. Stanley returned to his house and sat in his recliner. He knew he was too restless to watch television. After a few moments, he went into the bedroom and took off his bloodied shirt. As he threw the dirty shirt into the hamper beside the open closet door, he noticed that the Samsonite two-suiter wasn't on the closet shelf. He looked through the clothes in the closet. There seemed to be a few things missing, but he wasn't sure. He looked for Maya's photo album, where she kept the family snapshots, including the ones of the grandchildren Junior sent down from time to time. When he couldn't find the album, he knew that Maya was gone. Her checkbook was missing from the little corner desk in the living room where she worked on the household accounts, and so was her little recipe file box.

She was gone. No question about it.

Stanley looked up the number and direct-dialed his son in Hamtramck. Junior's voice was a little garbled at first because his mouth was full of food.

"It's me," Stanley said, "and I'm calling long distance from Florida. Have you heard from your mother?"

"Just a sec, Dad." Junior finished chewing. "Are you calling from the jail?"

"No, I'm home. I'm calling from home."

"Mom said you were in jail when she called me. How'd you get out? She said you were arrested for molesting some little kid."

"It was all a mistake, son. Maya didn't see what she thought she saw, and that's all been cleared up now."

"Is Mom still there, Dad? I'd like to talk to her."

"No, she isn't here. I just wondered if she called you. I don't know where she is."

"In that case, she's already left, Dad. She said she was

coming back here to Detroit, that's what she called to tell me, and that was that. Now, I realize you own the house up here and all that, but I told her we didn't have any room for her. Christ, Dad, we've only got two bedrooms and one bath, so where'll we put Mom?"

"She's driving up, then? I don't think she can find her way to Detroit, and the Escort's due for an oil change, too."

"If she's already left, there's nothing we can do about it, I guess. But when she gets up here, I'll send her back after a couple of days. We really can't put her up for more than one or two days. Maybe I can make reservations for her at the Howard Johnson's, or some motel near the house. Too bad you didn't get out of jail soon enough to stop her from leaving. A woman Mom's age shouldn't be driving all the way across the country by herself."

"She'll get lost. There's no doubt about that."

"No, I don't think she'll get lost, Dad. She can always ask the way to Michigan at a gas station. D'you want to talk to the kids while you're on the phone?"

"No. Did you call the jail, Junior, and try to get me out?"

"I didn't call anybody. I was trying to talk Mom out of coming up here, and then she hung up on me. I'm trying to eat dinner now. I've really had a bitch of a day. Mom was in a hurry and told me she'd give me the details when she got here. What happened, anyway?"

"Nothing happened. When your mother gets there, she can give you her version of the details. And you can also tell her for me that I won't take her back. Tell her to keep the damned Escort and look for a job. You can also tell her not to cash any checks with the checkbook she took with her either, because the account is now closed!"

Stanley hung up the phone. His face was flushed and his fingers trembled. He went into the kitchen and heated water to make a cup of instant coffee. Before the water boiled, the phone rang. At first he wasn't going to answer it, figuring it was Stanley Junior calling him back, but when it kept ringing he finally picked it up on the eighth ring.

"Listen, Dad," Junior said, "and please don't hang up. If the trouble's all cleared up, and if Momma calls me again from wherever she is on the road, I'll just tell her to go back home. Okay? Of course, she knows what she saw, and all that, but I think I can talk her into going back, especially now that you're out of jail. I'd like to see her, of course, and so would the kids, and all, but we really don't have any room here for her—and that's a fact."

"I won't take her back, Junior. Mom's your problem now, not mine. If that's the way Maya thinks about me after all these years, I don't want the woman around. She never liked it down here in Florida anyway. So from now on, she's your—"

"Let's talk a minute, Dad."

"There's nothing else to talk about. She made up her mind, and I've made up mine. Just make sure you keep sending me the rent money every month, and don't give it to Maya. I still have to pay the mortgage down here. Understand?"

"Okay, Dad, but I think we'd better discuss this later, after you and Momma have a chance to cool off some. We'll work some—"

"It's already worked out, Junior. Just give my love to the kids. You called *me* this time, and you're on long distance, you know."

"Right, Dad. Do you need any help from me? Can I get you a lawyer? If you need a lawyer, I can check around here, and see if—"

"I don't need no lawyer, because I'm not in any trouble. Your mother's in trouble, not me. Get a lawyer for Maya. Good night, son." Stanley hung up the phone.

Stanley tried to calm down. He drank his coffee at the

kitchen table. His heart was beating rapidly, and he could almost feel it inside his chest. He was disappointed in his son, as well as in Maya. If the situation had been reversed, and he had learned that Junior was in jail for molesting a child, he would have been on the phone, or gone to the jail with a lawyer immediately. And no matter what they said, he wouldn't have believed Junior guilty of doing something like that. But Junior hadn't even called the jail to find out what they were doing with his father.

With Maya gone, his life would be a little harder now. He would have to cook his own meals, clean the house, and do his own laundry, but he would rather do that than take her back. That's what their marriage had come down to anyway, a division of labor, just two people sharing the same house. For months Maya had tried to talk to him about moving back to Hamtramck, and every time she brought it up he had refused to discuss it.

"We made our decision when we came down here," he told her, "and we're settled in now. If you want to go up there on a visit, you can go by yourself. I don't ever want to see ice and snow again. Just call Junior and tell him you're coming back to visit for a couple of weeks or a month—and see what he says!"

Maya hinted to Junior on the phone a few times that she would like to visit, but she didn't get an invitation, and she didn't come right out and ask for one because she knew she wouldn't get one, and Stanley knew she wouldn't ever get one. So this "incident" with Pammi was the first real excuse she had to leave, her first opportunity, and she had taken it because Junior couldn't turn her away if Stanley was in jail. Well, as far as Stanley was concerned, she could stay there, too. He had his pride, and he wouldn't take her back. He might if she begged him, but he didn't think she would do that. In her own way, she was as stubborn as he was; she didn't like Florida, and she didn't need Stanley any more than he needed her.

Well, he could take care of himself. It was all over, and he was too exhausted to think about it any longer. Without finishing his coffee, Stanley went into the bedroom to lie down for a moment, to quiet the rapid beating of his heart.

A minute later, Stanley was asleep, and he didn't awaken until morning.

It was still dark when Stanley got up at five A.M. and shaved. He scrambled two eggs in butter and toasted himself two slices of bread. He made instant coffee instead of using the Mr. Coffee machine, because he didn't know how to work it and he couldn't find the directions in the kitchen drawer where Maya kept all of the warranties for their appliances.

Stanley was disappointed in his son, but no longer angry with him. The boy (Junior was almost forty years old) hadn't turned out as well as he should have, even though Stanley had paid for Junior's two years of community college. Junior had been fired from both Ford and Chrysler because he had been unable to adjust to working on the line. After a series of low-paying jobs, he had finally found a job selling new cars for Joe "Madman" Stuart Chrysler in Detroit. The last time Stanley had talked to his son on the phone, the boy had been on the verge of tears. Junior worked for an unrealistic and demanding sales manager who'd had an old-fashioned cardboard outhouse built, complete with a cutout quarter moon on the door. The salesman with the lowest sales each week had to stay seated in the "shithouse" during the weekly sales meetings and pep talks. Any salesman who ended up in the shithouse for three weeks in a row was fired automatically. Junior spent one or two meetings a month in this mock-up and had barely escaped the terminal third week on two different occasions. For some time, it had been in the back of Stanley's mind to suggest to Junior that he move down to Florida when he got fired, as he was bound to be sooner or later, so he could get a fresh start in life. But that was out now. And if Junior fell behind in the rent payments, Stanley would have him evicted. It was just a token rent he paid anyway; the Hamtramck house should be renting for $325, or even $350 a month.

After breakfast, Stanley got a notebook from the desk and made a list of things he had to do. He used to make a similar list the first thing every morning when he had worked in the Ford paint shop, and the methodical planning of his days there had worked well for him since.

First, he would close his bank account, move to another bank, and put the account in his name only. He would also cash in his three ten-thousand-dollar CDs and pay the early withdrawal penalty. He could then take out three new CDs under his own name. He hated to lose money to the penalty, but if Maya cashed any of them he would lose every cent.

Should he buy a new car? No, he could wait on that for a while. The municipal bus ran into downtown Riviera Beach every hour, and he could ride it into town. He had never been without a car, as far back as he could remember, but he could watch the list of repossessed cars that the banks posted every week until a good deal came along. It didn't pay to rush into buying a car, whether it was new or used. And maybe a used car would be the best buy after all. It was the same when Saul, Maya's old Airedale, died. She had wanted to buy a new puppy to replace the old dog, but he had reminded her that at their age any dog they bought now would probably outlive them and that there would be no one left to take care of it when they were gone.

Stanley had hated the flatulent Saul and didn't want another stinking dog hanging around the house and begging at the table. At his age, he wouldn't outlast a new car, either, so why not buy a cheaper, secondhand one?

On the way back from the bank he would stop at the supermarket and buy a dozen or so TV dinners. They were simple to fix. All he had to do was put them into the toaster oven for twenty-five minutes at 425° and his dinner would be ready. He had often asked Maya why she didn't fix TV dinners instead of preparing time-consuming meals from scratch every day, but she wouldn't hear of it. Probably because she didn't know what else to do with her time, he supposed.

Before going into town he would do his laundry, and when he came back he could put it into the dryer. There was nothing to that. He knew how to use the washer and the dryer. Then, while the laundry was drying, he could go down to the park and tell the Wise Old Men that he was a bachelor now.

Stanley's mind froze.

They would know that already. They would also know by now that he had been arrested as a child molester. He was innocent, of course, but Sergeant Sneider had told him that there were two other old geezers involved with Pammi, and it was quite possible that one, or both, of them were Wise Old Men. Whoever it was would lay low now, but any man once accused—as he was, even though he was innocent—would always be suspect. He didn't think any of the Wise Old Men would actually say anything to him about it, but they would think about it—and figure it was him—and he didn't want to sit there while they looked at him sideways and speculated about his guilt. No, it would be a long time before he could go to the park again—if ever. On the other hand, the longer he stayed away from the park, the more they would consider him guilty.

He couldn't win either way.

Stanley separated his clothes from Maya's and put her dirty clothing into a brown paper grocery bag. He sure as hell wasn't going to wash *her* things. When she got around to sending for her clothes, he would pack them up and send them to her dirty. He looked through the pockets of his bloodied shirt and came across the news clipping Troy Louden had handed him. He hadn't forgotten about it; he had merely put it out of his mind, which wasn't the same thing. This errand had priority over everything else he had to do, but he was reluctant to deliver a message like that. It wouldn't do the young man any good. But he had said that he would do it, so he might as well. There was a Big 5 writing tablet on Maya's desk. Stanley printed out the message in block letters:

IF YOU DON'T DROP THE CHARGES, I'LL KILL YOUR BABY AND YOUR WIFE AND THEN YOU.

The printed message looked sinister all right, but it also looked unreal. Stanley then printed ROBERT SMITH under the message and sealed it in one of Maya's pastel pink envelopes, along with the clipping. Then he printed Collins's address on the envelope. There was only one Henry Collins listed in the West Palm Beach section of the phone book.

Even if the message didn't help Troy, it couldn't hurt him any. If Mr. Collins brought it in to the police station, Troy could deny that he sent it. How could he? He was in jail. Stanley put the sealed envelope into his hip pocket, collected his checkbook, certificates of deposit, and passbook, but he paused at the door. It was eight A.M., and the sun was blazing. He put on his billed cap and his sunglasses, and got his walking stick from the umbrella stand beside the door, but still he hesitated. Mrs. Agnew was out in her yard, watering the oleanders that grew close to her house. She would turn her back on him the moment he stepped outside. He could count on that. But all the other neighbors on the two-block walk to the bus stop would peer through their windows and point him out as the dirty old man who had molested little Pammi Sneider. Except by sight, Stanley didn't know his neighbors very well. But Maya knew them all because they often met at each other's houses in the morning when the bakery truck stopped on their street. The housewives would come out in their wrappers and buy sweet rolls and doughnuts and take turns meeting in each other's houses for coffee. Maya had picked up gossip this way about the various neighbors, and had often tried to tell him about how Mrs. Meeghan's dyslexic son was failing in school, or about Mr. Featherstone's alcoholism (he was a house painter), but Stanley had always cut her off. He didn't care anything about these people, didn't know them, didn't want to know them, and didn't want to know anything about them. If they had been men he worked with, or something like that, he might have been interested in their private doings, but he wasn't interested in these housewives or their husbands or their noisy children.

But he realized now that these women would be gossiping about him and about Maya's leaving him, because that's what they did best—pry into other people's lives. Stanley steeled himself and walked to the bus stop, without looking either to the right or the left.

Stanley got off at the Sunshine Plaza Shopping Center when the bus stopped in front of the Publix. The bank wasn't open yet, so he drank a cup of coffee in Hardee's and slipped a dozen packets of Sweet 'n Low into his pants pocket. When the bank opened (it was really a Savings & Loan Association, but it also operated as a bank), Stanley had no trouble cashing in his CDs and collected a cashier's check for the money in his savings and checking accounts. He had expected an argument. But why would they argue? They made a handsome profit off him when he cashed in his three one-year CDs early. As he left the bank officer's desk, Mr. Wheeler said:

"We're sorry to lose you as a client, Mr. Sinkiewicz, but I suppose you need your money for bail—"

"Bail? What're you talking about?"

"It was on the radio this morning—your, ah, trouble, and all, you know. So I assumed you required funds for a lawyer, and to post bond."

"No." Stanley shook his head. "That matter was all a mistake. It's all cleared up now."

"I'm glad to hear it, Mr. Sinkiewicz," Mr. Wheeler said, smiling. "It was a pleasure to serve you."

Stanley walked over to U.S. 1 and waited for the bus to West Palm Beach. He realized now that all the time he had been talking to Mr. Wheeler, the banker had been staring at the bandage on his lip. He had probably wanted to ask about it, but didn't have the nerve. And all the time, Wheeler figured he was dealing with a child molester out of jail temporarily, on bail. If there had been something about his arrest on the radio, maybe there had been something on the local TV newscast, too. Stanley felt his heart pound again, and he slumped on the bus-stop bench.

The bus came at last, and he rode into West Palm Beach, getting off at the downtown Clematis Street stop. He deposited his cashier's check of $38,314.14 in a money-market checking account and withdrew fifty dollars with his new temporary checkbook before leaving the new S & L. Interest rates on CDs had dropped, and he could earn almost as much interest in the new money-market account as he could from buying new CDs. Besides, he wanted to have his money readily available in case he wanted to buy a car. He also filled out forms to have his UAW pension and Social Security checks transferred to his new account.

Before leaving the S & L, he asked the young woman who had opened his new account how to get to Spring Street, in West Palm Beach. She gave him complicated directions that would entail two bus transfers, and he couldn't understand what she was talking about. Being without a car gave a man an entire new way of looking at the world. He thought he knew West Palm fairly well, just from driving around and going to the library, but he didn't know it at all when it came to public transportation. He walked to the Greyhound bus station and got a Veteran's cab. The driver, a black man wearing a woman's nylon stocking cap with a little topknot in it, didn't know where Spring Street was, either. He had to call the dispatcher on his radio for directions. It was a three-fifty ride to Mr. Collins's house, where Stanley got out and told the driver to wait for him.

Collins's house was a two-bedroom, lemon-colored concrete-block-and-stucco building on a short dead-end street with eleven other houses constructed from the same plans. A pudgy young woman was listlessly spreading sand on a dying front lawn. There was a baby, eighteen months or perhaps two years old, in a plain pine playpen on the front porch. The barefooted woman wore faded blue shorts and a lime-colored elastic tube top. The pile of yellow sand was about six feet high, and she was taking a small shovelful at a time from the pile and sprinkling it awkwardly on the lawn. She was perspiring freely. Stanley checked the house number against the address on the envelope.

"Excuse me. You Mrs. Collins?"

She nodded, a little out of breath, and looked incuriously from Stanley to the cab, then back at Stanley. The driver had his door open and was reading a comic book that had Bugs Bunny on the cover.

"Is Mr. Collins home?"

She shook her head. "No, he ain't. He's out gettin' estimates on the car. He had a accident yesterday, and he has to get three estimates before he can go to the insurance company for the money. At least that's what they told him on the phone. Tomorrow he has to go back up to Jax, so he has to get the car fixed today. I don't know when he'll get home."

Stanley felt a great sense of relief. It was much easier this way, dealing with a young woman instead of a truck driver. "I don't have to see your husband, Mrs. Collins. I found this envelope downtown on Clematis Street. I figured it might be important, and since there wasn't any stamp on it, I got a cab and brought it on out." He tried to hand the woman the envelope, but she wouldn't take it.

"I'm pretty busy right now, and I can't spend no time listening to you tryin' to sell me something. I'm tryin' to spread some of this sand around this mornin' before it gets too hot, and it's almost too hot to be out here now."

"You better take it. I don't want nothing for my trouble, but as you can see, the meter's ticking on my cab, so I can't stay and talk with you."

She dropped the shovel on the ground, wiped the palms of her hands on her shorts, and took the envelope. As Stanley started to back away, she tore it open and frowned as she read the short message. She looked up, puzzled, and started to unfold the news clipping.

"I don't understand this at all. Who are you?"

"I'm a retired foreman," Stanley said, pausing beside the taxi, "and I was shopping downtown when I found that envelope, that's all. All I am, I guess, is a good Samaritan. But I'll tell you something else I've learned living down here in Florida. If it was chinch bugs and army worms that killed your lawn, sand won't get rid of them. You'll have to get an exterminator out here to spray your lawn, and it'll run you about thirty-five dollars."

Stanley tapped the driver's comic book with the end of

his stick, got into the back seat of the cab, and closed the door. Mrs. Collins rushed over. "Just a minute! What's all this mean? I don't understand what this is all about!"

"I don't know either," Stanley said, pushing down the door lock. "It's addressed to your husband, so maybe he knows. Let's go, driver."

The driver closed his door, put down his comic book, and made a U-turn back toward Pierce Avenue. The woman stayed at the curb, staring at the retreating cab for a moment, and then unfolded the clipping again.

Stanley caught the bus back to Riviera Beach and got off at the International Shopping Mall. He watched a demonstration class of middle-aged aerobic dancers perform in the plaza section for about a half-hour, then had a slice of pizza and a Diet Coke at Cozzoli's while he waited for the movies to open at one o'clock. He got an Early Bird ticket and sat through two showings of *The Terminator* before coming out into the mall again. Because of daylight savings time, it still wasn't dark enough to go home, so he wandered around the mall until the nine P.M. bus left for Ocean Pines Terraces.

It had been awful to walk those two blocks that morning, with all the neighbors looking at him, so he wanted to make certain it was dark before he went home. He was exhausted from the long day, and he had missed his afternoon nap. There was so much shooting going on in the movie, he hadn't been able to sleep in the theater, either. Stanley went to bed and fell asleep immediately. He forgot to put the damp wash in the dryer, and the next morning the laundry was covered with mildew and he had to wash it all over again.

CHAPTER 7

That afternoon, after taking his nap, Hoke knocked on the door of each occupied apartment and introduced himself as the new manager. The schoolteacher, a Ms. Dussalt, had already left the island to spend a month of her summer vacation with her parents in Seffner, Florida. One of the Alabama couples claimed that their toilet kept running after it was flushed. Hoke showed them—both of them—how to jiggle the handle to make it stop.

"And if that doesn't stop it," Hoke said, "take off the lid, reach down in there, and make sure that the rubber stopper's covering the drain."

"That's inconvenient," the woman said. Her tiny lips were pursed, and her abundance of hair had recently been blued.

"That may be," Hoke said, "but if I called a plumber out here for thirty-seven dollars and fifty cents an hour, he'd tell you the same thing."

"At the rentals you all charge, we shouldn't have to spend five minutes or so jiggling the handle every time we use the bathroom."

"I can move you to another apartment if you like. But you've been living here for two weeks already, and if I move you you'll have to pay a thirty-five-dollar cleaning charge for moving before your two months' rent are up."

"That's all right, Mr. Moseley," the woman's husband said quickly. "I don't mind jiggling the handle."

Hoke used his passkey to check Ms. Dussault's apartment, and turned off her water heater. He made a note in his policeman's notebook to turn it on again a day before she would return. The salad man wasn't home, but the college professor was in. He wanted to talk, and Hoke had a difficult time in getting away from him. He was a tall, rather stooped Ohioan in his middle thirties, with long chestnut hair in a ponytail down his back, secured by some rubber bands. He wore a "Go 'Gators" T-shirt, blue-denim cutoffs, and Nike running shoes without socks. He said his name was Ralph Hurt, but everyone at the University of Florida called him Itai, because *itai* meant "hurt" in Japanese. He had once spent an entire year in a Zen monastery in Kyoto, and had talked so much about his experiences in Japan that his colleagues in his department had come up with the nickname. Itai had a year's sabbatical leave at three-quarters' pay, to write a novel.

"You teach English, then? My dad told me you were a biology teacher."

"I am. But I couldn't get a grant to do the research in my field, so I told the board I'd write a novel instead. Sabbaticals are given out on a seniority basis anyway, so the board didn't give a rat's ass what I did so long's I put something down on paper as a project. So I said I'd write a novel, and now I'll have to write one to have something to show my department chairman when I get back. It doesn't have to be a publishable novel, although that would be nice, but I'm going to have to come up with two or three hundred pages of fiction."

"What is your field?"

"Ethiopian horseflies. I'm probably the only American authority on Ethiopian horseflies. Most of the original work on Ethiopian Tabanidae was done by Bequaret and Austen, back in the late twenties, but these early studies were incomplete. Other hot-shots in the field are Bigot, Gerstaeker, and, of course, Enderlein, but there's still a lot to be done. And there hasn't been much recently. The problem, you see, is that these flies can be as troublesome after they die as they are in life. The fact that the fly is only caught in the act of aggression seems to lead to a lamentable display of force by collectors."

"You mean it's slapped down on when it bites?"

"Exactly. As a consequence, it's almost impossible to get an Ethiopian *Haematopta* intact, you see. What I really wanted to do was to go to northern Ethiopia and do my own collecting. There's only so much a man can learn from plates, and I only have a half-dozen preserved specimens up at Gainesville to study. A man could write a long and very important book on wing variations alone, if he had the specimens. But I've only got one wing specimen that's half-way intact. I didn't know you were so interested in horse-flies, Mr. Moseley."

"I'm not. But I guess it must be an important field of study."

"It is, definitely. There's no such thing as a group of immaculately preserved specimens, and until there is, all we have is a somewhat spurious appearance of accuracy in the studies published so far. At any rate, in lieu of going to Africa, I have to write a fucking novel to get my year off. Please excuse me. Sometimes I don't watch my language, although I'm careful around students."

"I don't always watch mine either," Hoke admitted.

"The novel's coming along, though. I'm writing about a college professor at Gainesville, a history professor, who's having an affair with one of his students—an orthodontist's daughter from Fort Lauderdale. She works part-time in a wicker furniture factory, and they meet there at night to make love."

"Does she have bad teeth?"

"Yes. How'd you know that?"

"I don't know, but it seems to me I've already read a novel like that in a paperback—or maybe it was a movie?"

"You must be mistaken, Mr. Moseley. This is a true story, based on my own experiences. But I've disguised it by making the hero a history professor instead of an entomologist. The girl actually worked in a seat-cover shop—for cars—and her father was a peridontist, not an orthodontist."

"That's a fairly thin disguise."

"You're probably right, but entomologists aren't expected to be particularly inventive. The manuscript won't be publishable anyway, and the department chairman won't even read it, so it doesn't matter. He'll just count the pages, and if there're more than two hundred he'll be satisfied. Writing it, though, is a kind of therapy for me. I'm lonely down here, and I'd much rather be in Ethiopia, collecting. Maybe you can come down some evening and have a drink? I can tell you a lot more about horseflies, or we can talk a little about Zen—"

"I don't think so. My father owns the El Pelicano, and he told me he'd rather not have me socializing too much with the tenants."

"That's absurd. Well, take these along anyway." The professor got a three-volume set of H. Oldroyd's *The Horse-Flies (Diptera: Tabanidae) of the Ethiopian Region* from the pile of books beside his desk and handed them to Hoke. The three books were heavy; altogether, Hoke figured, they weighed ten or twelve pounds.

"I'll get these back to you as soon as I can, Dr. Hurt."

"Itai. Just call me Itai, and there's no hurry. If you have

any questions, I'm home most of the time, at least when I'm not on the beach."

Hoke returned to his apartment and put the three volumes on his dining table, a small, round affair with a green Formica surface and aluminum legs. There were four straight chairs with foam rubber seats, covered with plastic sheeting, and they too had aluminum legs. The floor was covered with brown linoleum with a square tile design, with narrow beige lines that were supposed to look like grout. There were no rugs in any of the apartments, because sand would get into the carpeting as the tenants came in from the beach, and there was no daily maid service to vacuum up. There was a narrow galley (it wasn't big enough to be called a kitchen), with a Formica counter between it and the living-bedroom. Two sturdy oak stools stood at the counter. The bathroom had a shower but no tub, and this room was so narrow that when Hoke sat on the toilet his knees touched the wall. The two single Bahama beds were in one corner of the living room, with the top third of one bed pushed beneath a square coffee table that held a clear glass lamp, two feet high, filled with seashells. When the El Pelicano was a hotel, only one door was required, but now Florida law required two doors for apartments. When Frank converted the rooms into efficiency apartments, he had added the extra door right next to each entrance door, but this useless exit was blocked inside each apartment by the dining table. The two doors, the galley, and the windows took up most of the wall space on three sides. There was room enough on the remaining wall, however, for a picture. The framed print, a cheap reproduction of Winslow Homer's "The Gulf Stream," was the same in all eight apartments, and was bolted to the wall to prevent its theft. Also bolted to the wall and chained in the galley were a toaster oven and an electric can-opener.

Like the picture, these were highly pilferable items. A window air conditioner occupied the bottom half of one window, but the view of the ocean from the other window by the Bahama bed was excellent. Hoke usually sat at the table instead of the counter, because when he looked up he liked to see the semi-naked black man lying in the damaged boat floating in the current. The black man seemed indifferent to his fate, whatever it was going to be, and appeared to be contented with his hopeless condition, drifting along with the Gulf Stream.

The stew in the big iron pot, simmering on the small stove, smelled wonderful to Hoke, but although he was hungry he planned to put off eating for as long as possible. If he ate too early, it would be a long time until breakfast, and he was limiting himself to only one bowlful.

Hoke opened Volume I of *Horse-Flies of the Ethiopian Region* and read the introduction. He didn't understand most of the technical terms, but the plates in the book were beautifully delineated, with an attention to detail that seemed painstakingly precise. By studying the plates closely, Hoke could see what Dr. Hurt—Itai—meant by damaged specimens. Some of the segments on the antennae were missing, and so were parts of the legs. The delineator had not guessed, or filled in the missing parts, but that, Hoke supposed, was what real science was all about.

In science, if it wasn't there, you couldn't just guess at something and fill it in, whereas detective work was just the opposite. You took what you had, the facts you could find, and then tried your best to fill in those missing parts until you came up with a complete picture. Well, he wouldn't have to worry about detection any longer. No more guesswork. These books, which he had been so reluctant to accept, were just the right sort of reading. He could read them when he didn't feel like working out a chess problem (after he got settled in, he planned to buy a board and chessmen and a book of problems), and he wouldn't get emotionally involved with the horseflies. He might have to buy a biology dictionary, however, to learn the definitions of some of the special words entomologists used. Maybe Itai had one; if so, he could borrow the professor's, a little later on—

There was a knock on the door, a rat-tat-tat of one knuckle.

Hoke opened the door, and there was his daughter Aileen. She exposed her crooked, overlapping white teeth in a wide grin. She was wearing jeans, a pink T-shirt, and tennis shoes. As she encircled Hoke's naked waist to hug him, and stood on tiptoe to kiss him, Hoke pulled back and looked over her shoulder.

"Did Ellita drive you up, or what?"

"I drove up myself. I didn't have any trouble at all."

"But you don't have a license!"

"Sure I do!" Aileen giggled and put her leather drawstring purse on the table. She opened the drawstring, found her wallet, took out a Florida driver's license, and handed it to her father.

"This is Sue Ellen's license," Hoke said. "If a trooper'd stopped you, you couldn't have passed as your sister. You girls don't look anything alike."

"But I wasn't stopped, Daddy. Now that I've proved I can drive, you ought to help me get a learner's permit so I can at least drive around in the daytime."

"I don't want you driving yet, honey, you aren't aggressive enough to drive in Florida. Where'd you park my car?"

"Over there—in the mall lot."

"Give me the keys. I'll move it to the manager's slot next to the entrance."

After they got the car, and Hoke reparked it by the entrance, he asked her what were in all of the cardboard boxes in the back seat.

"I brought my things, too, Daddy, along with stuff for you. I'm going to stay with you for the rest of your leave."

"Who told you that?"

"We had a family conference, me, Ellita, and Sue Ellen. Sue Ellen's got her job at the car wash, and Ellita'll be having her baby soon, so I had to be the one—and I *wanted* to be the one—to come up and look after you. Besides, Ellita's mother's going to move in before the baby comes."

"I can take care of myself. You girls are going out to California to live with your mother."

"No." Aileen shook her head. "We voted against that. Sue Ellen decided she isn't going back to school in September. She's sixteen and she's got a good job, so she can drop out legally. We don't want to live with Mom and Curly Peterson. And you know that Curly doesn't want us around."

"Just take what you need upstairs, and we'll leave the rest of the stuff in the car for now."

"Won't someone break in and steal them?"

"This is Singer Island, not Miami. Besides, there's no room for all of that stuff upstairs. When your grandfather converted the hotel to apartments, he had to use the closets for kitchens. So except for a few hooks by the galley doorway, and that little alcove in the bathroom, there isn't much room to store anything."

Aileen paused in the small lobby, holding her train case in her right hand. "What about the room behind the counter, Daddy?"

"That was the old office, when this place was a hotel. It's full of odds and ends now, a couple of rollaway beds and some other crap."

"If I cleaned it out I could make it into a bedroom, or we could store some of our stuff there."

"Never mind the 'we.' You can stay tonight, but I'm sending you back on the bus tomorrow."

"I'm not going back. You need someone to look after you; we decided." She walked into the apartment ahead of him. "I know you aren't sick, or anything like that, but you're still acting funny, and Ellita doesn't want you living all by yourself."

"What I do is none of Ellita's business."

"She's your partner, Daddy, and she's concerned about you."

"I'm quitting the department. I already told her that. I just haven't put my papers in yet because I've had a lot of other things to do. So Ellita won't be my partner much longer."

Aileen began to leaf through the books on the table. "These books are all about Ethiopian horseflies."

"I know. I've been studying them."

"Horseflies? I don't know, Daddy. You say you're all right and all that, and I believe you because you look fine—rested and all. But if I called Ellita and told her you were studying a three-volume set of books on Ethiopian horseflies, I think she'd be up here like a shot—"

"Don't get smart. There's a college professor who lives here, and he lent them to me for a few days. He's writing a novel."

"Really? What about?"

"It's about—I haven't read any of it. But don't bother him about it, either. A man writing a novel doesn't want to be bothered by some nosy kid asking a lot of dumb questions."

"Okay, Daddy, I won't say anything to him. That stew smells awful good."

"I guess you want some stew, too." Hoke said it in a way that would let her think he didn't care whether she ate any of it or not—but he did care. Aileen never seemed to gain any weight, but she was a voracious eater, so he knew she would want at least two helpings of stew. There went his plan. The stew wouldn't last two people for any five meals, and Aileen always ate a substantial lunch, too. And she liked to eat sweet things between meals. He didn't know what to do with the girl. He hated the idea of calling his ex-wife and asking her to take Aileen back—especially if Sue Ellen refused to go, too. Sue Ellen was bullheaded, and if he insisted that she return to her mother, Sue Ellen might just move out of the house and find a room somewhere in Miami. She was already making more than $150 a week at the Green Lakes Car Wash, and if she started to work overtime on Saturdays she would be more than able to support herself. But at sixteen, Sue Ellen shouldn't be living all by herself in Miami. Christ, how in the hell could a man simplify his life?

Aileen came up behind him, put her long arms around his waist, and rubbed her cheek on his hairy back. "I missed you, Daddy. I—we were all so worried about you. But you're going to be fine. I'll take good care of you, you'll see."

"I'm fine now. Just look in the cupboard above the sink, and set the table. You'll find plastic plates, two plastic bowls, and some wooden-handled silverware in the drawer beside the sink. So set the table, and I'll dish up the stew."

After they finished eating, Aileen excused herself and left the apartment, saying that there was something she needed in the car. She was gone for more than fifteen minutes. While she was gone, Hoke put the leftover stew in the refrigerator and washed the dishes and silverware. When she came back empty-handed, Hoke asked what it was she had forgotten in the car.

"Chewing gum." She opened her mouth to show him the gum. "But while I was downstairs I took the old broom that was behind the counter and swept the lobby. It really needed it, and so do the hallways, upstairs and down."

"Jesus." Hoke shook his head. He remembered then that on top of acting as a rental agent, he was also responsible for keeping the apartment house clean; for keeping the small lawn mowed; and for checking that all of the garbage was put into the dumpster outside, if and when the tenants left stuff lying around. Maybe it might not be a bad idea to keep Aileen around for two or three days until he could get things policed up, and *then* he could send her back to Miami.

Aileen took her Monopoly game out of one of the cardboard boxes she had brought upstairs earlier and began to set it up on the dining table. "Let's play some Monopoly, Daddy. What do you want to play? The slow game or the fast game?"

"The slow, regular game, I guess. What's the hurry?"

CHAPTER

8

After Stanley rewashed the laundry and put it into the dryer, he sat in his recliner and wondered what to do with himself. He had forgotten to stop at the supermarket to buy the TV dinners, but there were all kinds of canned goods in the storage cabinet. There were also eggs, milk, hamburger, and a few tomatoes in the refrigerator, so he could get by without going to the market for a few days.

He didn't want to leave the house and have people stare at him and whisper. Perhaps one of the Wise Old Men would come by and offer him some moral support? He dismissed this thought at once. He had never invited any of the old men to his house, and none of them had invited him to visit them either. Most of these retirees were a lot like him, he supposed. Their wives ran them out so they could clean up, and the park had just been a place to go—either there, or one of the malls. Stanley didn't have a close relationship with any one of them.

As he had gotten older, Stanley recalled, especially after he had been assigned full-time to the paint shop, he had lost most of the friends he once had on the line. He had lost interest in drinking beer in a noisy tavern. It was more comfortable to sit at home in his underwear, and a lot cheaper to drink a six-pack at home after work. The number of men he had known well dwindled as many of them were replaced by robots; and the new employees were all so much younger than Stanley that he hadn't had anything in common with them. The new men had called him Pop, or somctimes Grandpop, but they hadn't asked him to go bowling with them after work. At one time, Stanley had been keen on bowling, but he hadn't bowled a line now in —hell, it must be fifteen years, at least. In fact, he had given his bowling ball to Junior when he left Hamtramck for Florida.

In other ways, it was kind of pleasant to have the house to himself in the morning. He certainly didn't miss Maya. He didn't have to leave the house and wander around for hours. He could watch "Donahue" himself if he wanted to, instead of getting Maya's secondhand opinion about what the people had said that morning about sexual deviance. He had never been satisfied with her summaries; she always seemed to leave out something important or get it wrong somehow.

He decided he would do all his shopping at night. The market was open until eleven, and the bus ran until ten. In the late evening, he would be much less likely to run into any of his neighbors at the supermarket.

Stanley got his deck of Jumbo index playing cards and laid them out for a game of Klondike on the kitchen table. With the big numbers, he didn't need to wear his reading glasses. He played for almost an hour before he tired of the game, but he didn't beat the cards a single time. There were ways to cheat and win, but Stanley never cheated because he would only be cheating himself.

At ten-thirty the mail came. Stanley waited until the postman got to the next house before opening the door. There was another offer for supplementary insurance for people on Medicare (he got one or two of these solicitations a week) and a circular from Sneider's Union Station offering a free car wash with an $11.95 oil-and-lube job. If he still had the Escort, he would have taken Sneider up on that one, but Maya had the car. No catalogs today. Sometimes Maya received a short letter from one of the grandchildren, usually asking for something or other, which she immediately bought and mailed to them. But Stanley never got any personal mail. He no longer read the children's begging letters either, because they made him so angry. Louise, Junior's wife, encouraged her kids to write Maya and ask for things, Stanley suspected, because brand names were never misspelled, unlike the longer, and even shorter, words in their letters.

Stanley tossed the mail in the trash can. He folded the dry laundry and put it away. The blood on his shirt hadn't washed out altogether, so he put it back into the hamper. He would rewash it a third time the next time he did the laundry, and if it didn't come out then he'd just throw it away. He had plenty of shirts.

Finally it was noon, so he could fix lunch. He heated a bowl of tomato soup, but he wasn't hungry. When Maya fixed it, she put whipped cream in it, but there wasn't any Cool Whip in the refrigerator. He didn't finish the soup. By the time he washed the saucepan and his bowl and spoon, it was only twelve-thirty. Stanley changed the sheets on his twin bed and put the dirty sheets into the hamper. He took a long shower, put on clean underwear, and stretched out on his sweet-smelling bed for a nap. With the venetian blinds closed and the window air conditioner turned to High-Cool, he fell asleep almost immediately.

He was awakened at five by the telephone. When he heard the phone he didn't know how long it had been ringing. It was on the kitchen wall, and Stanley, who was wearing his socks but not his shoes, slipped on the terrazzo floor and almost fell when he rushed to answer it. He picked up the receiver.

"Hello."

There was no answer.

"Hello. Who is this?"

The person at the other end hung up. Stanley hung up, too. He hated it when people did that. If they had a wrong number he expected them to say so, not just hang up without a word. But what if it was intentional? Someone trying to harass him. He could expect that—if someone thought he was a child molester. Well, he wouldn't let that bother him . . . but it *did* bother him. He poured a six-ounce can of prune juice into a glass, added ice cubes, turned on the television, and watched a rerun of "Kojak." He had missed the first few minutes, and it was one he hadn't seen before.

A little after six, just after the news came on, a taxi pulled up outside and stopped at the curb. Stanley went to the window, then hurried to open the front door as Troy Louden came up the walk.

"Evening, Pop. Let me have a five, will you? I've got to pay the cabbie."

Stanley took out his wallet and gave Troy a five-dollar bill.

"Better give me one more, Pop—for a tip."

Troy paid the driver and then came back to the house.

"Sit down, sit down, Troy," Stanley said, indicating the recliner and switching off the TV. "It's good to see you, son! I delivered your message, the way you said, even though I didn't want to. Mr. Collins wasn't to home though, so I gave it to his wife."

"I know, Pop, that's why I'm here. To thank you. The message was just an empty threat, but it worked out just like I told you it would. Collins came down to the lock-up and told them that he'd been mistaken. The knock on his head had confused him, and being dazed that way, he only *thought* I had a gun. The sergeant wasn't too happy about it, but Collins had this bandage on his head so he couldn't say that Collins had intentionally filed a false arrest charge, either. When they let me out, I told the sergeant I wanted to see Collins and tell him there was no hard feelings, but he'd already left. Did you tell Mrs. Collins your name? When you talked to her, I mean?"

"No, I just told her I was a messenger."

"Did you get my clipping back?"

"She kept it. I guess she showed it to Mr. Collins when he got home. He was out getting insurance estimates for his car."

"That's okay, Pop. It was a nice little story, but I've still got a few more clippings."

"Would you like some coffee, Troy? I don't have any beer, but—"

"Coffee'll be fine, but let me fix it. You had dinner yet?"

"I was going to wait till after the news."

"Watch the news, then. I'll fix dinner for both of us, and you stay out here while I work in the kitchen. Hell, that's the least I can do for you."

Instead of watching the news on television, Stanley sat at the pass-through counter while Troy prepared dinner. He delivered a bitter diatribe against his wife for leaving him, against his son, and Sergeant Sneider, and his neighbors, and Mr. Wheeler at the bank. Troy didn't interrupt him until Stanley told him about the mysterious phone call.

"That must've been me, Pop. I borrowed a phone at the station and called to see if you were here. I didn't have any money for a cab or a bus, but I knew if you were home you'd take care of it. I didn't say anything else because I didn't want the sergeant listening in, you know? Ordinarily, I wouldn't've come directly to your house in a cab, but would've taken the bus, got off a couple of stops away from your house. Cab drivers keep a log, so I can be traced to your address. But inasmuch as I'm leaving for Miami, it won't matter. I didn't want to leave for Miami without thanking you—"

"I'm glad it was you, Troy. I don't like the idea of getting scary calls like that."

"You still might get a few crank calls, Pop. But don't worry if you do. People who phone instead of facing you in person aren't the ones you have to worry about. You might get some eggs or rocks thrown at your house at night, too. But that'll be teenagers. They'll hear their folks talking, you see, and they'll consider you fair game. But after the word on your innocence gets around, it'll all blow over. That is, if word does get around. It doesn't seem likely that this Sneider guy and his wife will go around the neighborhood telling everyone that their daughter's a pre-puberty hooker."

"I wish you hadn't told me that."

When dinner was ready, Stanley set the dining-room table. Troy had cooked individual meat loaves, parsley potatoes, and beets *â l'orange*, using a covered bowl of leftover beets he had discovered in the refrigerator. There was no lettuce, but Troy had arranged a decorative pinwheel of alternating tomato and cucumber slices, garnishing the platter with stuffed deviled egg halves. He made eight cups of coffee in the Mr. Coffee machine and showed Stanley how to work it in the future.

"Seems to me, Troy," Stanley said, with his mouth full, "you can do most anything. I never had to learn how to cook, so I never got around to it."

"What you need," Troy advised, "is a housekeeper. A half-day would be plenty. She could clean your house, fix your breakfast and lunch, and then leave your dinner in the fridge to warm up at night."

"I couldn't afford that. I'm on a fixed income."

"Wouldn't cost you much. If you got an illegal Haitian

woman, you could pay her a buck an hour and change your luck on the side."

Stanley put his fork down on his empty plate. He had eaten the beets, a vegetable he detested. "Know what I been thinking, Troy? I was kinda hoping you'd stay here with me for a while. I've never lived alone before, and I'm just rattling around this house. It's only two bedrooms, and the porch, but it seems like a big place for a man all alone. There's a single bed in the guest room, and you can have that all to yourself. And if you want to find a job of some kind in town, you can live here free. Won't cost you a cent."

Troy grimaced. "I don't like the confinement of a steady job, Pop. I thought I explained that to you. I've got a little deal working in Miami, however, which'll bring me in some quick cash—quite a lot of it, if it all works out. But I won't be sure till I get down there and check it out. I'll need to borrow a few dollars from you to get to Miami, for bus fare, because the desk sergeant advised me to leave town. In fact, he was pretty emphatic about it."

"I can let you have thirty dollars. That's about all I've got on me now, but if you want to wait till tomorrow I'll cash a check and give you some more. But I sure wish you'd stay with me for a few days. Hard work never hurt nobody, and a smart young fella like you could get a job easy in Riviera Beach—"

"That's enough!" Troy said. The white scar on his forehead had turned pink. "Who in the fuck are you to tell me how to live? You don't know a damned thing about living. You don't understand your wife, your son, or even how your mind works, and that's because you've never had to use it. I've learned more about living in thirty years than you have in twice that long." Troy got up from the table, took his coffee into the living room, and sat in the recliner.

The old man followed him and put his hand gingerly on

Troy's shoulder. "I'm sorry, son. I didn't mean to rile you none. You don't have to get a job to stay here. I didn't mean that. I never got along good with my son, but I've been able to talk to you, and I've got enough money coming in each month that the two of us can live here pretty good. I'm worried about you, that's all. Going down to Miami, broke as you are, you might get into some trouble."

"I might at that." Troy grinned. "But I don't think so. If everything works out, I won't need any money for a year or so, maybe longer. But I appreciate the offer. Maybe I'll come back from Miami and spend a few days with you—in a couple of weeks or so. How does that sound?"

"It sounds fine. I'll write my phone number down for you, and you can call me when you're coming and I'll get some steaks and stuff."

"Good. How about some kind of dessert?" Troy put his cup on the cobbler's bench that served as a coffee table. "Anything you like. I'll fix it."

"No thanks, Troy, I'm not much on sweets."

"Suit yourself." Troy tapped the cobbler's bench with a forefinger. "I worked in a shoe repair shop once, a program for young offenders in L.A. I really hated the smell of cobbler's glue."

"Now that's a good trade—" Stanley started to say something else, but changed his mind.

Troy cleared the table and washed the dishes, pots, and pans. If Troy had asked him to help, Stanley would have been glad to, but the thought of volunteering never occurred to him. Finished, Troy reentered the living room, drying his hands on a dish towel.

"It's a peculiar thing, old-timer, but a man your age can learn something from me, although it should be the other way 'round. First I'll tell you something about me, and then I'll tell you about you."

"A man can always learn something new." Stanley filled

his pipe. "There's an extra pipe if you want to smoke. I don't have no cigarettes."

"I don't smoke."

"Smoking is a comfort to a man sometimes. I like to smoke a pipe sometimes after dinner, but I don't smoke during the day—"

"Smoking comforts ordinary men, but I'm not an ordinary man. There aren't many like me left." Troy drew his lips back, exposing small even teeth. "And it's a good thing for the world that there isn't. There'll always be a few of us in America, in every generation, because only a great country like America can produce men like me. I'm not a thinker, I'm a doer. I'm considered inarticulate, so I talk a lot to cover it up.

"When you look back a few years, America's produced a fair number of us at that. Sam Houston, Jack London, Stanley Ketchel, Charlie Manson—I met him in Bakersfield once—Jack Black. Did you ever read *You Can't Win*, Jack Black's autobiography?"

"I been a working man most of my life, Troy. I never had much time for reading books."

"You mean you never *took* the time. I've just named a few men of style, my style, although they'd all find the comparison odious. Know why? They were all individualists, that's why. They all made their own rules, the way I do. But most of us won't rate a one-line obit in a weekly newspaper. Sometimes that rankles." Troy paused, and his brow wrinkled. "There was a writer one time . . . funny, I can't think of his name." Troy laughed, and shook his head. "It'll come to me after a while. What I'll do is pretend I don't want to remember it, then it'll come to me. Anyway, this famous writer said that men living in cities were like a bunch of rocks in a leather bag. They're all rubbed up against each other till they're round and smooth as marbles. If they stay in the bag long enough, there'll be no rough edges left, is the idea. But I've managed to keep my rough edges, every sharpened corner.

"But you, old-timer, you're as round and polished as an agate. You've been living in that bag for seventy-one years, man. They could put you on TV as the perfect specimen of American male. You're the son of a Polish immigrant, and you've worked all your life for an indifferent capitalistic corporation. Your son's a half-assed salesman, and you've had the typical, unhappy sexless marriage. And now, glorious retirement in sunny Florida. The only thing missing is a shiny new car in the driveway for you to wash and polish on Sundays."

"I've got a car, Troy! A new Escort, but Maya took it when she left."

"I'm not running you down, Pop. I like you. But life has tricked you. You fell into the trap and didn't know you were caught. But I'm a basic instinctive man, and that's the difference between us. Instinct, Pop." Troy lowered his voice to a whisper. "Instinct. You've survived, but mere existence isn't enough. To live, you have to be aware, and then follow your inclinations wherever they lead. Don't care what others think about you. Your own life is the only important thing, and nothing else matters. Want some more coffee?"

"I better not. I got me a little bladder problem. If I drink more than one cup it gets me up at night."

Troy got another cup of coffee. He returned to the living room and grinned at the puzzled expression on the old man's face.

"If I were in your shoes, Pop, I'd enjoy the situation. Quit feeling sorry for yourself. All of a sudden you've departed from the norm, and now people are noticing you. Yet you're upset because your neighbors are disturbed. Why should you worry about what they say or think about you? You survivors think you're living out here in Ocean

Pines Terraces. What you're doing, you're dying out here."

"I worked hard all my life, and I was a fine craftsman. I took pride in my work—"

"Did you? You hated it, Pop. You told me you got sick every day from the smell of paint and turpentine, but what about the bathroom back there? Did you get sick when you painted the bathroom?"

"No, but that ain't the same as working on the line."

"Sure it is. The paint's the same and the smell's the same. But you didn't get sick because you were working for yourself, and you painted it the color you wanted. I don't want to hurt your feelings, but maybe you should take off the blinders. Where's the phone book? I want to find out when the bus leaves for Miami."

"Right there." Stanley pointed. "Under that pile of *Good Housekeeping* magazines, on the counter."

While Troy looked up the number and called, Stanley's mind raced, trying to think of something to say in his defense. He wanted Troy to have a good opinion of him.

"Two-thirty, Pop. If you'll let me have the thirty bucks now, I'll be on my way."

"You don't have to leave just yet." Stanley put his pipe down, looked into his wallet, and handed Troy thirty dollars. "Sit down awhile, Troy. There's plenty of time. I can always call you another cab when the city buses stop running. I don't want you to think you've hurt my feelings, either. A man don't mind hearing what others think about him, even if they've got it all wrong."

"I don't, Pop, and I don't care what people think of me."

"Well, I like to listen to you, anyway. I liked that part about the rocks in a leather bag. That makes a lot of sense. But a man's born where he's born. And if he's raised in a city, he can't help being a city man."

"I was raised in a city, too. Los Angeles. But if you follow what I'm saying, it's all a matter of awareness and instinct.

Today the times are so damned good it's hard to be an individualist. What you should've done, the first time you came home and puked up your guts, was quit striping cars."

"I couldn't quit, Troy. It was the best job I ever had. I was newly married, too. I guess I can't really explain it, but most people in Detroit'll work for an auto company if they can. The union did a lot for us, too, you know."

"Have you got an alarm clock? Maybe I'll take a little nap before the bus leaves."

"Sure, you can sleep in my wife's bed, Troy." Stanley led the way into the bedroom and switched on the bedside lamp. "I'll just sit up, and wake you in plenty of time for the bus."

Troy put his arm around Stanley's shoulders, then dropped it. He pinched the old man's skinny buttocks, and Stanley flinched.

"Ever fool around, Pop? Want to go to bed with me? I wouldn't mind a little round-eye. It'll make me sleep better."

"No, no." Stanley shook his head and looked at the floor. "I never done anything like that."

Troy shrugged, sat on the side of the bed, and pulled off his boots. "I won't press you. But I advise you to keep away from little girls. Next time you're liable to land up in Lake Butler. And some of those cons up there would rather have a clean old man than a young boy." Troy unsnapped the buttons on his shirt. "If you've got an alarm clock, go to bed. You look like you need some sleep yourself. I won't bother you."

"I don't need any sleep. I had me a long nap this afternoon. I'll wake you in plenty of time."

Stanley closed the bedroom door. He poured a cup of coffee and pulled the plug on the machine. If he was going to stay up anyway, the coffee couldn't bother him too much.

What made Stanley uneasy was the way Troy had hit the nail on the head about his alleged allergy to the smell of paint. When Maya had wanted the all-pink bathroom, he had wondered about it at the time. He had enjoyed painting the bathroom, taking his own sweet time, and he had done a beautiful job in there. But the bathroom was small, and he had often worked with the door closed. And he hadn't been sick or nauseated during the three days it took him to complete the job.

But he didn't recall actually hating his job at the plant, either. He'd been too happy to have a good job, especially when a lot of men in his neighborhood had been laid off. There had been days when he had been sore about something or other, but that was only natural with any kind of work. Besides, Troy had never had a regular job, he said. What could he know about the comfort and security it gave a man to know that he had a paycheck coming in every week? With a paycheck, a man could plan things, build up some savings, even buy on credit if he wanted something bad enough. He knew exactly how far the money would go every month. Except for strikes. The budget went to hell then. But after the strike, he would be better off than before, with a higher paycheck and other fringe benefits. Reuther had been a genius; that's probably why they had killed him. There were a lot of things he would like to talk about with Troy if he would only stay a few days . . .

At one-thirty, Stanley made a fresh pot of coffee in the Mr. Coffee machine. It wasn't so hard. At two he awakened Troy.

"I made some fresh coffee, and I already called for the cab."

Troy, fully dressed, joined him in the kitchen and poured a cup of coffee.

"What's your all-fired rush to get to Miami, Troy? Staying here a couple of days won't hurt you. If the police don't know you're here, they won't be out here checking on you."

"I'm not worried about the cops, I'm looking for a fresh stake. I wouldn't mind staying here a couple of days, but I want to visit the West Indies. Sit down a minute, Pop. There's this guy down in Miami I met in New Orleans. He's a Bajan nonobjective painter, and he told me about a job in Miami that could make us both a bundle."

"What kind of a painter?"

"A Bajan. Barbadian, from the island of Barbados. They call themselves Bajans."

"I mean the other. Nonobjective, you said."

"Right. It's different from abstract. In abstract art, part of something is recognizable, but in nonobjective art nothing is."

"I don't understand—"

"Hell, you told me you were a painter, a striper."

"I am. But I never heard of nonobjective art. It don't make any sense."

"Now you've got it. It isn't supposed to make any sense, Pop. But James, that's his name, can't draw worth shit, so he became a nonobjective painter. He's a remittance man, in reverse. His father's a black man, and his mother's white, an Englishwoman. His father owns some kind of catchall store in Bridgetown. Dry goods, English china, peanut butter, and he also has the island concession on two different European cars, James told me. That's the way they work down there. His old man has the peanut butter concession, so anybody wants peanut butter he has to get it from James's father. James is the only legitimate son, although he has a few illegitimate brothers and sisters. When his father made enough money, he went to England and got himself an English wife before he came back.

"James's father wants him to go into business with him, but James talked his family into letting him study painting in the United States. His old man sends him an allowance of two hundred bucks a month, and he keeps this allowance low so that James'll give up painting and come back to Barbados. Evidently, legitimate sons are a premium in Barbados, and having light skin is good for business, too.

"If he wanted to paint on the side, James told me, his old man wouldn't care, but full-time nonobjective painting is too much for his father to tolerate. His aunt sent him some extra dough on his twenty-sixth birthday, and he used it for a sketching trip to New Orleans. I met him on the levee one day. He had a sketchbook, and he was trying to draw the *Dixie Queen.* It was like some little kid drawing. We got to talking, and we became friends. He mentioned this setup in Miami when he learned that I was experienced in that line. He's desperate, you see, to study art in New York at the Art Students League, on Fifty-seventh Street. He thinks if he could get a one-man show in New York, he'd get some recognition, and then he'd never have to go back to Barbados.

"To cut this short, I dropped James a card that I was on my way to Miami, and I'm a few days late already—because of what happened in Jacksonville."

"What happened in Jacksonville, Troy? You never told me nothing about that."

"I don't think you want to know about it, Pop. It was just a misunderstanding I had with some guy I met in a bar."

The cab pulled up at the curb, and the driver honked his horn. Troy opened the front door and waved to the cabbie to let him know he had heard.

"Thanks for everything, Pop. I'll send your money back to you in a few days."

"Never mind the money, Troy. I—I suppose it's too late for me to go with you, ain't it?" The old man's lower lip quivered.

Troy rubbed the flat place on the bridge of his nose. "It's

never too late to do anything, Pop. I can't promise you anything, but if you want to come to Miami with me, the cab's waiting."

The cabbie sounded a long blast on his horn. Troy opened the door again. "Don't blow that horn again." His voice carried in the night air, and the driver jerked his hands away from the wheel as if it were red hot.

"I can't go right this minute, Troy. But I can come in a day or so."

"Get a pencil and paper. I'll give you James's address."

Stanley got a ballpoint and a piece of paper from Maya's desk. Troy scribbled the address. "That's James Frietas-Smith, with a hyphen between the names. I've never been there, but the house is in the neighborhood they call Bayside—not far from downtown. There's no phone, so come right out to the house. There's a big house in front, belongs to the Shapiros, and James has the garage apartment in back."

"I can find it. I can't come today, but Thursday or Friday for sure. At least I'm pretty sure."

Troy winked and kissed Stanley lightly on the lips. He opened the door, stepped outside, and snapped his fingers. "Pop! The writer's name. The guy who made the statement about the rocks in the bag. Somerset Maugham, the Englishman. And he lived to be a helluva lot older than you."

Troy got into the cab, and Stanley turned off his porch light. He wondered if any of his neighbors had seen Troy kiss him, but he didn't much care if they had. It had been a sweet kiss, the way his son had kissed him when he was seven or eight years old and left for school in the mornings. Then one morning Junior had stopped kissing him, and even pulled away when Stanley had tried to hug him. Boys were like that. Junior would still let Maya hug him in the house, but if she tried to kiss or hug him in public, the boy had a fit, and pulled away from her, too. But Troy had liked him well enough to kiss him good-bye, and the old man was touched by it. Well, maybe he would go to Miami, and maybe he wouldn't. Despite what Troy said, a man couldn't do anything he felt like doing without thinking it over first.

CHAPTER 9

On Sunday, Hoke and Aileen went to his father's house for dinner. Sunday dinner was always served at three P.M., because the Moseleys usually had a late breakfast and skipped lunch. It was an early dinner for Inocencia, too, so she could finish up and go home to her own family in time to attend evening church services. There was a standing rib roast for dinner, and if anyone got hungry later, they could make sandwiches. Frank had always followed this practice on Sundays, even after he became a widower, and he hadn't changed the tradition when Helen came into his life.

Hoke and Aileen got to the house at one, so Aileen could swim in the pool before dinner. Aileen didn't like to swim in the ocean. She was afraid of jellyfish, and had once been bitten on the toe by a bluefish in Vero Beach. The El Pelicano didn't have a pool, so her grandfather had given her his permission to use his pool any time she wanted to walk the mile and a half to his house on Ocean Road. Frank and Helen rarely swam in their pool, but they had white cast-iron chairs and an umbrella table beside the pool, and they often sat out there in the early evenings to have a drink and watch the traffic on the intracoastal waterway. There was an old back-scarred manatee that often came to the dock in the evenings. When it did, Helen fed it a few heads of iceberg lettuce. Because iceberg lettuce was eighty-nine cents a head, Helen had tried to feed the manatee Romaine, which was much cheaper, but the manatee didn't care much for it, so she had gone back to giving it iceberg. While Aileen splashed in the pool, Hoke looked for the manatee, but it never showed up.

Hoke was wearing a new yellow poplin jumpsuit, tennis shoes, and a pair of Ray-Ban aviator-style sunglasses he had owned for ten years or more. He occasionally missed the tug of his gun at the back of his belt, where he usually wore it, but he no longer carried it, or his badge, or his handcuffs. On the right leg of his jumpsuit there was a square cargo pocket that closed with a zipper, but the outline of the gun was clearly visible when he put it into this pocket, so he had decided to quit carrying his weapon. Inasmuch as he was on leave, and not in Miami, he wasn't required to have his gun on his person at all times. Still, he felt a little funny without it.

Frank was in his den, watching a lacrosse game on cable, and Helen was in the living room. She sat at her fruitwood desk, addressing envelopes and enclosing mimeographed letters requesting donations for the Palm Beach Center for Abused Children. She was on the last few envelopes when Hoke joined her in the living room. He poured three ounces of Chivas Regal at the bar, added two ice cubes, and gave himself a splash of soda. Helen looked over her shoulder and smiled. "I'm about finished, Hoke. Could you fix me a pink gin, please?"

"Tanqueray or Beefeater?"

"It doesn't make any difference when you add bitters, so I'd just as soon have Gordon's."

Because it did make a difference, Hoke poured three ounces of Tanqueray into a crystal glass, added ice cubes, and put in a liberal sprinkling of Angostura bitters. He took a cocktail napkin from the stack and put the napkin and drink on the edge of the desk where Helen could reach it.

"Thank you." Helen sipped her drink. "This is Tanqueray."

"There is a difference, then."

"I know that, but what I meant was that it didn't make any difference to me. There, that's the last of the list. I wanted to have these letters printed, but I was argued out of it. The committee thought if we had them mimeographed instead, the letter would be more convincing as a dire need for funds. In my opinion, mimeographed letters look tacky. I'm not sure anyone'll read them."

"Copiers are best. A Xeroxed letter looks like the typed original nowadays."

"I may suggest that to the committee next time, although there's no urgent need for funds. We only have one abused child in the program so far, and we're sending him up to the Sheriff's Boy's Ranch in Kissimmee for the rest of the summer while his mother dries out in Arizona. She's paying the tab for both ranches, the one in Kissimmee and the one in Tucson."

"When did you get interested in abused children, Helen?"

"I'm not, really. But I thought I should serve on some kind of committee, and this is less onerous than some of the others. What I really want to get on is the Heart Fund Ball Committee, but there's a waiting list a mile long for that one."

"I met a man on the beach the other morning, Helen, who told me you still have an apartment at the Supermare. A guy named E. M. Skinner. D'you know him?"

Helen laughed, shook her head, and dampened the flap of an envelope with a sponge. "I know him all right. He has the penthouse, and he was president of our condo association for almost a year before we got rid of him. When the condo first opened, he was the only owner who wanted to be president, so we all voted for him. But he was a busybody and started making all kinds of foolish rules, so the other members of the board, especially Mr. Olsen and Mary Higdon, got him voted out. Mr. Olsen's our new president now, and Mr. Skinner's no longer even on the board. One of the rules he wanted, for example, was a wristband with your apartment number on it. You were supposed to wear it at the pool at all times. This band, he claimed, would keep tourists and strangers from using our pool without permission. The manager, Mr. Carstairs, knows everyone in the building and doesn't need to check a wristband to see if you're a resident or not." She put her envelopes down. "But I'm a little annoyed that Mr. Skinner told you about me. Why would he tell a stranger he met on the beach that I still have my apartment there?"

"I told him I was Frank's son, that's why. But I was surprised that you still had an apartment there."

Helen looked toward the hallway, and then lowered her voice. "I'll tell you a little secret, Hoke, but don't mention it to Frank. Okay?"

"How secret is it?" Hoke sipped his drink. "Frank and I are a little closer now than we've been in some years, and I don't want to jeopardize our relationship. After all, he's made it possible for me to stay here on the island—"

"I'll tell you, and if you want to tell him you know, it won't hurt him any. It might embarrass him a little, but that's all. When we went to Nassau on our honeymoon we were supposed to get married there, but we didn't. We both needed our death certificates from our former spouses in order to get a license. We didn't bring them along, so we couldn't get a license without them. We'd already sent out announcements that we were married, so we had our honeymoon anyway. Then, while we were there—a week in Nassau's like a month anywhere else, you know—and we got to talking, we decided not to go through with a wedding. After all, what difference would it make? Except for making our lives more complicated legally? In the long run, marriage would cost us both money, you see. Of course, everyone thinks we're married because it was in the newspapers, but by remaining single I still get my homestead exemption on my condo at the Supermare, and he gets an exemption on this house. That saves us twenty-five thousand a year apiece. We also save on our income taxes. They're punitive for married people, as you know. Anyway, that's the secret, or our little secret, and if you want to tell Frank you know, go ahead. But please don't tell anyone else."

Hoke grinned, leaned over, and kissed Helen on the cheek. "I'll carry your secret to the grave, Helen. I, too, have lived in sin, and it's better than being married."

"Sin has nothing to do with it. It's just common sense and economics. I have plenty of money, and I don't need Frank's. We've both made out separate wills, and that'll take care of everything if one of us dies."

"Inasmuch as Frank is thirty years older than you, it shouldn't make much difference."

"Frank's in pretty good shape, Hoke."

"Thanks to you. I was glad when you two got married, Helen. Although I knew about the girl friend he had in Lantana. He used to see her two or three times a month, even when my mother was still alive."

"Well, he doesn't have a girl friend in Lantana any longer. And that's no secret. I put an end to that by threatening to tell her husband."

Hoke finished his drink and shook his head. "Don't tell me anything else, Helen. I'm trying to simplify my life, and everything I'm learning today makes it more complicated."

Helen laughed. "Let me show you one more secret. Come on. Follow me."

"Do I need another drink first?"

"No." She laughed. "Come here."

Hoke followed Helen to the kitchen, and then through the kitchen exit to the two-car garage. Helen pointed to a girl's Schwinn ten-speed bicycle that was leaning against the garage wall. The bike was painted Latin red, and there was a brass nameplate on the slanting bar of the frame. THIS BICYCLE WAS MADE ESPECIALLY FOR AILEEN MOSELEY was engraved on the brass plate.

"Frank bought it for Aileen so she can ride up here any time she wants and use the pool. Do you think she'll like it?"

"Of course she will. But it'll make it that much harder for me to get rid of her. Oh, I don't mean that the way it sounds. I love Aileen, but I think she should be living with her mother. Now that she has a bike, it'll be that much harder for me to persuade her to go out to California."

"There's no hurry about that, Hoke. We both think Aileen should stay with you for a while. You've had a difficult time for a few days, and you need her—or someone—with you for a few months. When school starts, she can catch the bus into junior high in Riviera Beach."

"I don't think Patsy'll take her back anyway. There isn't a helluva lot of room in our efficiency, but she seems happy enough."

"Why shouldn't she be? I'd've given anything to live alone with my father when I was her age. And in a way, I'm doing that now, living with Frank." Helen blushed and turned away. "I hardly ever saw my father when I was a girl. I was away at school most of the time, and he was too busy making money to have any time for me."

"Well, at least I'm not making any money." Hoke grinned. "Apparently the less money you have, the more likely you are to have your children living with you. That ballplayer my ex-wife married makes three hundred and twenty-five thousand dollars a year with the Dodgers."

They returned to the living room, and Hoke poured a shorter drink. He added ice cubes but skipped the splash of soda. Hoke and Helen were almost the same age, and he had always been comfortable around her, although he had rarely talked to her alone. She was blonde and plump, but not heavy, and she had been a positive influence in his father's life. The old man was thinner and much happier since he married—began living with—Helen. She dressed him better, too. Frank wore slacks and colorful sport shirts now, instead of the wrinkled seersucker suits he had favored, and she had thrown away the black leather bow ties he had worn every day to the store.

"Would you like another pink gin, Helen?"

"I don't think so. We're going to have wine with dinner, so one'll be plenty."

"When was the last time you visited your condo at the Supermare?"

"About a month ago. Why?"

"Was anything missing? Skinner told me that you had some burglaries there recently. The thief's been hitting the empty apartments."

"That's the first I've heard about it, but I haven't been going to any of the monthly meetings."

"Do you have a bolt lock on your door?"

Helen nodded. "A regular through-the-doorknob lock, and a bolt lock too."

"If you want me to, I'll check it out for you."

"I don't keep any jewelry there. Just furniture and furnishings, and a few clothes. Frank and I change clothes there once in a while when we go to the beach. And I have to live there, or be physically present, on January first, to get my homestead exemption."

"When's the last time you went to the beach?"

Helen laughed. "About four months ago. During the season. It's too hot for me in the summer."

"We'd better drop by and check it out."

"I've got some extra keys. I'll give them to you, and you can drop by some morning when you go swimming. In fact, you can use the apartment any time you like, or swim in the pool. I'll call and tell Mr. Carstairs that you're my guest. But Aileen can't use the pool, or even hang around the building. No children are allowed."

"Don't people there have grandchildren?"

"Sure they do, but they're not allowed to visit. The no-children rule was one of the major selling points for an apartment at the Supermare. A lot of people don't want to have grandchildren around, Hoke, or even their own adult children. Not everyone's like Frank and me." Helen got the extra keys from the center drawer of her desk and put them into an envelope. She handed the envelope to Hoke, and he dropped it into his front pocket. "You'd better get Frank now, Hoke. Take him a drink, and by the time he's finished, dinner should be ready."

"What does he like? He used to drink bourbon on the rocks, or with a little Coke—"

"Give him a Beefeater on the rocks, but put an olive in it. He thinks vermouth ruins a martini."

"He's right."

Helen went into the kitchen, and Hoke fixed his father a stiff gin on the rocks. It occurred to him for the first time in his life, as he headed toward the den, that one of these days, if he was lucky, Frank might leave him the El Pelicano Arms in his will. And if he did, he would be able to stay on the island until he died without any more worries. Even if Frank didn't leave him the apartment house, and left everything to Helen, he was sure that Helen would let him stay on as manager.

But he had better prove that he was worthy of the job by renting out those two empty apartments as soon as possible . . .

Aileen was shown the new bicycle before dinner, and she kissed Frank, Helen, and Hoke. Hoke had told her that she would not be allowed to drive his car again; now she could go almost anywhere she wanted to go on the island with her bicycle.

"I'll get you a basket for the handlebars," Hoke said, "and you can do our shopping at the supermarket."

"I don't need a basket. I can carry groceries under one arm, and steer with one hand."

"Just don't ride through the mall parking lot," Hoke said. "A lot of sick Yankees back out without looking, and they might run over you."

Aileen ate swiftly so she could ride her new bike, but still she put away two helpings of rare roast beef, with mashed potatoes and gravy, before she excused herself from the table.

After dinner, Frank and Hoke went into the den with their coffee. Frank turned on the cable to a women's mud-wrestling match in Buffalo, New York. Frank, who'd only had the cable channels for a few months, had never known about lacrosse, mud wrestling, four-wall volleyball, and knife-, star-, and hatchet-throwing contests until he signed up for cable, so he was still interested in these new—to him—sports. He was also fond of Dr. Ruth's sex show in the evenings, and rarely missed her program.

At a quarter to five, Hoke got to his feet. "I've got to go, Dad. I left a note on my door saying I'd be back at five. Someone might be there looking for an apartment."

"Stick around, son. There's a man coming over after a while I want you to meet. Let Aileen ride back on her bike; she can tell anyone there to wait for you."

Hoke found Aileen outside and told her to take herself and her wet bathing suit back to the apartment house.

"If someone's there, you can show them an empty apartment, but tell them to stick around till I get back."

"I know how to show the apartments, Daddy."

"I know you do, honey, but I want to screen people. I don't want any Latins to get in there for two months or more. Or some drunk. Okay?"

"What's the matter with Latins? Ellita's a Latin."

"Nothing's the matter with them, but our efficiencies are for one or two people, not for families of six or more. There're only two single beds, you know."

Aileen let this pass. "I put a sack of mangoes in the front seat of the car, Daddy. Helen said we could have all we wanted from the tree in the back yard."

"Fine. How're the brakes on the bike?"

"I *know* how to ride it, Daddy—and I won't ride through the parking lot."

Hoke fixed another Scotch and soda in the living room, but he didn't return to the den. He went into the kitchen. Inocencia had cleaned up in there and had gone home. Before leaving she had made four roast beef sandwiches and put them into a sack for Hoke to take home. Hoke took the bag of sandwiches out to his car and put them on the seat next to the mangoes. As he closed the car door, a black Buick Riviera pulled up behind Hoke's Le Mans in the driveway.

"I'm leaving in a few minutes," Hoke called over to the man who got out of the car. "So you'd better let me back out first, then you can pull in ahead of me."

"I'm only going to be here a few minutes myself. You're Sergeant Moseley, aren't you?"

"That's right, but I don't live here. I'm just visiting my dad."

"You're the man I've come to talk with." He introduced

himself as Mike Sheldon, chief of police for Riviera Beach. "Your father called me yesterday and said you'd resigned from the Miami Police Department."

"Well, I haven't resigned yet, Chief. I'm still thinking about it. My problem right now is what's best for me, Chief. You know how it goes. I can either take my pension money out in a lump sum, or I leave it in till I'm fifty-seven and then start drawing it monthly. I haven't got around to sitting down with a pencil and paper and figuring out what's the best thing to do."

"If you take it out in a lump sum, you'll have to pay income taxes on it as earned salary this year."

"I know that, but my income for the next six months will be negligible, so I still have to go over the figures."

"I was in the same position." Chief Sheldon rubbed a deep white scar on his chin. He was a heavyset man in his late forties, and his face was severely sunburned. His nose was peeling, and when he took off his dark sunglasses, as he did now, the freckled skin below his blue eyes was paper-white. "I've only had this job for six months. The old chief was indicted, you know, and I had to make up my mind in a hurry when the city commission offered it to me. I was a homicide lieutenant up in Trenton—that's in New Jersey—and I'd put in for chief at three or four small towns, answering ads in the journal. Riviera Beach made me the best offer. So I had to make the same kind of decision you're up against. I left my money in the pension fund. I'm making less money as chief here than I did as a lieutenant in Trenton, but life's a lot easier here on the Gold Coast. Money isn't the most important thing in a man's life."

"Not unless you don't have any."

"Your father said you'd had it with Miami, but you might be open to an offer here in Riviera Beach."

"That's impossible." Hoke shook his head. "The police

station's on the mainland. I've decided never to leave the island again."

"Never's a pretty long spell. Just hear me out. I looked over your record from when you were still a patrolman here on the Riviera force, before you went down to Miami. You were a good officer here. No reprimands, and five commendations, which isn't bad for three years. Then I called your Homicide Chief, Major Brownley, in Miami, and he said you were one of his best detectives—"

Hoke laughed. "You called Major Brownley? He doesn't know I'm quitting! As far as he knows I'm on a thirty-day leave without pay. I told you I hadn't put any papers in yet. He must've shit his pants when you called him."

"He was a little disturbed at first, yes. But I was discreet. I just told him I wanted to offer you a lieutenancy as my Homicide Chief here, but when I mentioned the salary he just laughed. All I can offer you, except for the lieutenant's bars, is fifteen thousand a year."

"I make thirty-four as a sergeant in Miami."

"That's what he told me. But then, if you're fed up with Miami—and I can't blame you for that—the higher rank and the job itself might be more to your liking. We don't have many homicides, although we do have a lot more abuse cases and missing persons every year, and they come under Homicide, too. A lot of things have changed in Riviera since you left here. Ten years ago, most of the residents were WASPs; now we've got sixty percent blacks."

"You must be kidding. I don't think there're more than one or two black families living on the island."

"That's here on Singer. They can't afford to live over here. But there's been a big influx in town. For a couple of years we had a drop in population, but now it's on the upswing with more blacks moving in. The WASPs have moved out to North Palm Beach, or to those new suburbs in West Palm. That's one of the reasons I was hired. I had to deal with a lot of black crime in Trenton."

"Major Brownley's a black officer."

"I figured that when I talked to him on the phone. But he told me you'd worked in Liberty City and Overtown, so you've dealt with black crime."

"What you need is a black lieutenant, Chief. You don't need me. I've never taken the lieutenant's exam in Miami, and I'm not sure I could pass it if I did."

"That's no problem. If you were a sergeant already on my force, you'd have to pass the exam before you could get a promotion. But if you come on the force from outside, I can appoint you as a lieutenant immediately, based on your experience and my personal evaluation. The city commission gave me the job, and so far they've been letting me run it my way. Why don't you sleep on the idea tonight, and then come by the station in the morning? I'll show you what the job entails. You'll have a free car, you know, and that's worth at least four thousand bucks a year. And you'll only have two detectives to supervise—a black and a Puerto Rican."

"I already told you, Chief, I can't come over because I've made up my mind not to leave the island."

"You aren't making a helluva lot of sense, Sergeant Moseley."

"Maybe not. But I'm living in a six-hundred-dollar-a-month apartment, rent-free, and I'm making another four hundred in salary, so I can survive without ever going into town. Everything I need's right here on the island—laundromat, supermarket, restaurants, and the best beach in Florida. Complete with no hassles. The worst that can happen to me is to step on a tin can on the beach and cut myself."

"No job's any safer than Homicide, Moseley. When you report to the scene, the victim's already dead, and the killer's long gone. Or he's still there, crying and saying he didn't mean to do it."

"But then there's all the paperwork and the headaches. It was time for a change. But I want to tell you I appreciate the offer, Chief Sheldon."

"It wasn't exactly unsolicited." Sheldon shrugged. "After all, your father has a lot of clout in this town. He used to be on the city commission, and he owns half of Singer Island. I'm not saying you aren't highly qualified—"

"I think some of that's exaggerated. Dad used to own a lot of the island, but all he has left now are a few beachfront lots—"

"Which appreciate about a thousand bucks per beach foot every year."

"I suppose. What about those burglaries in the condos? Who's handling them?"

"At the Supermare? Right now, Jaime Figueras. He's a homicide detective, the Puerto Rican I told you about, but I gave them to him. He hasn't found out much of anything. Who told you about them?"

"Things get around. If you live on the island, you find out about everything sooner or later. I might be able to help him. Why not ask Figueras to drop around and see me at the Pelicano? Tell him to bring an inventory of the missing stuff. That is, if you don't mind a little civilian help."

"If you haven't resigned yet, you're still a police officer, and I need all the help I can get. I'll send him around tomorrow."

"We'd better go inside and see the old man."

"I don't need to see Mr. Moseley. He asked me to talk to you, and I have. I'll just back out and go."

"Better see him for a minute. If you leave without talking to him, it'll hurt his feelings. Have a drink, at least, and then tell him you've got some pressing business. But he's funny about things like that."

"A man can always use a drink."

They went inside, and the chief had two drinks and made some small talk with Frank before leaving. He didn't mention his offer to Hoke, and Frank didn't ask him about it.

But after the chief was gone, Frank said, "Did you take Sheldon up on his offer, Hoke?"

"No. I couldn't take it because I'd have to leave the island and work in the Riviera Beach station. And please, Dad, don't do any more favors for me. I'm happy at the El Pelicano. But I sure didn't know that the black population was up to sixty percent in Riviera."

"Seems like more than that. But it's been good for the hardware store. They have to fix up those old fifties houses they move into, and my business has increased almost twelve percent in the last year."

"Why don't you sell the store, Frank? You and Helen could take life easy and do some traveling or something. You don't need the money."

Frank grinned. "Going to the store gives me a chance to leave the island every day, that's why. I'm just as stubborn as you are. And I already saw the world on that trip Helen and me took on the *Q.E. II* last year. It wore me out, and I don't want to see it a second time."

"I'm sorry, Dad. I shouldn't've mentioned it."

"I'm the one who should apologize. I shouldn't've called Chief Sheldon, not without checking with you first."

"Don't worry about me, Frank. I'm fine now, and I appreciate you getting Aileen the bicycle. I'll just say goodbye to Helen, and then I'd better get back and see about renting those empty apartments."

As Hoke drove back to the El Pelicano Arms, he turned over in his mind the information he had picked up. He had discovered that Frank wasn't married to Helen, which was something he wouldn't have thought possible a few years back; and he had been offered a job that he would have leaped at if it had been offered to him six months ago. But he couldn't take it now. If he did, he could still reside on the island, but he would be spending most of his time investigating knifings and shootings in Riviera Beach—that is, when he wasn't waiting around in the Palm Beach County courthouse to appear as a witness. He had liked Chief Sheldon; they had similar backgrounds in police work, and Hoke knew exactly how Sheldon's mind worked. But Hoke had almost insuperable problems just trying to manage a place like the El Pelicano Arms.

The rents were too high, for one thing. And he needed a coin-operated washer and dryer for the residents to use, because it was a two-block walk to the laundromat. Both of the Alabama couples had complained about that. The ice machine in the lobby was broken, and he couldn't get a man to come out until next Tuesday, if then. He would have to find a new service, one that would come out on weekends. But worst of all, he was under the old man's thumb again.

When he'd been married to Patsy, and still on the Riviera Police Department, he and Patsy used to have dinner with the old man every damned Sunday, and now he would be expected to spend every Sunday afternoon with Frank again. There was no way out of it. Frank would expect it, and no excuse would be acceptable.

There was a blue Camaro with Dade County plates parked in Hoke's manager's slot at the El Pelicano Arms. Hoke pulled in behind the car and blocked it so it could not back out. Then he walked over to the mall and used the pay telephone to call the towing service. After the tow truck had showed up and towed the Camaro away—it would cost the Camaro owner sixty dollars to redeem his car—Hoke felt good for the first time that day.

CHAPTER 10

Unlike Troy Louden, Stanley Sinkiewicz was a homeowner with responsibilities. He couldn't just pick up and leave in the middle of the night, and he would never have gone down to Miami by himself to spend money on an expensive hotel room. But Troy had invited him to stay with him, and he wouldn't be all alone down there in the city. He wanted to get away from the Terraces for a while, even if it was only for a week or so, to let "the incident," as he now thought of it, blow over. He wouldn't get in Troy's way, and he wouldn't wear out his welcome down there. From all accounts, Miami was a dangerous place, but nothing would happen to him if he was down there with Troy and that Bajan fella.

But the first thing he would have to do was to buy a car. A man without a car would be helpless down there, and he didn't know anything about the bus routes, or how to use the new Metrorail, either. In a city that widely spread out, a car was an absolute necessity.

He rode the bus into West Palm Beach and made arrangements at his new bank to buy a brown Honda Civic, a repossessed 1981 model with 42,000 miles on the odometer and a new roof rack. He felt guilty about buying Japanese, but being six years old the Civic was only $1,800, not counting taxes.

He paid with a check and filled in the insurance transfer from his Escort at the bank, applying its coverage to the Honda. This transfer meant that Maya no longer had any insurance on their Escort, but that was her problem now, not Stanley's. He also got another five hundred dollars in traveler's checks and another forty in cash at the bank before driving home in his new—practically new—car.

He found the mortgage book in his wife's desk and wrote out two monthly mortgage checks in advance. He didn't know how long he would stay in Miami, but at least he had this worry off his mind. He called the telephone company and, after being transferred three times to people who didn't seem to understand what he wanted, managed to get his telephone placed on a hold, or standby, basis. This way, if someone called, the caller could hear it ring, but the phone would not actually ring at his home, nor would he be able to make any calls from his home until it was taken off standby. The fee for this was nine dollars a month. Stanley argued with the supervisor he had finally been transferred to, telling her that it was outrageous to charge him this much money for an inoperable phone, but the company wouldn't budge. Stanley then sent a check for the current phone charges—and for ten dollars more—to the address the woman gave him, which was different from his regular billing address.

The business with the phone company was such an ordeal, Stanley decided to do nothing about paying any of his other utility bills in advance. If they cut off his water and electricity while he was gone, he would pay up and get them reconnected when he returned.

He then drove into Riviera Beach, mailed the mortgage payments, and signed a "hold mail" card at the post office for an indefinite period, writing on the card, "Will pick up at PO when I return from vacation."

If Maya had still been with him—instead of running away—these were all little chores that he could have delegated to her. And he knew his life would be complicated in a lot of other respects by her desertion. But it was worth it. He wouldn't have been able to take Maya to Miami with him anyway, even if she had been willing to go. Being without a wife gave a man a whole different way of looking at the world, and it looked even better now that he had a car to drive again. If it came to a toss-up, a car or a wife, most men, or at least the ones Stanley had known in Detroit, would certainly give up their wives.

After packing some white shirts and some wash pants in a cardboard box, and putting on a new blue-and-white seersucker suit he had bought when he first came to Florida, but had never worn, Stanley wondered what to do about the storm shutters. If he closed them, and turned off the electricity, everything would be mildewed when he returned. He decided not to pull them down, but to crack all of the windows a little for circulation after he turned off the air conditioning. He drove over to Sneider's station to have the tank filled and asked Mr. Sneider to pull down the storm shutters from the outside if there happened to be a hurricane while he was gone.

"If you'll do that for me, Mr. Sneider, I'll give you a dollar for your trouble when I get back."

"No problem, Mr. Sinkiewicz. It's the least I can do for a neighbor. You takin' I-95 into Miami?"

"I thought I would."

"They've been having some highway robberies down there, you know. They throw a mattress or a set of box springs on the off-ramps, and then when you stop another guy throws a concrete block through your window and robs you. It's been in the papers. So what you should do is carry a tire iron on the other bucket seat in front, so you can chop off the man's fingers when he reaches in for your wallet and wristwatch."

Stanley checked the trunk, but there was no tire iron. Sneider got one from the shop and handed it to him. "I'll lend you this one, Dad. You can return it when you get back. But if I were you, I'd stay in the center lane on I-95 and keep your doors locked. When I drive down to Miami in my tow truck for parts sometimes, I carry a shotgun loaded with birdshot. I don't want to kill nobody, but a load of birdshot in the face will discourage most of these robbers."

"I could stop at Moseley's Hardware and buy a shotgun—"

"The tire iron'll be enough. I use my shotgun for dove hunting, too, but for you, I wouldn't go to that extra expense just for a trip down I-95."

"How's little Pammi, Mr. Sneider?"

"I sent her up to Camp Sparta for the rest of the summer. She called last night to tell us she won fourth place in the archery contest. They know how to straighten little girls out in Camp Sparta. You get a little girl, or a little boy, interested in sports, it gets their mind off their private parts."

"I never had the advantage of going to a summer camp when I was a kid."

"Me neither. But there was a time there in the service, for about five years, when I didn't own a damned thing that couldn't be left out in the rain. Kids have it good nowadays, but they're too dumb to know it."

Hoping he hadn't neglected anything important, Stanley drove to I-95 and headed south for Miami, seventy miles away, and without a single stoplight on the interstate.

* * *

The painting on the upright easel in the garage had a meaning so private that the artist himself, James Frietas-Smith, didn't know what it was.

James always worked slowly, on one large canvas at a time, and without a preconceived notion of what the final product would look like. He piled on paint and then more paint until every inch of the canvas was covered with multiblobs of color three-quarters of an inch thick.

James stepped back about ten feet and studied the painting for a few minutes. The composition definitely held the eye within the rectangle, and the magenta blobs on the right balanced the three wide smears of lampblack on the left. But the overall picture needed a touch of luminosity. James squeezed a large tube of zinc white. The thick paint oozed out like dilute toothpaste onto his palette knife. Moving in close to the canvas and spreading his short, slightly bowed legs, James applied the globule of white to the center of the canvas. He brought his pursed lips close to the blob and blew steadily, flattening it into the shape of an amoeba with the jet of air he forced through his lips.

That was all it needed, he thought, as he stepped back and looked at the picture again. Finished. A wave of depression engulfed him as he wiped his fingers on a turpentine-soaked rag. It was always this way when he completed a picture. Always. Painting them was a joyful suspension of life, but it was a downer to finish them. Who would buy a picture like this one, anyway? The canvas was sixty inches wide and forty inches high, and a frame would make it larger still. James always made his own stretchers, tacking down the canvas and sizing the surface with white lead himself. The money he invested, including the tubes of paint, was a large sum for a man in his financial position. And if he were to consider the time consumed in actually painting and finishing a work (the cost of framing was out of the question), he would have to charge a great deal of money for each finished picture. But so far, he couldn't sell any of them; he couldn't even give them away.

The primary colors he was fond of would overpower most living rooms, and the hotels he had tried were not interested. A few weeks ago, before his trip to New Orleans, James had stacked four of his paintings on top of his little Morris Minor, tied them down with rope, and driven to a half-dozen small hotels in Miami Beach. The two managers who consented to look merely shook their heads; the rest of them wouldn't even come out to the parking lot. He didn't intend to let them humiliate him again. He would just have to wait until he was somehow discovered, and his work recognized by someone.

The picture was finished now, but what could he do with it? Maybe the best thing to do would be to scrape off the paint and begin another. But he didn't feel like starting another painting. Not now. Not when he was frightened half to death—and part of his fear, he noticed, had somehow managed to work its way into the new painting. He didn't recall using so much magenta in anything else he had done.

The temperature in the four-car garage was in the high eighties, but James's hands were cold and clammy. He wiped his palms on his blue-denim cutoffs and sighed. If this thing with Troy Louden didn't work out, he would be in the hands of the Allambys for certain. James shivered and left the garage studio for the bright sunlight of the jungly back yard. James didn't know the precise origin of the expression "in the hands of the Allambys," although he presumed it had been a slave-owning family of unusual cruelty during the early years of Barbados. But Bajans, when they still used the archaic expression, knew for certain that when a person was "in the hands of the Allambys," hope was gone, the worst that could happen to a man had already happened, and from that day forward the man was lost . . . doomed.

Like many Barbadians whose families had been on the island for a dozen generations or more, James wasn't completely Caucasian, even though in Barbados he was considered a white man. His hair was reddish brown and curly. His eyes were blue. His nose, although high at the bridge, was wide at the base, and his large round nostrils flared slightly when he got excited. His even teeth were white and strong, and his lips were pronounced and thick. His jutting hips and the carelessly swinging arms that gave an island rhythm to his loosely disjointed walk also hinted at his ancestry and upbringing. But only once since he'd come to the United States—in New Orleans—had James been recognized as a man who was half black.

Every time James recalled the incident in New Orleans, a wave of shame, fear, and revulsion hit him, like a man with a case of the dog bitters. He had gone into one of those intimate, candle-lit, side-street, open-air restaurants to sample some of the city's famous French-Creole cooking. The patio setting was attractive, with flowers growing in ceramic pots along the intricate wrought-iron fence. There were colored lights trained on the fountain in the center of the courtyard. The waiter had seated James at a glass-topped wrought-iron table, with a pink plastic table setting and pink linen napkin. He handed James a menu printed in French and left him alone for five minutes.

When James had looked up again from the menu, he was confronted by two white-jacketed men who were studying his face by the flickering light of the double-candled hurricane lamp on his table. The headwaiter nodded briefly to his table waiter and then said softly and firmly, "We'll serve you this time, sir, but don't come back again. Many of our patrons prefer not to dine with black men."

No one overheard the headwaiter, but for a moment

James had been petrified with fear. Without protesting, without even ordering, he had slunk out of the restaurant. He hadn't eaten anything that evening. He had walked for hours, thinking about the things he should have said to the waiters. He could have shown them his Barbados passport; he could have forced a showdown of some kind—but he hadn't. Two days later James had left New Orleans on the Greyhound bus and come back to Miami, even though his vacation money would have stretched for another week.

He had a good setup here in Miami, and he was sorry now that he had gone to New Orleans in the first place. If he had only stayed put, when his aunt had sent him the birthday check, he wouldn't be involved now with Troy Louden and that horribly mutilated woman! James could hardly look at her face without feeling sick to his stomach, and he couldn't meet her eyes at all. Her face was so badly disfigured, he knew that the horror he felt in his heart would show in his eyes.

And now another man was coming in on the deal—Pop Sinkiewicz, Troy Louden's old cellmate. Another professional criminal and ex-con. Troy had told James that Sinkiewicz had done a little time with him for trying to crack a small safe, and that James should be nice to the old man because he would be financing their operation. How many more would be in on it before Troy was through? He had never dreamed that Troy would come to Miami in the first place. James had been rather vague about the job at the time he had suggested it to Troy in New Orleans, but he hadn't been able to concentrate fully on his painting since he received the postcard from Troy saying he was on his way to Miami.

The postcard alone had been an omen. A symbol, and an ugly one, too. As a nonobjective painter, James thought often about symbols, even though he avoided them in his work, and just the sight of that four-color postcard had shaken him before he read it. Naturally, James hadn't told Troy about the incident in the courtyard cafe; he would never tell anyone about that, ever. Yet the card from Troy had featured a typical New Orleans wrought-iron gate, and filling the background behind the gate (not in front, which would have made a big difference, symbolically, but *behind*) there was a bed of roses—yellow, pink, and dark red. What had made Troy take that particular card at random out of a drugstore rack? There were literally thousands of postcards he could have chosen. Did the gate represent prison bars? Or did it mean the color bar? The symbols meant something awful; he knew that much.

Suppose, just suppose, everything went wrong? The robbery would fail—or *could* fail—despite Troy's assurances to the contrary. Then where would he be? In prison, that's where, and if he went to prison, would the authorities list him as a black man or a white man? But that wasn't as important as *going* to prison . . .

Oh, man, he wouldn't be able to stand being in prison either way.

On the other hand, Troy knew what he was doing. This sort of thing was old stuff to Troy, and if everything worked out smoothly, as Troy claimed it would, James would be off to New York with four or five thousand dollars—maybe more—in his pocket. And if there was a place that deserved to be robbed in Florida, it was the Green Lakes Supermarket.

On the tenth of every month James received a check for $200 from his father, mailed from Bridgetown, but it wasn't enough, not nearly enough to live on and buy expensive art supplies, too. When the Green Lakes Supermarket had announced its grand opening in the newspaper, James had driven out there and applied for a part-time job as a bag boy. He had worked on Fridays until eleven, and all day Saturdays. The minimum wage, plus his tips, had added almost forty dollars a week to his income. But this extra money wasn't enough either, not when he had to buy art supplies and pay for the upkeep on his Morris Minor. To supplement his supermarket pittance, James had done a little pilfering every Saturday he worked at the market. He hadn't taken much, only little items he could stuff into his pockets—a can of sardines, a can of tuna, some candy bars, apples, toothpaste, and once a pound of hamburger, which had turned bad before he got home that night. Then on his way back inside the store after delivering a load of groceries to a customer's car in the parking lot, James would drop off his pilfered items behind the front seat of his Morris, which he always parked close to the store's entrance.

At four P.M. on the last Saturday he worked at the market, the day manager crooked a finger at him as he came back in from the lot, pushing a half-dozen carts he had collected. The day manager was in his early forties and wore a Fu Manchu moustache, a red tie, and a pink button-down shirt.

"You're fired, James."

"Why?"

"For stealing, that's why! Now get the fuck out of here, you goddamned thief, and don't stop at the cage for your check on the way out!"

Two of the girls on the checkout line heard every word.

"Yes, sir," James said, and hurried out of the store as the two checkout girls giggled.

That was a week before his twenty-sixth birthday, and before he received the sizable and welcome check from his Aunt Rosalie. Now he had no money, and a lot on his mind.

The Green Lakes Supermarket had suited Troy perfectly when James had driven him out there yesterday to show it to him. After spending fifteen minutes in the store, with James outside in the car, Troy had rejoined him with two apples he had bought. He handed one of the apples to James and bit into the other.

"Lush," Troy had said. Then, gesturing toward the entrance, "It's just like you said, James."

From a professional's point of view, the layout of the store and the location of the market were ideal. Eventually there would be an entire Class B shopping center in the Green Lakes subdivision of Miami, with thirty different stores, but at present only the supermarket had opened, and the rest of the buildings were still under construction. The supermarket would anchor one end, and there would be a K-Mart at the other. The twenty-five-acre parking lot had been completed, but had not yet been striped for parking spaces. The new supermarket was about 250 yards away from State Highway 836, which led to the Miami International Airport cutoff. Troy couldn't have selected a better location, or a better time, for a successful robbery if he had been allowed to design one himself. The employees were new, and security was lax, and as James had said, the safe was supposed to be locked but in practice never was until the store was closed for the night.

When they got back to James's garage apartment, after the quick surveillance of the supermarket, Troy had borrowed the Bajan's last five dollars, taken the Morris Minor, and driven away. James hadn't seen him again until he returned later that night with the woman—

"Pardon me, son."

James leaped two feet off the garage floor and whirled in midair before he landed again. "Man!" he said to Stanley Sinkiewicz, "you shouldn't sneak up on a man like that, man!"

"I didn't mean to scare you none, son. I knocked at the door of the big house in front, but when no one answered I just came around here to the back."

"That's all right, sir." James had recovered his breath. "I live back here over the garage. The Shapiros own the big house, and they let me live here free for taking care of the place while they're up in New England for the summer."

"You're James Frietas-Smith, with a hyphen?"

"Yes, sir."

"You're the fella I'm looking for, then." Stanley stared curiously at James. Stanley had never seen a Bajan before, but the young man, except for the size of his splayed bare feet, looked about the same as any other well-tanned Floridian wearing cutoff shorts and a paint-stained T-shirt. "My name's Stanley Sinkiewicz. Senior," he added. "I'm a friend of Troy Louden's."

"Yes, sir. We been expecting you, Mr. Sinkiewicz. Troy and Miss Forrest have gone over to her motel to get her suitcase. She's moving in with us, too." James forced a smile. "They should be back just now."

"Miss Forrest? I haven't met her—"

"I only met her last night myself, Mr. Sinkiewicz. She's Troy's friend, not mine. If you're parked out front, you better pull into the yard back here and park over there." James pointed to the utility shed.

Stanley nodded. "The grass out front needs cutting. It didn't look like nobody lived here, and I was afraid for a minute there I had the wrong house."

"I'm supposed to cut the grass every two weeks, but I was away on a trip and missed a few weeks."

Stanley got his car and parked it by the shed. He brought his box of clean clothes and toilet articles into the spacious four-car garage, and James tried to take the box away from him.

"I'll take that upstairs for you, Mr. Sinkiewicz."

"I'm not in any all-fired hurry, son." Stanley surrendered the box and looked at the huge paintings stacked against and hanging from the garage walls. "Troy told me you were an artist. I'd like to look at your work, if you don't mind?"

"I don't mind at all." James put the box on the steps that led upstairs to the apartment, and crossed to the easel. "I finished this one just now, but I haven't got a title yet. Sometimes when I can't think of a title I give it a number. But I haven't thought of a number, either."

Stanley studied the painting, frowning with concentration. He put on his reading glasses and moved in a little closer. "I wouldn't know, myself—although it looks a little scary."

"It's a nonobjective painting," James explained, "and some kind of emotion is all you're expected to get out of it. Two years ago there was a German painter staying over on the Saint James coast—that's in Barbados—and I showed him some of my work. He told me I was probably the only primitive nonobjective painter working today. He's the same man who advised me to go to New York and study at the Art Students League. And when we finish our job, that's where I'm going."

Stanley nodded. "You could use a little more study, I guess. I used to do some painting myself. One thing you need's a steady hand." Stanley pointed to a canvas on the wall, a crosspatch of thin vertical red lines and thinner horizontal black lines on a lemon background. "Now that picture over there. You put all them lines on with a straightedge, didn't you?"

"Yes, sir. That was just an experiment, Mr. Sinkiewicz. But even Mondrian used a ruler to get certain effects."

Stanley shook his head. "If you've got a steady hand, you don't need no straightedge. You got any clean canvases and a striping brush? I'll learn you how to do it."

"Yes, sir." James didn't want to have the old con spoil one of his unused canvases, but he didn't want to offend him either.

James removed the newly finished painting from the easel and replaced it with a recently sized blank canvas. "There's a can of brushes on the workbench, Mr. Sinkiewicz. Take any one you like."

Stanley moved to the cluttered workbench. He opened a can of turpentine and held the spout to his nose. He sniffed experimentally, inhaled deeply, and screwed the lid back.

"Do you like the smell of turpentine, son?"

"I don't mind it. But I don't particularly like it."

"One good thing about turpentine. It always smells the same."

"Yes, sir," James said uneasily. "It always smells the same."

Stanley rummaged around in a coffee can full of brushes and selected a short-handled camel's hair brush about a half-inch in width. "This ain't no regular striping brush, but it'll do. A real striping brush is wider, and slants back aways, and the bristles are longer on one side than on the other. I'll just stir up some of this cadmium orange and turpentine, and then I'll show you how to make a straight line without looking at the canvas."

As Stanley mixed the new tube of cadmium orange with turpentine, James scowled and bit his lower lip. The paint had cost him $4.95 in U.S. dollars, and the old man had squeezed out half the tube.

"All right, young fella," Stanley said, his cheeks flushing, "just watch me now."

Stanley held the paint-loaded brush at his side, resting his forearm on his hip, and stared up at the cobwebby ceiling. He took two swift steps in front of the canvas, turned, and winked at James. James's jaw dropped. The bright orange line on the canvas was exactly one-eighth of an inch wide, and straight as a die. The line was as vibrant as a tightly stretched guitar string. It looked to James as if it would hum to the touch, and the old man had drawn this perfect rule in less than a second!

"That's what I mean by a steady hand," Stanley said, with a short laugh.

James clucked and shook his head. "I don't know how you did that, Mr. Sinkiewicz. I couldn't draw a line that straight, even with a yardstick."

"There's a knack to it, son. Here. Take the brush and I'll show you how to hold it. You've got to put the right amount of paint on the brush, too. With a little practice, you can learn how to do it."

For the next forty-five minutes James and Stanley were engaged in painting straight lines. The once-white canvas was an almost solidly colored orange rectangle when Troy Louden pulled into the driveway outside the garage and honked the horn of the Morris Minor. They both went outside to meet him. Troy embraced the old man, hugging him to his chest, and kissed him wetly on the cheek.

"By God, I'm glad to see you, Pop! To tell you the truth, I wasn't sure you were going to pry yourself loose from up there. If you hadn't come today, I was going to call you tonight. You've met James, I see."

"He sure has, Troy," James said. "Mr. Sinkiewicz has been teaching me how to paint a straight line."

"That's nice of you, Pop." Troy frowned at James. "I hope you thanked him."

"Yes, I did."

"It'll take him a while to get the hang of it," Stanley said. "A man can't learn nothing overnight."

Troy punched the old man lightly on the arm, and then snapped his fingers. "Jesus. I was so glad to see you I forgot to introduce you to Dale Forrest. Hop out of the car, honey, and meet Mr. Sinkiewicz."

Stanley had seen the woman in the car the moment he had stepped out of the shady garage, but he had hurriedly looked away again. As Dale Forrest advanced toward him timidly, holding out her limp right hand, Stanley forced himself to look at her face again. The young woman had a voluptuous figure, with long straight legs. She wore green-denim clamdiggers and a short-sleeved white silk blouse with the top three buttons undone to reveal her cleavage. Her heavy breasts, without a brassiere, strained against the thin silk. Her skin was a golden bronze, and her hair was almost the same shade, although bright highlights shimmered at the crown. Her long thick hair softly framed her face, and there Dale's beauty stopped.

There were four knobby irregular bumps on her forehead, as if someone had been beating on her with a hammer. Instead of eyebrows, Dale had two hairless dents above her eyes, both of them crisscrossed with red scars where stitches had recently been removed. She had filled in these crescent-shaped depressions with black makeup, which made them more obvious. Her nose was crushed almost flat, and the left nostril was partly missing, as if cut away with a razor blade. Both of her sunken cheeks contained rough and jagged scars, and some of these holes looked large enough to contain marbles. Her jaw had been broken, and reset off-center, and her tiny recessed chin jutted to the right at a puzzling angle. Although Dale still had her lower front teeth, her six upper front teeth were missing, and her gummy smile was like a grimace of intense pain. Stanley recognized that the grimace was a smile, but when he looked at it he felt like crying. Her scarred and puffy lips reminded him of the sewn end of a sack of potatoes.

"I'm happy to make your acquaintance, Mr. Sinkiewicz," Dale said. She shook Stanley's hand, then dropped behind Troy as if she were trying to hide.

"Likewise," Stanley said, clearing his throat.

"James, boy!" Troy said. "Where'd you put Stanley?"

"We haven't been upstairs yet, Troy. But I thought I'd give him the bed out on the porch, if that's all right with you?"

"That'll be fine. Get Dale's bag out of the car."

The six-bedroom, two-story house faced Biscayne Bay, and the Shapiros, the elderly couple who owned it, spent three winter months there every year. They had, at one time, kept the garage apartment as servants' quarters, but they no longer employed live-in servants, even when they were in residence, so the garage apartment hadn't been redecorated for more than ten years. Even so, the garage, like the bayside house, was constructed of the coquina stone that was once quarried in the Keys, and its exterior showed almost no deterioration. All of these residences along the bay, put up in the late 1920s, when there had been a good view of Miami Beach, were built to last, and they had. In return for staying on the premises, and for looking after the grounds, James Frietas-Smith had the rent-free use of the apartment and garage, with his utilities paid for by the Shapiros.

The empty garage below the apartment was huge, and with all four doors swung up against the ceiling there was ample light for his painting. The apartment above, however, was shabby, filled with discarded furniture and other items from the large house in front. In addition to the screened porch on the east side, furnished with a sagging three-quarter-sized bed and several odd pieces of antique furniture, there was a living room, a bedroom, a bathroom with a tub but no shower, and a kitchen large enough to include an old-fashioned breakfast nook, as they were called in the 1950s. The view from the porch and from the breakfast nook provided a good prospect of the bay. All of the rooms were large, with high, paneled ceilings. The pink wallpaper, with tiny rosebuds of darker pink in the design, had pulled away in various places and hung down in scattered tatters. A musty, nose-tingling odor of dust, mildew, and stale bacon grease pervaded the rooms, and there was no air conditioning. There was a large overhead ceiling fan in the living room, but it didn't work any longer.

"You can have the bedroom, Pop," Troy said, "if you don't want the porch, but Dale and I don't mind it in there, and you'll have a better breeze on the porch at night."

"Whatever you think, Troy."

"Good. The bathroom's at the end of the hall next to the kitchen, and I'll have James put some clean towels in there for you. You don't mind sleeping here in the living room, do you, James? You can sleep on the Empress couch."

James shrugged. "I don't care where I sleep." He took Dale's overnighter into the bedroom, and she followed him in. When James came out again, she closed the door and stayed in the bedroom.

"Take your jacket off, Pop," Troy said. "We've got some errands to run this afternoon, so you might as well be comfortable."

Stanley had put on his suit jacket after getting out of his car, but he shucked out of it now and removed his tie. Troy took them and handed everything to James.

"Hang these up for Pop, James. Okay, old-timer, let's get going."

"Where to?"

"James." Troy snapped his fingers. "Have you got any more money?"

"The five I gave you was my last cent."

"Well, it doesn't make any difference, I guess, now that Pop's here." He put a hand on the old man's thin shoulder. "Pop, you'd better give James twenty bucks or so, to go to the store. Talk to Dale, James, before you go, and find out what she needs. She can cook dinner for us. We should be back around six or six-thirty."

"I don't know where you're going, Troy, but I'd like to

go along," James said as he accepted two ten-dollar bills from Stanley.

"And I'd like to take you, too, James, but Pop and me've got some business to discuss. Ask Dale if she knows how to cook pork chops."

Troy crossed to the bedroom door and rapped on it. "Dale, honey." The door opened, and Troy planted a long kiss on the woman's ruined mouth. "Pop and me are going out for a while. James'll get you what you need, and you can fix dinner for us. All right, sweetheart?"

"Yes, sir, Mr. Louden."

"There's a good girl." He patted her exquisite buttocks.

Stanley followed Troy down the stairs. Troy wanted to drive, so Stanley handed over the keys to his Honda.

CHAPTER

11

At seven-thirty that Sunday evening, Hoke and Aileen ate one roast beef sandwich apiece and decided to save the other two for Monday's lunch. Hoke wasn't hungry, and neither was Aileen, but they chewed methodically through the sandwiches, washing them down with tall glasses of iced tea. Aileen wanted something sweet afterwards, and Hoke told her to eat one of the mangoes, suggesting that she either eat it over the kitchen sink or take it into the shower—preferably the latter—because it was so ripe.

Aileen took the mango into the bathroom, closed the door, and moments later the shower was running full force. Hoke cleared the table, rinsed the plates and glasses, and put them on the sideboard. Because the water was running at the sink and in the bathroom, he didn't hear the first knock, but when he turned off the faucet, he heard a very loud pounding at the front door. Hoke opened the door, trying to hold back his rage. There was no need for anyone to bang so hard. Louis Farnsworth, the salad man at the Sheraton Hotel, was at the door. Hoke would have said something sharp to him, but there was a woman standing there too.

Farnsworth was a thin man with a pot belly. He wore his white pants above the pot, and it looked as if he had a bowling ball below his belt. His hair was gray and thinning, and he had a sour expression on his lined face. The young woman behind Farnsworth was shorter than he was, but she outweighed him by sixty or seventy pounds. Her face was round, and her cheeks were so fleshy they sagged almost to her lips. Her puckered mouth was a small round O, and she stood there blinking pale blue eyes. She—or someone—had plucked away most of her eyebrows. She had given herself—or someone had—a home permanent that didn't take, and her brownish hair had frizzed up all over her head. A port-wine-colored birthmark covered most of the left side of her face, including the left eyelid. Her heavy breasts inside her white T-shirt sagged nearly to her waist, and she wore a waitress's brown mini-skirt with a skimpy red apron.

"You didn't have to break the door down," Hoke said.

"I'm sorry," Farnsworth said. "I guess you didn't hear me knock the first time. I knew you was in there because I could hear the water running."

"Okay—what can I do for you, Mr. Farnsworth?"

"I need me another key. This here's Dolly Turner. She's just come down from Yeehaw Junction, and she's got herself a dishwashing job at the hotel. Until she gets a couple of paychecks and can rent her own place, she's gonna bunk in with me. So I need us another key."

"Why can't you both use the same key?"

"We're on different shifts, that's why. What's the big problem about a second key?"

"No problem." Hoke went into the kitchen and opened the drawer where he kept his books and the extra keys. "You're 204, right?"

When Farnsworth didn't reply, Hoke brought him the extra key with the apartment number written on an attached cardboard tag. "That'll be a buck-fifty deposit,"

Hoke said. "When you return the key, you get the buck-fifty back."

"I didn't pay no deposit on my key," Farnsworth protested.

"That's because you paid a one-month security deposit rent, along with your first month's rent. If you lose your key, I can take it out of that. But each extra key's a buck-fifty deposit."

Dolly Turner looked sideways at Farnsworth. He took out a blue-green package of Bugler and some white papers, and rolled an economical cigarette. Dolly had a black wool Peruvian handbag with a white embroidered llama on one side. She rummaged in the interior, which was filled with odds and ends, including a flannel nightgown, and managed to find $1.38 in change.

"That's twelve cents short," Hoke said, after counting the pennies.

She glanced over at Farnsworth again, who took a long drag on his thin cigarette, and then watched black ashes flutter to the floor.

"That's all I got on me," Dolly said, in a tiny voice, "but I'm supposed to get paid next Saturday, if I work out all right."

"Okay. I'll trust you for the rest. But we don't make any profit on lost keys. It costs a buck-fifty to have one made."

Aileen, wrapped in a bath towel, came out of the bathroom, noticed the couple in the doorway, and quickly dodged back inside. Farnsworth and Dolly Turner left, and a few minutes later, Aileen, in jeans and a T-shirt, came out of the bathroom.

"Who was that with Mr. Farnsworth, Daddy?"

"Dolly Turner. She's going to be living with him until she's saved up enough money to rent her own place. She just got a job at the Sheraton, and he was good enough to take her in."

"But they aren't married. Isn't it against the law to rent to an unmarried couple?"

"They aren't exactly a couple. He's renting the place, not her, so she's merely his guest."

"But isn't it against the law for two people to sleep together if they aren't married?"

"No. They can sleep together. There's no law against that. But fornication between them is against the law. In fact, the missionary position is the only position allowed by law in Florida, and even then you have to be married. But it's a law that's rarely enforced."

"What's the missionary position?"

"That's when the woman lies on her back, and the man gets on top."

Aileen giggled. "That ain't the only way they do it up in Vero Beach."

"*Isn't*, you mean, or anywhere else. But that's the Florida law. It just isn't enforced, that's all."

"If they did, it would sure spoil things in the parking lot at Beach High." Aileen laced up her running shoes and went to the door. "I'm gonna go out for a while and walk off that sandwich and mango."

"Aren't you going to ride your bike?" Aileen's new bicycle was wedged between her Bahama bed and the wall.

"I'm just gonna walk around the mall. But tomorrow I'm gonna clean out that old office downstairs and keep it down there. The apartment's too crowded, and if I leave it outside somebody'll steal it, chain and all."

"That's a good project for you. The dumpster people come on Tuesday, so I'll help you tomorrow. Most of the stuff in there is junk anyway. If we clean it up, maybe we can use it as an office again."

After Aileen left, Hoke was restless. He slapped his chest

with both hands, and then he slapped his front pockets. He shook his head when he realized that he was feeling for his cigarettes, although he had no real desire to smoke one. He hadn't had a cigarette since the first day of his mid-life crisis, and he didn't really want one now, except that was what he had always done when he was bored or restless—smoke a cigarette. To give his hands something to do he went into the kitchen and cleaned the burners with a wet Brillo pad. As the foam formed between his fingers he recalled a description of eating pussy he had read in a novel last year. The description had been exaggerated, but the fact that he was thinking about pussy again was a good sign. He would have to do something about that, as soon as he got things organized around the El Pelicano. The best place for pickups used to be the Sand-Shell Villas, in its small dark bar in Singer Island Shores. A lot of New York secretaries, usually in pairs, took a villa on the beach during the off-season at the attractive package rates, which included round-trip fare from Kennedy. They were easier to pick up with two guys, but now that he had his own apartment, he could probably break up a pair and bring one home for the night—except for Aileen. He would have to do something about Aileen soon. If she absolutely refused to go out to her mother in L.A., he would have to persuade her to go back to Green Lakes. After all, Ellita could use Aileen's help as well as her mother's when the baby came. But that was still a few weeks away. He wanted Aileen out of his apartment sooner than that—

There was a light tapping on the door. Hoke washed his hands at the sink and dried them on a dish towel as he crossed to the door to open it. Dolly Turner, clutching her wool handbag, blinked vacantly at him a few times, then took two hesitant steps inside as Hoke backed away from the door. She reached into her bag and handed him the extra key to 204.

"I want my deposit back."

"Leaving already? I thought you two were an ideal couple."

Dolly worked her tiny mouth in and out and shook her frizzed head. "He wanted me to do something."

"What did you expect? When Mr. Farnsworth didn't come up with the twelve cents, I figured he wasn't into altruism."

"What?"

"Kindness to strangers, with no strings attached."

"I don't mind the regular way, I expected that. But I'm not gonna do nothing that ain't natural."

"How're you going to get back to Yeehaw Junction?"

"I'm not going back. He didn't get me my job, and I'll just sleep on the beach till I get paid. It won't cost me nothing to eat in the hotel kitchen."

"You won't be able to sleep on the beach, Miss Turner. The public beach closes at ten, and the beach is patrolled at night. You'd get picked up for sure. Why don't you keep your key and go over to the mall till about ten or ten-thirty, and then come back. Tell Mr. Farnsworth you're afraid of catching AIDS—"

"What's AIDS?"

"Mr. Farnsworth knows. By ten-thirty, he'll probably be ready to settle for something rather than nothing. If not, knock on my door again. I'll be up till at least eleven, and I'll give you your deposit back and let you sleep in my car. But just for one night. Tomorrow you'll have to find someone else or make other sleeping arrangements."

"I wouldn't mind sleeping in your car right now."

"Do it my way. You should've thought of these things before you left Yeehaw Junction, but you can think about them now, sitting on the bench over at the mall."

"I had to leave. When my daddy died, I didn't have no place to stay." She began to cry.

"It's a hard world, Miss Turner, but it's not as bad as you think. You've got a job. You can eat, and you've got two places to sleep—either with Mr. Farnsworth or in the back seat of my car. And even if you do something unnatural with Mr. Farnsworth, you still won't actually have to *sleep* with him afterwards. He's got two Bahama beds in his apartment, just like I have, so you'll have a comfortable bed all to yourself."

"You've given me something to think about." She wiped her face with the back of her hand.

Hoke opened the door a little wider. "Good. As I said, I'll be up till at least eleven, so go over to the mall and think about your options."

"I think maybe I'd better go back down the hall and talk to Mr. Farnsworth again."

"Whatever."

Hoke closed the door behind her, wondering if he had handled the situation diplomatically. The girl was only twenty-one or -two, and he was no expert on giving advice to the lovelorn. Perhaps he should have returned her deposit, and let it go at that. But if he had, she would have ended up in the Palm Beach County Women's Detention Center without her new dishwashing job, and with the beginning of a rap sheet. He wondered what he would do if he were in Dolly's position—there was a double rap on the door—but he was a man, and would never be in Dolly's position. Hoke shook his head and picked up his car keys from the dining table. That was quick, he thought. I'll tell Dolly to keep her head down in the back of the car, even though the night patrol cars hardly ever check the apartment house parking lot. He would wake her at six, take her a cup of coffee, and she would be fine.

Dr. Ralph "Itai" Hurt was at the door. He wore a light-blue muscle shirt exposing stringy arms, swimming trunks, and canvas skivvy slippers.

"Good evening, Professor."

"Itai. Just call me Itai," he said with a half-smile. "You aren't eating dinner now, are you?"

"No, we finished a while ago."

Itai nodded. "That's what I figured. I'm a little embarrassed about this, Mr. Moseley, but I've got a strong sense of *locus parentis,* held over from when kids were still 'kids' at college until they were twenty-one. I still volunteer advice sometimes to eighteen-year-olds, and they're pretty quick to tell me it's none of my business. Now that kids are considered adults at eighteen—"

"I know. It's easier to put them in jail. I suppose you want your books back. They're over here on the table—"

"No, no, that isn't what I've come to see you about. I want to talk to you about your daughter for a moment. I've been thinking about it, and I know how young she is, so perhaps you won't think I'm out of line if I—what's the word—'rat' on her."

"We don't call them rats anymore. The new term is 'confidential informant.' What's your beef with Aileen, Professor?"

"None at all. There are, as you know, some hibiscus bushes right outside my window where I work—"

"How's the novel coming along?"

"Not bad. I got a page and a half today. Actually it's a page and a quarter, but that's because I stopped halfway through the last sentence. When I finish the sentence tomorrow it will be about a page and a half. Hemingway said that was the way to do it."

"It works that way on Incident Reports, too. Look, what's on your mind, Itai?"

"Incident Reports? Right. Well, your daughter's been vomiting behind the hibiscus bush. That's what I wanted to tell you."

"When?"

"The last time? Just a while ago. But she's also been down there throwing up after breakfast in the mornings. Is she sick? Has she said anything to you about being sick to her stomach?"

"No. She eats a lot for being so skinny. More than I do, in fact. But she seems healthy enough."

"She isn't healthy, Mr. Moseley. I suspect she's got bulimia—a form of *anorexia nervosa.* Remember that singer a few years back, Karen Carpenter? That's what she died from. She kept vomiting, sticking her finger down her throat until she lost so much weight she finally starved to death. It's fairly common at the university. Even Jane Fonda had bulimia as a girl, she said, although she managed to kick it later on."

"I don't see how Aileen could catch anything like that. She hasn't been around anyone with a disease like bulimia, or I'd've known about it. She's never complained about being too full, either. If anything, she seems hungry most of the time, like any other normal teenager."

"If you threw up everything you ate, you'd be hungry, too, Mr. Moseley. It's called an eating binge. Then they get rid of it, and they still stay thin, or get thinner. How old is Aileen now, exactly?"

"Fourteen. Almost fifteen."

"Does she menstruate?"

"I think so. I haven't noticed any of the pads and whatnot around here yet, but down in Miami, living with three females, I'd sometimes see the Carefree boxes they came in —you know, in the garbage. But I don't know for certain about Aileen."

"At fourteen, she should be. But once you develop bulimia, and stick with it, even if you've started menstruating, you'll stop again. Just like female runners stop when they get up to six miles a day. And that's what they like, you see. When they stop menstruating they consider it a good sign. Their diet's working and they're getting thinner."

"Christ, how thin does she want to get?"

"This is a psychological disease, Mr. Moseley. If they've got bulimia, they'll never believe that they're thin enough. So if that's what this is with Aileen, she needs treatment right away. I don't want to alarm you, but I thought I'd tell you what I thought. Because if I'm right, your daughter needs to see a shrink."

"Jesus Christ."

"I'll talk to her if you want me to, because I could be wrong, you know."

Hoke shook his head. "I think you may be right, Itai. I should've noticed the signs myself. She always disappears after every meal, saying she's got an errand, or she's going out for a walk—even down in Green Lakes."

"I've got some Early Times downstairs. Come down and I'll buy you a drink."

"I'd better wait for Aileen to come back."

"I know where she is. I can point her out to you from my window downstairs. After she throws up, she lies down on the bench by the parking lot. It makes you weak, you know, throwing up that way, so she always stretches out there to rest afterwards. Come on."

They went downstairs to Itai's apartment and the professor pointed through his window to Aileen. She was lying on her back on the concrete bench, with both hands clasped behind her head.

"You want to look at the vomit?" Itai suggested. "We can go outside, and I can show it to you behind the bush."

"Fuck no, I don't want to see the vomit! Where's the Early Times?"

Itai brought out the bottle and glasses, and they had two shots apiece, without water or ice.

"I feel like a bastard, Mr. Moseley. But this is pretty

serious business, and if the girl doesn't get psychiatric treatment she could actually die."

"What ever happened to the brother?"

"What brother?"

"Karen Carpenter's brother."

"I don't know. But he wasn't a bad musician. I imagine he found a job playing in a cocktail lounge somewhere. But they made so much money as a couple, he might've retired. Their records still sell pretty well. You hear them on the goldie-oldie stations sometimes."

"Bulimia must be a female disease. I never heard of a man getting it, did you?"

"No way! Most men'll diet for a few days at a time, but men don't have the intestinal fortitude to starve themselves to death the way women do."

"Thanks for the drinks, Itai. I appreciate you coming to me with this—and I owe you one."

"I feel like a prick, being the informant, and I may be wrong. But it won't hurt anything to look into it."

Hoke went back to his apartment, wishing he had hit up Itai for a third drink. He made a pot of coffee instead and waited for Aileen. She returned about fifteen minutes later. He told her to pour herself a cup of coffee and to join him at the table.

"You want to play some more Monopoly, Daddy? We can play the fast game—"

"No, I want to talk to you."

"I don't want any coffee."

"Sit down, anyway. When's the last time you had your period?"

"Oh, Daddy . . ." Aileen blushed and looked away.

"When?"

"I haven't started yet."

"That isn't true. Ellita told me once that both of you girls were menstruating. I'd been complaining to her about all the paper products that were coming into the house. She told me then, and I remember."

"I did a few times, but then it stopped. I talked to Ellita about it, and she told me not to worry about it. Every woman's not the same, she said. Some are regular and some aren't, at least at first. Let's play Monopoly, Daddy. It's embarrassing to talk about this grungy stuff."

"I want you to change into a dress and your good shoes."

"What for?"

"Because I said so. And do it now!"

Aileen took a backless sundress into the bathroom to change, and Hoke put her canvas carryall on her bed. She wouldn't need much, but he packed the bag with underclothing, jeans, and T-shirts, taking them out of the cardboard box at the foot of the bed. He then put Aileen's sweater into the bag; she would need the sweater in L.A.

Hoke's jumpsuit was too tight under the arms for his shoulder holster, so he strapped on his stiff ankle holster instead. At least he could get his pants leg over it. He put his .38 Chief's Special in the holster, his shield and ID case in his right front pocket, and dropped his handcuffs into his rear pocket.

"Let's go," Hoke said, when Aileen, dressed now and wearing a new pair of Mushrooms with her sundress, came out of the bathroom. He picked up her bag.

"What did you put in my bag?"

"Everything you'll need."

They went downstairs. As Hoke unlocked his Le Mans, Dolly Turner emerged from the shadows of the building and clawed at his arm.

"You said I could sleep in your car, Mr. Moseley, and now you're driving away."

The car door was open, and Hoke could see by the dome light that Dolly Turner's left eye was black and blue. It was swollen, and the discoloring did not blend in well with her birthmark.

"We're using the car right now, Dolly. You can sleep in it when I get back."

"There's 'skeeters out here," Dolly whined.

"Okay. Hold onto this bag, and hop into the back seat."

Hoke put Aileen into the passenger's seat in front, got in himself, and locked the doors. There was no release on Aileen's door; Hoke had had it removed to keep suspects from jumping out at red lights when he transported them in his car. Dolly sat in the middle of the narrow back seat, cradling Aileen's canvas bag in her ample lap.

Aileen sulked during the ride to the West Palm Beach International Airport, but after Hoke parked in the visitors' lot, and she realized she was actually being sent back to her mother, she said, "I don't want to go back to Momma, or to Miami either. Grandpa said I should stay with you!"

"I'm your father, not your grandpa. Fathers don't always know best, but they do the best they can. Let's go. You, too, Dolly."

When they got inside the airport, Hoke told them both to sit down. He handcuffed Aileen's right wrist to Dolly's left wrist. "Now you girls sit here while I get the tickets, and I'll be right back."

Hoke went to the Eastern window and used his VISA card to buy two one-way tickets on the red-eye flight to Los Angeles. There was a half-hour stopover in Houston, the clerk said, and the flight left West Palm at two A.M.

"Don't you have a flight that goes straight through?"

"Sure, but not till ten A.M. tomorrow morning. I wouldn't wait for it if I were you. The stop in Houston isn't very long, and if you're asleep you probably won't even be aware of it."

"I have a little problem. The 'D. Turner' isn't me. It's the nurse over there on the bench. She's accompanying a mental patient to L.A., and I don't want her to try and get off the plane in Houston."

The ticket seller, a long-armed young man with a fuzzy brown moustache, looked to where Hoke was pointing. He frowned when he noticed the handcuffs. "Which one's the mental patient?"

"Don't be funny. The young girl's the patient."

"I wasn't trying to be funny, it's just that I've never seen a nurse in a brown mini-skirt with a red apron. I just wanted to be sure which one so I could get word to the captain, that's all. She won't cause any trouble on the plane, will she?"

"Of course not." Hoke showed the clerk his badge and ID case. "This is a family thing, and we want to keep it quiet. The young girl's Curly Peterson's adopted daughter, and he'll meet the plane at LAX."

"The pinch hitter for the Dodgers Curly Peterson?"

"That's the one."

"I didn't know he had a daughter. Somehow, you don't think of a rich ballplayer, with all that dough they make, being dumb enough to get married. But a lot of 'em are married, I guess."

"And they have daughters. Sometimes sons."

"Right. You don't have to worry, Sergeant. I'll see to it that the captain's informed when the plane comes in. It'll be past my shift, but I'll stick around anyway to tell him. You couldn't pick a better airline than Eastern. We really do earn our wings every day."

"I appreciate it."

Hoke returned to the bench, removed Dolly's handcuff, and then locked Aileen's wrist to the bench rail. "Come with me, Dolly. I want to talk to you for a minute."

Hoke led Dolly over to the coin lockers, out of Aileen's earshot. Dolly's black eye looked worse under the bright lights than it had in the car, and there was a smear of blood on her T-shirt he hadn't noticed before. The white of her half-closed eye looked like a piece of red celluloid, and her fat cheek was puffy.

"Mr. Farnsworth really hit you, didn't he?"

She nodded. "But I got him back in a good place."

"Okay. Here's what I want you to do, Dolly. You fly out to L.A. with my daughter, and when you get there her mother'll meet you and keep you on for a few days as a trained nurse—"

"I ain't never had no nurse's training, 'cept for the things I did for my daddy and all."

"My ex-wife doesn't know that. Just tell her you're a trained nurse, and she'll want to pay you off—probably within a day or two—and then you ask her for fifty dollars a day."

"That much?"

"That's right, including today. You've already earned fifty bucks, and you aren't even in L.A. yet. Then, after she pays you off, go to the Welfare Department in downtown L.A. and apply for emergency relief. You can't get on regular welfare till you've lived there a year, but in California all new arrivals qualify for emergency relief. They'll fix you up with a room, food stamps, or a meal ticket, and then you can look for a job out there. It's easy to get a job in a kitchen in California, and you'll have a better future there than in Riviera Beach."

"Don't I need permission or something to leave the state?"

"No. Who told you that?"

"I don't know. I was born here, up in Yeehaw Junction, and I thought I had to get permission."

"Hell, no, Dolly. You can go anywhere you like. This is practically a free country. And if you don't like California, you can always ask them at the welfare office to send you back. But I know you'll like it out there. The important thing is to not let the girl get off the plane when it stops in Houston. My ex-wife, Mrs. Peterson, will be waiting for you at the L.A. airport. Okay?"

"Do they feed us on the plane?"

"Sure, you get two breakfasts on the red-eye. One between here and Houston, and another breakfast somewhere around the Grand Canyon. Meanwhile, I'll get you something out of the machine. Here's the key to the cuffs. Go back and cuff yourself to Aileen again."

"And a diet orange crush, if they have it."

"There's an orange juice machine, I'm sure."

"If they don't have an orange crush, I'd rather have a Classic Coke."

Hoke got some change from the change machine and bought two ham-and-cheese sandwiches, two bags of Doritos, and two half-pints of orange juice from the machines. He brought them back to the bench. He handed one sandwich to Aileen, and gave the rest to Dolly.

"If it was Sue Ellen instead of me," Aileen said, "you wouldn't send *her* out to Los Angeles. You've always loved Sue Ellen better than me. But someday you're going to be sorry you did this, just wait and see! I won't forget it, neither, handcuffing me like a criminal!"

"Eat your sandwich."

"I'm not hungry."

"You should be, after throwing up your dinner."

"Who told you that?"

"Never mind. I love both you girls the same, and if Sue Ellen had the same problem you have I'd send her to L.A. too."

"You always wanted a boy instead of me!"

"Is that what you think?"

"I heard you tell Ellita once you wished you had a son."

"That was in addition to you two girls, not instead of, for

Christ's sake. Is that why you're trying to stay thin? Are you trying to look like a boy instead of a girl?"

"You don't know or care anything about me!" Aileen's brown eyes filled with tears, and she shook her head to clear them away. "Nothing!"

"Don't cry, honey," Dolly said, offering the opened bag. "Have some Doritos."

Hoke went to the bank of pay telephones and used his Sprint card to call Patsy in Glendale. The phone rang ten times before Patsy picked it up. Hoke sighed when she answered.

"Patsy, this is me, Hoke."

"You caught me as I was going out the door, so make it short. I've got to pick up Curly at the studio. He's doing a commercial for the new California Chili-Size people. You know how much he gets for a thirty-second spot?"

"No, and I don't give a shit. This is an emergency, Patsy, or I wouldn't've called. Aileen came down with bulimia, and I'm sending her out to you with a trained nurse on the Eastern red-eye, Flight 341. I want you to meet the plane with a doctor and get her into a hospital right away."

"What's she got?"

"Bulimia. It's a wasting-away disease, and if she isn't treated by an expert she can die from it."

"Can't she be treated there in Florida?"

"No, it's a California-type disease. They know more about it there than they do here. Jane Fonda had it, and Karen Carpenter died from it. Aileen needs a specialist. Your doctor'll know who to call in for a consultation. So you'd better bring him along when you meet the plane. I don't know if you'll need an ambulance or not. Probably not, but you'd better ask him about that, too."

"How long's she had it?"

"I don't know. I just found out today myself. But she's a very sick girl. She only weighs about eighty pounds."

"She weighed ninety-five six months ago!"

"See what I mean? You got a pencil and paper?"

"Just a sec—"

Hoke repeated the flight number and gave her the time of arrival at LAX. "Please call me at Dad's house when she gets there, and let me know what the doctor says."

"Are you up at Grandpa's?"

"I'll wait for your call at his house. I'm staying at the El Pelicano, here on Singer Island, and I haven't got a phone."

"What are you doing up there?"

"I quit the force, and I'm managing the El Pelicano for Frank."

"What about my alimony? You owe me three checks already."

"Jesus Christ, Patsy, your husband makes three hundred and twenty-five thousand bucks a year!"

"More than that, counting commercials, but what's that got to do with our final agreement?"

"Let's talk about money later, okay? Right now you've got to get ahold of a doctor, so he can have Aileen admitted to a hospital when she gets there."

"When the girls lived with me, they were never sick for a single day."

Remembering the pediatrician's bills Patsy had sent him in the ten years the girls had lived with her, Hoke almost said something about it, but he restrained himself.

"In that case," he said, "you shouldn't have sent 'em back to me." He racked the phone before she could reply. Perhaps he had overstated Aileen's illness, but with Patsy he always had to exaggerate to get her attention. He only hoped now that he had elaborated Aileen's condition sufficiently so that Patsy would get the girl some help.

The wait for the two A.M. departure seemed interminable. Aileen stared at Hoke with loathing and tightened lips, but gradually her mood changed for the better. Hoke got the key from Dolly Turner and took off the handcuffs when Dolly said they had to go to the bathroom.

"Okay, Dolly, but don't let her throw up in there."

When they returned, Hoke didn't cuff them again. He returned the handcuffs to his hip pocket. When the flight was called, Hoke walked them to the gate. Aileen seemed resigned to the trip to L.A. She gave him a weak smile and took his hand.

"I love you, Daddy."

"I love you, too, honey. And just as soon as you're well again, I want you back. I hope you know that."

Aileen nodded. "I'll be back soon, Daddy." He hugged her, and kissed her on the cheek.

"If you happen to see Mr. Farnsworth tomorrow," Dolly said, "ask him to tell 'em over at the hotel that I've done quit and went out to Hollywood."

"I'll tell him."

Hoke drove back to the island, feeling embarrassed and guilty at the same time. It was embarrassing to have a stranger—a tenant—tell you that your daughter had a psychological disease like bulimia, and he felt guilty for not picking up on the signs himself. He had been so wrapped up in his own concerns, he had neglected both of the girls; and for that matter, he had been pretty abrupt with Ellita when he had talked to her on the phone.

Hoke parked in his slot at the El Pelicano and checked his mailbox in the lobby, the first time he had looked into it since Thursday. There was an advertising flyer from Es-Steem-Cleaners, offering a $21-per-room rug shampoo, and there was a Mail-Gram from Ellita in the box.

On Mail-Grams, Hoke knew, they telephoned the message and sent the letter the next day. But he didn't have a phone, so the Mail-Gram could have been in his box since

Friday or Saturday morning. The message was short: HOKE, CALL ME AT YOUR EARLIEST CONVENIENCE. ELLITA.

Hoke left the lobby and crossed the lot to the pay phone beside the brightly lighted 7/Eleven store. The Singer Island store was open twenty-four hours a day now, which made the 7/Eleven sign meaningless. It took Hoke three tries on the pay phone to get Ellita. To use his Sprint card he had to dial thirty-six numbers altogether: the 1-800, the 305 area code, and his Green Lakes number. Then he had to dial his Green Lakes number again, and finish with his authorization code number. Even when he took his time dialing, it was hard to keep all of the numbers straight in his head in the dim light of the booth.

Ellita answered on the fifth ring. "Allo?"

"It's me, Ellita. I know it's late, or early, but I just picked up your Mail-Gram."

"What time is it? I was asleep."

"A little after three."

"And they just delivered the Mail-Gram? I called it in Friday."

"It's my fault, Ellita. I just now got around to checking my mailbox. You could've called me at Frank's house. We spent almost all afternoon over there."

"I didn't want to bother him. When I called before to ask after you, he was a little cross, I thought. But a problem's come up, Hoke, and I wanted to talk to you about it. You remember when Dr. Gomez told me I should have the amniocentesis, and you told me not to do it?"

"You're damn right I did. You don't need a needle stuck into your belly, and he's only trying to gouge you for more money."

"Insurance pays eighty percent, Hoke—"

"I know, but the other twenty percent comes out of your pocketbook. Besides, it's the principle of the thing. We discussed this—"

"But here's the problem, Hoke. He wants me to sign a paper absolving him of responsibility for any birth defects in the baby—just because I turned down the amniocentesis. My mother says I should have it, and not sign the paper."

"Look, Ellita, it's the same as I told you the first time. You're a healthy woman, and you don't need to know whether you're going to have a boy or a girl—"

"It's a boy, Hoke. He kicks like a boy."

"All right, then. And if they discovered any birth defects, you'd have him anyway, wouldn't you?"

"Of course. He's my baby. I know I'm going to love him no matter what."

"Then sign Gomez's paper and let him off the hook. Your mother's old-fashioned and still thinks that doctors know everything. She's into authority figures, that's all. But don't let me influence you either way, Ellita. If you want to do it, go ahead. I'm just telling you what I think."

"I don't think I need it, either, Hoke, but I wanted to talk to someone about it first. I'll just go ahead and sign his paper."

"I'm sorry I didn't phone you earlier, but like I said, I just now got your Mail-Gram."

Hoke was going to tell her about Aileen's affliction, and sudden flight to California, but he decided that this was not the best time. It would be better to wait on that, until after he had heard from Patsy.

"I'm a little curious, Hoke. How come you checked your mailbox at three in the morning?"

"Oh? I thought I heard a disturbance downstairs, so I checked it out. But it was just a couple of cats fighting. While I was downstairs, I checked the box, that's all. How's Sue Ellen?"

Ellita laughed, but quickly suppressed it. "Sue Ellen? I don't know about Sue Ellen, whether she's all right or not."

"What do you mean? She isn't sick, is she?"

"No, she's fine, but she did something awful to her hair. She had it cut short on the sides, and then had it dyed green —right down the middle."

"That doesn't sound like something she'd do willingly. Do you suppose that—?"

"She dyed it for the concert, she said. The whole gang at the car wash is going to the Dead Kennedys concert at the Hollywood Sportatorium. And Sue Ellen wanted the new punk look, she said."

"That's okay, then." Hoke sighed with relief. "I thought she might be sick or something. I see a lot of young girls with dyed hair here on the beach."

"Green?"

"Sure. Green, blue, different colors. It's just a fad; next month, or next year, they'll dream up something else."

"You don't mind, then?"

"No, why should I mind? After all, Sue Ellen's the only girl working with those blacks and Cubans at the car wash, so she's got to prove she's just as tough as they are. So give her my love, and tell her to have a good time at the concert."

"I will. She was a little worried about what you'd think. She also paid thirty-five dollars for her ticket."

"That much? Well, why not? As the song says, she works hard for her money. Tell her to take a Saturday off sometime and come up here for the weekend. If she takes the bus, I can drive over and pick her up at the Riviera Beach station."

"Not this weekend. She's going to the concert."

"I know, but maybe next weekend. And tell her that Grandpa sends his love, too. Are you okay now, Ellita?"

"Sure, I'm okay. I'm feeling pretty good. I just wasn't going to sign Dr. Gomez's chit without talking it over with you first."

"Good. Go back to sleep, and I'll call you in a couple of days."

Hoke bought a four-pack of wine coolers in the 7/Eleven and drank all four bottles before he fell into a fitful sleep. His alarm woke him at six-thirty. He showered and shaved, put on a clean jumpsuit, and drove to his father's house to wait for a call from Patsy. He missed Aileen already, and he was glad that he had told the girl he wanted her to come back. Maybe Sue Ellen actually would come up for a weekend. Frank, he knew, would like to see her, green hair and all, and while she was here she could ride Aileen's bike.

CHAPTER 12

After Stanley and Troy left the house, Troy drove in silence until he was stopped by a red light. He turned and winked at the old man. "I think it's hot enough for a beer."

"I can always stand a beer. Sometimes two," Stanley agreed.

"I've been thinking about this little car of yours, Pop. We'll need a much bigger car for the rest of us. Besides, the clutch slips on James's little Morris."

Troy parked in front of a beer-and-wine bar on Second Avenue, and they went inside. Except for a middle-aged bartender and a few buzzing insects beating against the red neon Budweiser sign in the window, the dark bar was deserted. There were three booths and a half-dozen stools —most of the seats crisscrossed with gray duct tape—at the aluminum-topped bar. Troy ordered two long-necked bottles of Bud and told the bartender to bring them over to the booth with cold steins. Pop paid, and Troy filled the frosted mugs.

"Beer from a long-necked bottle tastes better than it does from a short-necked bottle," Troy said. "But I suppose you know that?"

Stanley nodded. Troy took a swallow, and so did Stanley.

"This is just right," Troy said. "Tell me something, Pop, what do you think of Dale Forrest?"

"I just met her, Troy, so I haven't thought much of anything about her. She seems like a nice enough girl, but what happened to her face? Was she in an automobile accident?"

Troy laughed. "No, not in an 'automobile accident.' It's a funny thing, but people call cars 'cars' until they refer to accidents, and then all of a sudden it becomes an *automobile* accident. Let me tell you something, Pop"—Troy snapped his fingers—"I'm going to help that girl. And if you feel any compassion at all for Dale, I want you to help me help her."

"Sure, Troy. I'll do what I can, but I don't—"

"You can do a lot, Pop, a helluva lot. Just to look at her now, you'd never guess that she was once Miss Bottlecapping Industry of Daytona Beach, would you?"

"She's got a nice shape." Stanley wet his thumb. "I can say that much."

"You noticed that, did you?" Troy grinned.

"I ain't making fun, son. It's just that it's easier to look at her figure than her face. That's all I meant."

"Maybe, Pop, I see something in Dale you don't see. I see the shining inner beauty of the woman. To me, what's inside is much more beautiful than a battered exterior. Do you know what I'm talking about?"

Stanley nodded. "Sure. Beauty's only skin deep. I won't argue none about that."

"Yes"—Troy nodded and took another sip of beer—"but it's much more than that, Pop, in a spiritual sense. I'm gonna fill you in some on Dale's background, and then you can appreciate what a beautiful woman she really is—not only in her body but in her soul. A man must help himself in this world, but sometimes he needs a bit of understanding from other people. I think Dale's taken a step forward into a better and richer life by listening to me, but now that this responsibility has been thrust upon me, I feel it right here, deep inside." Troy tapped his chest, took another sip of beer, and sighed. "Not only am I responsible for Dale Forrest, but I've got a duty to James Frietas-Smith, and an even greater debt to you."

"You don't have to worry none about me, son. I been looking after myself for a good many years now, and I can keep on for a few more."

"Exactly!" Troy thumped the table with his fist. "That's what I mean! Why should you? Why should any man your age have to look after himself? Because nobody loves you, that's why. Well, all that's changed now, Pop. You aren't alone in the world any longer. One man, at least, cares what happens to you, and that man is me! Why, you've got more get-up-and-go than any of these Miami yuppies. And certainly more than those slugs up in Ocean Pines Terraces. How many up there—think for a minute—would pack up and come down here to Miami to help me out the way you did? Just to help a friend in need?"

"Not many, I guess," Stanley said uneasily. "But I—"

"No excuses, Pop, please. I needed you and you came. It's that simple. Let's forget about it, and I won't embarrass you by trying to thank you. Instead"—Troy reached across the table and took Stanley's right hand in both of his—"I'll try to be the son you always wanted to have but never had . . ."

Stanley's eyes blurred a little. To cover his emotion, he drank the rest of his beer. He opened his mouth to say something, but Troy shook his head.

"Let me tell you about Dale Forrest, Pop. Right now, that girl and that young Bajan painter need our help, and we've got to do something to help them. Tell me the truth, Pop, what do you think of James's painting?"

"Well, I ain't any art expert, Troy, but I'd say that the

boy needs some lessons from an art teacher of some kind. He seems willing enough to learn, all right. I was showing him how to stripe, and he was catching on a little bit when you drove up with Miss Forrest."

"I've really got to hand it to you, Pop. You grasped James's problem immediately, and you stuck the needle into the nerve. James needs art instruction desperately, even though he's bulging with native Bajan talent. You and I can see to it that he gets to the Art Students League up in New York. And then, someday, we'll be sitting back, after James becomes a famous painter, and we can say, 'We helped that boy when he needed it most, and we're proud we did!' Isn't that right?"

"Just a minute, Troy." Stanley leaned forward and frowned. "I'd like to help that Bajan just as much as you, but I'm on a fixed income—"

"Christ, you didn't think I wanted money, did you? I'm the one who's putting out the money for James's studies in New York. It'll all come from my end. What I want from you is a steadying influence. I want you to give James and Dale the benefit of your wisdom and experience, that's all. You must've misunderstood me. I don't imagine you brought more than a few hundred dollars down here with you anyway. Right?"

"Well, I didn't know exactly how long I'd be staying. I brought along five hundred in traveler's checks. Of course, I've got my checkbook with me, and Visa card."

"That'll be enough. Your needs are simple, and while you're staying with me you're my guest, of course. The last thing I want you to worry about is money. But you have to let me tell you about Dale.

"A few months ago, believe it or not, she was on her way to stardom on the Gold Coast here. She was already the featured stripper at the Kitty Kat Theater, and she sang a solo, 'Deep Purple,' before her act. They have these live acts between showings of Triple-X movies at the Kitty Kat, see? Eight girls altogether, and Dale was one of the featured stars, with a life-sized cutout on a poster board in the lobby. She already had a slogan her manager wrote for her, 'You can't see Dale Forrest for the trees!' " Troy shook his head. "She was on her way up, no question about it.

"Her manager had a new gig lined up for her in East Saint Louis. The next step would've been burlesque on State Street, in Chicago. Then, inevitably, New York, and into television. Eventually, and I'm sure of it, she could have been one of those pretty girls on daytime TV, on one of the talk shows, leading guests on and off the stage. And then, blooie!" Troy slapped the table so hard the bartender jumped.

"Yes, sir!" the bartender said. "Two long-necked Buds, coming up!"

"What happened?" Stanley picked at the scab on his upper lip.

Troy sat back and lowered his voice. "She fell in love."

The bartender took some money from the pile of bills and change in front of Stanley. "Take a dollar for yourself," Troy told him.

"Thank you, sir."

"Now there's nothing unusual about falling in love," Troy was saying. "Dale's young. She won't be twenty-one for another five months, even though she looks older. And the guy she fell in love with was a handsome young cab driver. He was also a part-time student at the community college, taking a course in real estate. He was an athlete, too, Dale told me, playing slow-pitch softball every Sunday at Tropical Park. They were star-crossed lovers, Pop. Dale was already a flickering star, with only one way to go—straight to the top. But here was a guy who only wanted a real estate license so he could sit around in empty houses on Sundays instead of playing softball. Compared to Dale, the boy had no future at all. See what I mean?"

"I think so. She was riding in his cab and they had a car wreck."

"No, that isn't what happened. I'm just filling you in on the background so you'll see that marriage was out of the question. Here was a handsome man, but he had no real purpose in life. Dale was heading for stardom, but if she'd married him, she would've had to give up her dream. That's the American way, Pop. If a man can't support his wife, he's got no business getting married."

"That's right. But it's okay if his wife works part-time."

"I didn't mean part-time. It's nice for a woman to get out of the house for a few hours every day, but Dale would've had to give up show business."

"What happened?" Stanley refilled his glass.

"None of us are saints, Pop. All of us are human, so Dale started fucking the cab driver. If that was all there was to it, there wouldn't've been no problem. Once something like that starts, they get tired of each other after a while, and it would have ended. She would've gone on to stardom, and he, in all probability, would've finished his real estate course. But it also happened that Dale was fucking her manager. After all, he had discovered her, picking her out of a group of girls in a wet T-shirt contest up in Daytona Beach. He gave Dale her first break, and he was pushing her toward the top. He was entitled to screw her for his trouble, and she wasn't making any big money yet. In show business, that's the way things are done. You've probably seen the same thing in movies."

Stanley nodded. "On TV, too."

"But this is a real-life story. Dale isn't too smart; her manager wasn't too shrewd either. But he found out about the cab driver, and that's what happened to Dale's face. Her manager busted in on her in the middle of the night and beat hell out of her, and that was the end of her stage career.

No matter how beautiful her body still is, her face would frighten the customers."

"That man should be put in jail for ruining her face that way."

"Not so fast, Pop. You aren't looking at this objectively. Things are more complicated than that. It could be argued, for example, that Dale deserved to be worked over a little. After all, her manager was putting in a lot of time and effort in furthering her career. She had no business risking it with a cab driver. And the fact is, her manager didn't intend to mark her up that way, either. She was his bread and butter. But unfortunately, he was drunk at the time, and he forgot to take off his rings. He had a great big signet and a pinky, and that's what cut up her face so bad. And, being drunk, he kept on hitting her for a long time after he should've quit. You've got to admit she had a whipping coming."

"No, sir." Stanley shook his head. "A man should never hit a woman with his fists."

"What would you have done, if you were her manager?"

"I don't know, Troy. It takes a lot to make me mad, but I wouldn't've hit her, drunk or sober."

"Exactly. You'd have punished her, and so would I, but we've both got enough sense not to hit a woman where it'll mark up her face. Now that Dale's put herself under my protection, I can't look at her situation objectively. It's up to me to get her face fixed up again, so she can go on with her career. I just don't believe that a beautiful girl like Dale should suffer for one mistake, do you?"

"Of course, not. But what—?"

"Here's the answer, Pop, right here." Troy unsnapped the top buttons of his shirt and withdrew a brown envelope. He opened it and handed Stanley a color brochure of Haiti, with a photograph of the Gran Hotel Olofsson on the cover. "Haiti. That's the answer, Pop. When I met

James in New Orleans, he told me a lot about the West Indies, and he sold me on the idea of living in the islands. I went to a travel agent here and looked at folders on all the different islands, and Haiti looks best of all. Except for visiting border towns in Mexico, Tijuana and Juarez, I haven't been out of the United States."

"Me neither, except for Canada. I been in Canada lots of times, but not Mexico. Where is this Haiti?"

"The other side of Cuba. My original idea was to just go island-hopping, taking a plane from one island to another till I found one I really liked. But Dale has changed my plans. There's a plastic surgeon over in Haiti, a German doctor who lost his license in the States, but he can still practice in Haiti. A con I knew in Soledad told me about him—you know, in case you ever wanted to change how you look? He's supposed to be a top man. Well, I'm going to Haiti, Pop, and I'm going to find that surgeon for Dale."

Stanley tapped the folder. "That'll take a lot of money, won't it?"

"Don't you think Dale's worth it? And doesn't James deserve a chance to study art in New York?"

"Sure." Stanley nodded.

"And what about you, Pop? Wouldn't you like to see Haiti?"

"I don't rightly know. I'm not sure where it is, even."

"It's only two hours away from Miami, Pop, on Air France. And that's where you, me, and Dale are going next Sunday morning."

"I don't know about that. That's pretty short notice. Don't you need a passport and some shots and things like that?"

"Not to go to Haiti you don't. I already checked it out with the travel agent. You can stay sixty days without a passport or visa, and as long as you've got money and a return ticket they'll keep extending your stay. Indefinitely.

You don't need any shots, either. Round trips for the three of us, not counting taxes, will cost six hundred and sixty-nine dollars. Two-twenty-three apiece."

Stanley whistled softly. "That's a lot of money."

"Not for me it isn't. By Saturday night I'll have twenty-five, maybe thirty thousand dollars. Four thousand'll go to James, for New York, and then, after I pay you back two thousand, plus the vig, that'll still leave plenty for the three of us to go to Haiti, live in a nice hotel, and pay for Dale's operation. And while we're there, everything's on me, Pop. Transportation, hotel, drinks, anything you want, and for as long as you want to stay."

"What's this about paying me back two thousand?" Stanley straightened in the booth.

"I figure it's no more than right, Pop. I know it's only a short-term loan, but you're entitled to interest all the same. I'll need two thousand from you now, and on Saturday night I pay you back twenty-five hundred. I think that's fair, don't you?"

"Where're you gonna get all this money? The twenty-five or thirty thousand, I mean, to pay me back?"

"I'm holding up the new Green Lakes Supermarket, here in Miami. I thought I already told you. And I'm letting James and Dale help me."

"No, you never told me nothing like that. I can't loan you no money to commit a robbery! One of the main reasons I came down here was to keep you out of trouble. And why do you need two thousand anyway?"

"To pay for our airplane tickets, for one thing. There's a flight leaving Miami at twelve-forty Sunday, and we'll be on it, me, you, and Dale. I also need some cash to buy some things for the job. These are all ordinary business expenses. You know as well as I do, it takes a little money to make a lot of money."

"But if you get caught, you'll go to jail, Troy. And then where'll you be?"

"This job is foolproof, Pop. I've never seen a better setup than this one. Christ, this is what I do for a living. Hey—you're not prejudiced, are you, just because James is a black man?"

"Black? James? You said he was a Bajan. He don't look black to me."

"Well, he is black, as well as being a Bajan. He's at least a fourth black, maybe more, so that makes him a black according to southern laws. But that's just another reason he needs my professional help. If he tried to do this job on his own, as he intended to at first, he'd get caught. You ever hear of Affirmative Action, Pop?"

"Of course. We had it at Ford. Ford's an equal-opportunity employer."

"All right, then. Chew this over for a few minutes. Blacks in this country are only about ten percent, or perhaps a little more. But in prisons, about *forty* percent of the prisoners are black. In city jails, the percentage is even higher. Why do you think this happens, Pop? So many black men in jail?"

"I don't know. I never thought much about it."

"Well, I have. It's because there's no Affirmative Action plan for black ex-criminals, that's why. Without proper guidance and training, they almost always get caught and end up in prison. But I believe in Affirmative Action, and that's another reason why I want to help James. This particular job was originally his idea, but I planned it, and I'll see that it's carried out properly. James is a pretty desperate nonobjective painter, and he needs my help almost as much as Dale does. But I never thought you were prejudiced—"

"I'm not prejudiced, Troy. I'll admit that with Affirmative Action, you sometimes got a pretty dumb black foreman on the line. But some of the white foremen were just as dumb, I always thought. When you consider the aggravation and responsibility that goes with being a foreman, the extra money isn't worth it."

"That's true, Pop. I could never understand why the so-called correction officers worked for such low pay, either, but there's always someone dumb enough to take a guard's job. But you won't find many professional white criminals like me who'll train a black man under Affirmative Action. And this'll be my last professional robbery. When we go to Haiti, and after the surgeon starts work on Dale, which'll take several months, I'm going to start a business over there, one way or another. The Haitians make and wear these voodoo masks, you see. I figure Dale, with her figure and strip act, and wearing a voodoo mask, can get work at one of the tourist night clubs. That way, she'll keep up with her dancing while her face is healing, and be ready to take up her career back here when it's all over. We can rent us a beach house and eat fresh lobster for lunch every day. How does that sound?"

"It sounds fine, Troy, but two thousand dollars—"

"Two thousand loaned for twenty-five hundred back is a profitable deal, Pop. Besides, I don't even need cash. I'll just borrow your Visa card, and by the time your bill comes in a month from now, you'll have already been paid back your twenty-five hundred in cash. Of course, if that isn't enough interest for you, tell me what you want."

"It ain't the interest, Troy. I want to help you, but—"

"And James and Dale?"

"Them, too. But I don't want you to go to jail."

"You're worried about the loss to the supermarket? Is that it? Well, don't worry about that. They have insurance, so they won't lose a dime. In fact, they'll probably pad their loss, saying it was more than it was. In an operation like this one, nobody loses and everybody gains."

"Tell me a little more about the job."

"I'd rather not, Pop. The less you know, the better off you'll be. After this is all over, and you come back from Haiti, some cop might ask you about it. And if you don't know anything, you won't be able to tell him anything. I want to keep you out of this thing altogether, Pop. See what I mean? I want to protect you just like I'm protecting James and Dale."

"Let me think a minute, Troy. It's a lot to take in all at once, if you know what I mean . . ."

"Of course. Take all the time you want. There's no big rush about this. We've got till Saturday night. Want some pretzels?"

"A little too salty." Stanley shook his head. "But I'd like one of those small packs of barbecue chips."

Troy picked a dollar up from a small stack of bills and went over to the bar to look through the snack rack. Stanley took a sip of beer.

What would happen, he thought, if he turned Troy down? Everything between them would change, and quickly. If he still stayed on for a few days, the relationship between them would be strained, and he had truly been enjoying himself. It was all so interesting and exciting, being in the city with Troy, with James. Even Dale, now that he knew about her show business background, was a more exciting woman. On the other hand, if he lent Troy the money—which wouldn't hurt him too much, since it was out of savings, even if it wasn't paid back for a while—and Troy carried out this big robbery, Troy might end up in prison again. And he didn't want to be responsible for that, even indirectly . . .

Troy was back at the booth, handing Stanley a bag of Wise barbecue potato chips. "These are just as salty as pretzels, aren't they?"

"Maybe so, but the barbecue flavor gives 'em a better taste. They go good with beer." Stanley opened the bag, poured a handful of chips into his left hand, and offered some to Troy. Troy shook his head and made his lightning grimace.

"What happens, Troy, if I don't loan you the money?"

Troy shrugged, grimacing again, pulling his thin lips tightly over his small teeth. "James and me'll have to cowboy it, that's all. We'll have to drive around at night and hold up some liquor stores and gas stations. Two thousand isn't much. In two or three nights we'll have the stake. That's what I usually do when I need some quick cash. But James is inexperienced, and a little on the nervous side. That's why I asked you instead."

"In other words, you're gonna go through with this big robbery you planned, whether I help you or not?"

"You know I am, Pop. I already told you before, this is what I do. But I won't press you. If you don't think you're getting a good return on your investment, forget I asked you. And if you don't trust me—"

"I trust you, Troy." Stanley licked his fingers. "Hell, if I can't trust you, who can I trust? Besides, as they say, one hand washes the other."

"Now you're talking. Just let me borrow your Visa card, your union card, and voter's registration for ID. You can then drive back to the house, and I'll get a cab to take care of business."

"I don't have no voter's registration card. Down here in Florida, if you register to vote they make you serve jury duty."

"Your Social Security card'll do just as well."

"That ain't supposed to be used for identification. It says so right on the card."

"The man I'm dealing with will accept it, Pop. Trust me."

Stanley took out his wallet, found the cards, and handed them over to Troy. Troy slipped them into his shirt pocket. He snapped the flap shut. "I'll take the rest of the change here on the table for cab fare. You keep the travel folder and show it to Dale when you get back to the apartment. She hasn't seen it yet. You better cash one or two traveler's checks, too. But keep a record of every cent you give Dale for groceries. We can add that in on top of your twenty-five hundred next Saturday."

Troy dropped the Honda keys on the table and slid out of the booth. "Finish the rest of my beer, Pop—"

"Just a minute, Troy. Whatever happened to the cab driver?"

"What cab driver?"

"You know, the one who was carrying on with Dale."

"Oh, him? He visited Dale in the hospital, took one good look at her, and she's never seen him again. Some men are like that."

"That poor girl." Stanley shook his head and poured the rest of Troy's beer into his stein. "She's lucky she found you."

"I think she knows it, Pop." Troy kissed the old man on the cheek and left the bar.

Stanley trusted Troy about the money. After all, he thought, everything so far had happened the way Troy said it would, so Stanley had no reason not to trust him, and he could tell that Troy genuinely liked him. Stanley had worked with other men all of his life, and he could tell whether someone was sincere or not, and Troy was the only person who had paid any attention to him since he had moved to Florida. On the other hand, the credit limit on Stanley's Visa card was all the way up to $2,200. Without even asking him, the bank had automatically raised the limit by two hundred dollars when he had renewed the card two months ago. Any way he looked at the matter, he couldn't afford to outright lose two thousand dollars, even though, as Troy said, his intention was to pay back five hundred in interest just for using the money till Saturday. Stanley picked up his beer and his cane and crossed to the bar.

"Can I use your phone?"

"There's a pay phone in the hall, back there by the john. You need any change? It takes quarters."

"No, I've got change. But I can't read phone numbers too good, even with my reading glasses. Would you look up the eight-hundred number of Visa for me? And write it down?" Stanley put a dollar bill on the bar and pushed it toward the bartender. The bartender put the bill into a glass beneath the bar, then got the battered L–Z telephone book from the shelf to look up the number.

Stanley called the Visa number the bartender gave him and told the woman who answered that he had lost his Visa card.

"Do you have the number?"

"No, but I can give you my Social Security number and address."

"Let me have your name first."

Stanley gave her his name, Ocean Pines Terraces address, and Social Security number.

"When did you lose your card?"

"Yesterday, I think. But I didn't miss it till just now."

"All right. You'll get a replacement card in a week or so, but it'll have a new number. Not exactly a new number, but four additional zeros will be added in the middle. And this time, please write it down and keep it in a safe place, in case you lose it again."

"If someone finds and uses my card I won't be charged more'n fifty dollars, will I?"

"That's correct. But you should be very careful with your Visa card. It's not the same as money, it's better than money."

"Yes, ma'am. I might've just misplaced it, but far's I know now, it's lost."

"Yes, sir. Now if you do find it, don't use it. Just cut it in half and mail it in to us. Wait until you get your replacement card before you charge anything again."

"Yes, ma'am. I'm sorry I lost my card."

"We're sorry, too. But thanks for reporting the loss promptly, and have a rainbow day."

"Yes, ma'am."

Stanley folded the slip of paper with the Visa phone number on it and put it into his wallet. It would take the Visa people a day or two, perhaps more, to get the missing number on their lists, and by that time, Troy would have an ample opportunity to charge whatever he wanted. He felt a little guilty about reporting his card as lost, but if everything worked out all right, he could call Visa again and tell them he had found it after all. A fifty-dollar loss wouldn't hurt him too much, but a two-thousand-dollar loss, when a man was on a fixed income, was simply too much. What he would do, Stanley decided, was to just ask Troy for two hundred dollars in interest, instead of five hundred, when he got his money back. After all, the money Troy was going to make was primarily for Dale's and James's benefit, and Stanley felt sorry for both of them.

Stanley filled his car with gas and cashed a fifty-dollar traveler's check before driving back to James's garage apartment.

CHAPTER

13

Patsy didn't call Hoke at Frank Moseley's house until almost noon. On the advice of Curly Peterson's doctor, Patsy said, Aileen had been placed in a clinic at a Catholic convent in the Verdugo Woodlands section of Glendale. There she would be watched around the clock by the live-in sisters who ran the school.

"It's much better than a regular hospital, Hoke," Patsy said, "because as far as anybody knows, she'll be just another student there. Curly worries about his image, and it wouldn't look good for him if it got into the papers that his stepdaughter was starving to death. Not with his income."

"She isn't Curly Peterson's daughter. She's *our* daughter."

"Well, it wouldn't look good for you or me either, would it, if Aileen starved to death? Besides, Dr. Jordan'll look in on her every day. Curly said Dr. Jordan practically wrote the book on sports medicine, and he has a lot of confidence in him."

"She needs psychiatric help, not sports medicine. All those guys know how to do is shoot people in the knee with painkillers."

"That's easy for you to say. If you saw the bone spurs on Curly's feet, you'd want shots, too. But the Mother Superior will talk to Aileen every day, and she told me she's had a lot of experience with anorexics. Apparently some of the nuns have had it, and some of the convent girls come down with it on Novenas, she said."

"What are Novenas? One thing I know for sure, Aileen doesn't take any drugs—"

"I don't know what they are, and I didn't ask. I'm just telling you what the Mother Superior told me, that's all. The important thing is she knows all about anorexics, and she'll watch Aileen like a hawk and supervise her diet. She's got little black eyes like shiny caraway seeds."

"How serious is Aileen's case? And when'll she be cured?"

"It just takes time and patience, Dr. Jordan said. But first she's got to gain some weight and accept the idea that she's not too fat. I already promised her that when she gets up to one hundred pounds I'd take her home. So we'll just have to wait and see, that's all. She ate breakfast before the doctor gave her a shot, and that's a good sign. I already fired that weird nurse you sent out with Aileen, by the way. Where'd you find her, anyway?"

"On short notice, it was hard to get a nurse willing to fly out to L.A. I hope you paid her—"

"I did, and you owe me another hundred dollars."

"You'll get it, Patsy, just as soon as my pension money comes in. After my retirement papers go through, I'll take all my money out of the pension fund in a lump sum. And as soon as Aileen's well again, I want her back. But right now, money's tight."

"You *have* to take her back, Hoke. I go on all the road games with Curly, and we can't take her with us. If Curly told me once he told me a dozen times, he married me—not my daughters. Sometimes, when he's at bat, the camera points at me, and they tell the TV audience I'm his wife, and he likes that."

"I can understand all that. But if you handle the clinic and doctor bills, I'll take Aileen back, and gradually pay you back. Sue Ellen's got a good job in Miami, so I don't have to worry about her"—Hoke didn't mention the green Mohawk haircut—"but Aileen'll have to go back to school in September."

"Sue Ellen's got a job? That's hard to believe. I couldn't even get her to pick her clothes up off the floor in Vero Beach."

"What can I tell you, Patsy? She's getting minimum wage, plus tips, at the Green Lakes Car Wash."

"She has to go back to school, too, doesn't she?"

"No, she's dropping out. They like her at the car wash, and the manager gave her a permanent job."

"What kind of career is that for a girl? Only wetbacks work in car washes here in California."

"It's mostly Haitians down here. Sue Ellen's the only white girl there. But that gives her an advantage, she says. It won't hurt her to work for two or three years. Then, if she wants to go to college, she can take the G.E.D. test and go to Miami-Dade Community College. Don't worry about Sue Ellen. You've got enough to think about with Aileen. And please tell her to call Grandpa's house collect any time she wants, and I'll get back to her when they let me talk to her. Okay?"

After Patsy inquired after the health of Frank and Helen, and asked Hoke to give them her love, she rang off.

Hoke was vaguely dissatisfied and resentful after the conversation. Somehow, either on the phone or in person, Patsy had always managed to put him on the defensive. Hoke and Patsy were not Catholics, and he knew very little about the religion except that nuns were supposed to be tough disciplinarians. But maybe that was what Aileen needed. In religious matters, Hoke and Patsy were both nonbelievers, and they had never sent the girls to Sunday school, figuring that they could make up their own minds about that when they were old enough to think such things out for themselves. The nuns would undoubtedly go to work on Aileen, but Hoke had already warned the girls about religious cults and their brainwashing techniques, and he was sure Aileen could handle whatever propaganda the nuns tried to give her. Curly Peterson, the ballplayer Patsy had married, was probably a Southern Baptist, if he was anything, so it was probably the sports doctor—with his somewhat Biblical name—who had insisted on the Catholic clinic.

Hoke had eaten breakfast with his father, but Frank had been unperturbed by the news of Aileen's affliction. "When a girl's sick," he said, "she should be with her mother, and you did the right thing. When we find out exactly where she is, I'll wire her some flowers."

"Under the circumstances, it might be better to send her a basket of fruit."

"What? Oh, sure, I see what you mean. I've got to get down to the store."

Helen usually slept until noon, so Hoke managed to get out of the house before she called Inocencia for her breakfast tray.

Hoke became very busy at the El Pelicano. Before he could shave, Mr. Winters, a man in a khaki safari suit, had showed up wanting to rent an apartment for two months, and perhaps through October as well. He had a cashier's check for twelve thousand dollars, but no cash and no bank account. To obtain the first and last month's rent in advance, Hoke had to break his rule again and drive Mr. Winters to the bank in Riviera Beach so that he could cash the check and open an account. The drive to the bank was what Hoke would have called once a "two-cigarette" drive, one on the way over and another coming back, but he no longer smoked. Mr. Winters, or "Beefy" Winters, as the new tenant called himself, was an elephant trainer. He had been fired from the Ringling Brothers Circus in Kansas City. He tried to explain why, as they drove over the bridge into the city, but Hoke couldn't follow the complicated politics of the dismissal. Winters had also left his wife, who still worked for the circus "in Costumes." After returning to Sarasota, their winter home, Beefy Winters had cashed in their savings, and then had driven over to Singer Island to hide out from his wife until the season ended. He had a permanent winter job every year in Sarasota as a pharmacist, so he had decided to sit out the rest of the circus season in Singer Island and let his wife worry about where he and the money had gone. He was pretty sure that by the end of September she would take him back. He already missed the three elephants he trained, but not his wife—at least, not at the moment. But he would be glad enough to see her when the circus returned to its winter quarters in Sarasota.

Back at the El Pelicano, as Hoke gave him his key and a receipt, Beefy said that as a pharmacist he could make thirty thousand a year if he worked at a drugstore all year round, but circus life got into a man's blood.

"You have something in common," Hoke told him, "with Professor Hurt on the first floor. He's a horsefly man, and would probably enjoy talking to you about elephants and Africa . . ."

Hoke shaved, showered, and washed his dirty jumpsuit while he showered. He put the damp suit on a hanger and hung it over the showerhead to dry. The poplin material would be bone dry in about three hours. So far, the jumpsuits were the only items that had simplified his life. Everything else seemed to be as complicated as ever, and he still hadn't managed to slow his life down to the leisurely pace he had envisioned when he had accepted the management of the El Pelicano.

There were several cardboard boxes of Aileen's things in the apartment, and the small room was much too crowded. He decided to clean out the old office downstairs and store her bicycle and boxes there. The boxes had been opened, and he noticed the yellow-and-black Cliff Notes for *Catcher in the Rye.* He remembered reading the novel, and a simpler story would be difficult to find. Why would Aileen need the help of Cliff Notes to understand a boy like Holden Caulfield? He riffled through the pages of the Notes. Holden Caulfield was sixteen, but that was back in 1951, when the book was first published, so Holden was fifty-two years old now. Hoke took two boxes downstairs, one under each arm, thinking that Caulfield was probably either a balding broker on the stock exchange or one of those gray-faced corporation lawyers who had never been inside a courtroom. Either way, the thought was depressing.

Hoke unlocked the office door behind the short Formica counter. He put his cardboard boxes on the counter and looked inside the office. The room was about six by eight feet with an enclosed half-bath—a toilet and a washbasin, but no shower. If he cleaned it up and redecorated, and if he could somehow squeeze in a shower stall, he could probably rent this little room out as a one-person efficiency. Either that, or use it as an overflow bedroom for some family with an adult son or daughter. If he added a hot plate, he might be able to rent it to some permanent worker on the island—say, a dishwasher like Dolly Turner—for one hundred fifty or two hundred dollars a month. Then, if he didn't tell his father about it, he could pocket the money and Frank wouldn't know the difference. Fat chance. Frank would know about it within an hour; there were no secrets on the island.

The room was a mess now. A dusty metal desk took up

most of the space, and there were two rusty rollaway beds on top of it. Boxes of discarded sheets and battered cooking utensils were stacked haphazardly against the walls. Hoke tried the toilet, but it didn't flush. The water didn't run from the washbowl taps, either.

"Maybe the water's turned off, Sergeant Moseley?"

Hoke looked over his shoulder. A thin, dark man in his early twenties with a fluffy bandito moustache stood in the doorway. He had dark blue eyes, but Hoke recognized a Latin when he saw one. He wore a light tan summer suit with a yellow shirt and an infantry blue tie. He held a large brown envelope with the tips of his fingers.

"I'm Jaime Figueras," he said, shaking Hoke's hand. "You're a hard man to find, Sergeant Moseley. I came over about ten, hung around awhile, and then had a couple of beers at The Greenery. I decided to try again, and then if you weren't here I was going back to the station. How come you don't have a phone?"

"There's a pay phone fifty yards away in the mall."

"I didn't know that number. Besides, when you call a pay phone, nobody answers. And if someone does, he always tells you it's a pay phone and hangs up."

"I'm trying to simplify my life a little, that's all. If I had the only phone in the building, I'd be the message center for all my tenants. They'd also be knocking on my door at midnight wanting to use it. Anyway, what can I do for you, Figueras?"

"I haven't got a clue. Chief Sheldon said you might be able to help me out with these burglaries." He tapped the envelope against the Formica counter. "That's about it. He said you were a famous homicide detective from Miami, and that I could probably learn something from you."

"Famous? What else did he say about me?"

"That's about it. Except that you were Frank Moseley's

son, and that you used to be on the Riviera force before you went down to Miami."

"You're pretty young to be in plainclothes already."

"I'm twenty-four, and I've been a cop for more than three years now. I joined when I graduated from Palm Beach Junior College. I was going to transfer up to Gainesville, but I decided that two more years of education at the U.F. wasn't worth borrowing twenty thousand bucks, plus the interest. Besides, I was offered a job here, so I took it."

"As a cop, you'd make more money in Miami."

"I know. I went down there and talked to some of the Latin contingent on the P.B.A. But they discouraged me when they found out I was a *Mondalero.*"

Hoke laughed. "What did you expect? Cuban cops think that anyone who didn't vote for Reagan is a Communist sympathizer. If you voted for Mondale, you should've kept that information to yourself."

"I meant to, but I'm a Puerto Rican, not a Cuban. The trouble with Cuban-Americans, even when they're born here, is that they think of themselves as Cubans first, and *then* Americans. We love our island as much as they say they love theirs, but we know that without some kind of welfare, an island with a growing population can't support itself. All these Reagan cuts are killing us down there, man."

"You're probably right." Hoke shrugged. "You must've made the right choice, staying here in Riviera, or you wouldn't be a detective already. Want some coffee?"

"No, but I'd like to use your john. Like I said, I had a couple of beers in The Greenery."

Hoke put the two boxes inside, relocked the office door, and led the way upstairs. Hoke pointed to the bathroom door and took the envelope from Figueras. It contained two Xeroxed rosters listing the names of the residents with stolen items at the Supermare. The items each resident was missing were typed beneath the names. Many of the items were small objects, but there were also three paintings and a Giacometti sculpture on the list. The dimensions of the Giacometti weren't noted, but the paintings included a Corot, a Klezmer, and a Renaissance cartoon, artist unknown. The artists' names, except for the Klezmer, were vaguely familiar to Hoke.

"What've you done so far?" Hoke asked, as Figueras, zipping his fly, came back into the living room.

"I've talked to these people, and to the manager, Mr. Carstairs. These residents come and go, you know. Mr. Olsen—he's the president of the Supermare board of directors—he and his wife went on a two-week trip to the Galápagos a couple of months back, but they didn't miss their stuff right away. The cartoon was in the hallway, he said, and he never liked it much anyway. But it was plenty valuable. He didn't know whether it was missing before they left or not. His wife lost a diamond ring and a half-dozen elephant-hair bracelets. She had another diamond pin in her jewelry box, but that wasn't taken."

"What was the cartoon about?"

Figueras grinned. "I asked her the same question. It isn't a comic cartoon. It's a preliminary drawing of a Madonna and child, and it's supposedly after Raphael, Mrs. Olsen said. In other words, it's a brown-tone drawing, the kind the artist makes before he does the painting, and it's called a cartoon. 'After Raphael' means that it might've been drawn by Raphael but probably wasn't. It could've been done by one of Raphael's apprentices."

"It couldn't be worth much."

"I don't know. Mr. Olsen said it's worth quite a bit. Just as it is, without authentication, it's valued at twenty grand. And if it's ever authenticated, the value would triple. Mrs. Olsen isn't so worried about the diamond ring, but she wants the elephant-hair bracelets back because her granddaughter gave them to her last Christmas."

"Who gave you this list?"

"The manager. Carstairs. Then I talked to the tenants."

"Let's take another trip down there, Figueras. My father's wife's got an apartment there, and I promised her I'd check it out. She hasn't been in it for several months, so she might have something missing, too."

"Your stepmother has an apartment there?"

"Stepmother—come on. We're about the same age; she's just my father's second wife."

"Sorry."

"No cause to be. Technically, I guess she is my stepmother, but I've never thought of her that way. My kids call her Helen, not Grandma."

"Want to take my car?"

"No, you go ahead. I'll ride my daughter's bike down and take my trunks. After we check things out, I'll swim in the pool. I'd invite you, too, but a guest can't invite another guest."

"I got plenty to do back at the station. I really should come over here to the beach more often, but somehow, when I get through work and go home, I just don't think about it."

"You married?"

"No, but I got a live-in. Girl works at the International Mall. Suave Shoes. Nothing serious. She just wanted to get away from her parents and couldn't afford a place of her own."

"Lot of girls like that nowadays, it seems."

Figueras shrugged. "One, anyway."

Mr. Carstairs, a tanned, middle-aged man wearing khaki cargo shorts, a short-sleeved blue workshirt, and a pair of blue felt house slippers, was outside by the Supermare swimming pool. With a twelve-foot skimmer he was scooping dead dragonflies and bits of dried grass from the surface of the pool. When Hoke introduced himself, Carstairs put the skimmer down, nodded at Figueras, and lighted a menthol True.

"Your stepmother already called me about you, Mr. Moseley. The pool's open from nine to nine, but there's no lifeguard so you swim at your own risk. And no children are allowed."

"That's what Mrs. Moseley told me. Suppose I want to swim earlier, say, six or six-thirty in the morning?"

"I don't enforce the rules. I live over in Riviera, so I don't get here till around eight. But Mrs. Andrews, who lives right over there in 101-A, has threatened to shoot anyone who goes in before nine A.M. with her BB gun." Carstairs laughed harshly, and it brought on a paroxysm of coughing. His body doubled over and his face turned bright red. He clutched the back of an aluminum beach chair for support, coughed some more, and finally managed to take another short drag on his cigarette. That seemed to work; he stopped coughing.

"You okay?" Hoke asked.

Carstairs nodded, catching his breath. "It's the damned menthol. I might as well have stuck with the Camels. 'Course I don't think she'd really do it, Mrs. Andrews, with the gun. But she said she would, and ever since she made her threat at the monthly meeting, nobody's taken a chance. She brought her Red Ryder BB rifle to the meeting to show she had one."

"In that case," Hoke said, "I'll abide by the rules." He took one of the folded lists out of his pocket and handed it to Carstairs. "You got any more additions to your list? Any more reported thefts?"

Carstairs ran a finger down the list and shook his head.

"No, this is complete. But a lot of people are still away for the summer. When people get back, there may be more. I haven't inventoried any of the unoccupied apartments because I don't know what's supposed to be there in the first place. And even if the apartments are messed up, the owners could've left them that way when they went north."

"I understand."

"As a matter of routine," Figueras said, "I checked both pawnshops in town, but nothing showed up. These aren't the kind of things people would pawn anyway. A Corot, for example, worth maybe a hundred thousand bucks, wouldn't be fenced, either. A painting that valuable's usually held for ransom from the insurance company."

"I don't know what else to tell you, Mr. Moseley," Carstairs said. "We've got a twenty-four-hour guard on the gate, but the owners voted down a TV surveillance system. Most of the people living here are old enough to go to bed early. After ten at night, the gate guard checks the lobby and the pool area every hour or so."

"Have you got keys to all of the apartments?" Hoke asked.

"Sure. It's the law. I've got a master through-the-door-knob key, and those who've added bolt locks are required to give me the extra key. I keep 'em on a board in my office."

"What about the exterminator?"

"He's on a monthly schedule. I send out a mimeographed notice for the day and hours he's here, and they're supposed to let him in to spray. When he finishes all of the occupied apartments he comes back to me, and then I go with him while he works through the unoccupied units. If people are here, and don't let him in, they don't get sprayed, that's all. Our contract's with Cliffdweller's Exterminators, and they're bonded. They do most of the condos on the island."

"What about U.P.S., and other deliveries?"

"The gate guard signs, and then takes the packages up himself. And that includes pizza deliveries. That way"—Carstairs laughed—"the guard gets the tip the delivery man should get. Why not? We only pay the guards four bucks an hour."

"When he's on an upper floor making a delivery, the gate isn't covered."

"That's true. But it's locked. Nobody has to wait very long, and all the owners can open the gate with their plastic cards. There haven't been any complaints—except from pizza delivery men." Carstairs laughed harshly and fell into another spate of coughing. He sat heavily on a webbed beach chair, gasping for almost a minute before he recovered his breath. "Not everybody living here knows about these burglaries, but when the place begins to fill up again in November, and it turns out that some more absentee owners have been ripped off, there'll be hell to pay, and I'll be blamed. I like this job. I managed a condo in North Miami Beach for three years before coming up here, and they all complained down there because they thought I was overpaid. Twenty-two thousand a year, and they thought I was overpaid. Here, everybody thinks I'm *under*paid, and I get plenty of tips and sympathy."

"How much do you get here?"

"The same twenty-two a year. It's the going scale for a condo this size, but these wealthy people, who think I'm scraping along, don't ask me to do much of anything. Down in N.M.B., some of those old ladies even expected me to drive 'em to the fucking grocery store. I do real well here at Christmas, too. Absentee owners send me fruit from that place in Oregon. Last year I got four lugs of Comice pears."

"Next time you have a meeting," Hoke suggested, "why not have Detective Figueras give the owners a little pep talk on security. Anybody who's away for six months or more and leaves jewelry in his apartment is also leaving a cold trail if it's stolen."

"Would you do that, Officer Figueras?" Carstairs asked.

"Sure. It might take the pressure off both of us. Just call me at the station a day or two before you have a meeting."

"Thanks, Mr. Carstairs," Hoke said. "We're going to look around a little."

The manager nodded and lighted another cigarette with his Zippo. Hoke and Figueras got into the elevator, and Hoke punched the PH button.

"Thanks for the volunteer lecture," Figueras said. "But it's a little late now, isn't it, for a talk on security?"

"If they aren't doing the things you tell 'em, it might get Carstairs off the hook. He seems like a decent guy."

"Yeah, he does. But he ought to switch back to Camels soon. Those menthol cigarettes are killing him."

The elevator stopped at the roof exit, and the door opened automatically. They stepped onto a railed redwood deck that covered a fifty-foot square of the flat roof. Part of the deck had aluminum roofing, in blue and white panels. There was a metal blue-and-white patio set of table and four chairs beneath the roof section. The table and all four chairs were bolted to the deck to prevent strong winds from blowing them away. One twin-glass floor-to-ceiling window faced the deck, but the red vertical Levolors were closed. Hoke pressed the white button beside the double-door entrance to the penthouse. Figueras took out a crumpled package of Lucky Strikes and a book of matches from his jacket pocket, looked at them for a moment, and put them back. While they waited, Hoke looked out over the ocean. From this height it resembled an ironed sheet of Mylar. Out in the Gulf Stream, four or five miles away, three tankers steamed south. Thanks to them, Hoke reflected, the soles and toes of hundreds of feet would collect little pieces of tar when they walked on the beach. All of the motels and apartment houses kept metal containers of benzine and paper towels by the outside showers so that bathers could clean it off their feet. The tar was worse this year than Hoke could ever remember it.

Mr. E. M. Skinner, wearing royal blue slippers and a yellow silk happi coat over his purple silk pajamas, opened the door. He blinked in the strong sunlight.

"I was taking a nap," Skinner said. "I thought I heard the bell, but I wasn't sure. Today's Hirohito's day off."

"Hirohito?" Hoke took off his sunglasses.

Skinner smiled. "My Japanese houseboy. Actually, he's a Nisei, and his real name's Paul Glenwood. I sometimes call him Hirohito just to kid around. Come in, gentlemen."

"This is Detective Figueras," Hoke said. "He's the Riviera officer investigating the burglaries you were telling me about down on the beach."

Skinner nodded and shook hands with Figueras. "I think Carstairs mentioned your name to me." Hoke walked inside before Skinner could shake his hand and looked around the living room.

The room was large but seemed bigger because it was so sparsely furnished. There was a polished parquet floor, with no rugs to hide it. At the northern end of the room there was a grouping of leather overstuffed chairs and small black lacquered tables. A bar, covered in black leather and with two red-cushioned rattan stools, was directly behind the grouping. The other end of the room, apparently a dining area, was furnished with a glass-topped mahogany table and eight cushioned, wrought-iron chairs. A Nautilus machine, with four brown leather roller pads, incongruously occupied the space between the conversation area and the dining setup. There was a long pass-way counter into the kitchen, but the counter had a pull-down door, and it was closed. Hoke could see only part of the kitchen through the opened doorway. There were a half-dozen closed doors along the hallway, so Hoke concluded that Skinner had separate rooms for work and for play, and at least three bedrooms.

"I was telling Sergeant Moseley, Mr. Figueras," Skinner said with a thin smile, "I don't have my daily martinis until five, but that restriction doesn't hold for you. What will you gentlemen have?"

"I guess I could stand a beer," Figueras said.

"Nothing for me, thanks," Hoke said.

Skinner went behind the bar and rubbed his hands together. "Michelob okay?"

"Anything that's cold," Figueras said.

Skinner opened the bottle and poured part of it into a glass, then set the glass and bottle on the bar. Figueras had his Luckies and matches out. He looked at the bar, and at the tables, but there were no ashtrays. For the second time, Figueras put his cigarettes away. One of the small lacquered tables held two elaborately carved wooden fishes. There were floor-to-ceiling windows on three of the walls, but the closed vertical Levolors darkened the room. The track lighting above the bar was on dimly. There was a chandelier above the dining table, but it wasn't lighted.

"When you first heard about the burglaries, Mr. Skinner," Hoke asked, "did you check your own apartment for missing items?"

"I didn't have to check. I'm here all year round. And when I'm not here, Hirohito's here."

"You two are never out at the same time?"

"I didn't mean that. I mean, Paul lives in. He has his own bedroom. Sometimes when I go out at night he drives me. When I go to a party in Palm Beach I like to have two or three drinks, and I won't risk a D.U.I. Two double martinis, even watered down with ice, will register a big point one-four on the Breathalyzer, I've heard."

"It depends on the size of the person," Figueras said, taking a sip from his glass. "But they've been cracking down on drunk drivers. People who used to get a warning are now either doing a little jail time or community service."

"What kind of community service would I do," Skinner said, smiling, "if I happened to get caught? Not that I ever will, of course."

"It's up to the judge. But a Palm Beach corporation lawyer, two weeks ago, was assigned to work for sixty days putting on a new tar-and-pebble roof on school buildings in the county. Working with boiling tar, out in the sun all day, is pretty rough community service for a lawyer. But a barmaid I know got off easy. She licked stamps in the judge's office when he ran for reelection. They haven't established any firm guidelines yet, so it's still up to the whim of the judge."

Hoke cleared his throat. "So you haven't missed anything?"

"Not a thing. And if something was missing, Paul would tell me."

"I notice you don't have any paintings."

"I have paintings. A man has to have some collectibles for diversification. But I keep my paintings in my strong room, together with my certificates and Krugerrands and so on. No one goes in there but me. Not even my houseboy has the combination. I had the strong room put in while the Supermare was still under construction."

"What kind of paintings?"

"Well, I've got five Picassos—drawings, not paintings—and two Milton Averys."

"Could we take a look at them?"

"They're investments, not for showing. I'd be glad to show them to you, but they're wrapped up in brown paper and sealed. When Milton Avery died, my Averys almost doubled in value, but I don't like either one of them. Collectibles are just a hedge against inflation, as we say."

"Figueras," Hoke said, "would you mind going outside on the deck to finish your beer and smoke a cigarette for a few minutes?"

"Why?"

"Because I asked you in a nice way, and I know you want a smoke." Hoke put his sunglasses on the bar.

Figueras gave Hoke a look and poured the rest of the beer into his glass. Then he lighted a Lucky, took the glass of beer with him, and went out through the front door. As the door clicked behind Figueras, Hoke took a step forward and hit Skinner in the stomach with his right fist. The blow was hard and unexpected, and air whooshed from Skinner's lips in a strangled scream of fear, pain, and surprise. He clutched his stomach with both hands as he dropped to the floor, and kept making little *ah, ah, ah* sounds as he struggled for breath. This man, Hoke thought, has never been hurt before. Except for a toothache, maybe, he has never known any real pain. Certainly Skinner was handling his pain in a craven way. He drummed on the floor with his heels until his slippers fell off. When he regained his breath he began to cry, and he crawled backward away from Hoke. His fingers, scrabbling behind him, could get very little purchase on the polished floor. It took almost half a minute before his back hit the black leather chair behind him. His eyes popped wildly as he stared up at Hoke, and tears ran down his cheeks. He pressed his fingers into his stomach gently. "You—you broke something inside . . ."

Hoke nodded. "Lots of little things. Capillaries, for the most part, and some muscle shredding, but I was an inch or so below the solar plexus. Haven't you ever been hit in the belly before?"

Skinner shook his head. "Jesus Christ, that hurt! It still hurts!"

Hoke took Skinner's right hand and pulled him to his feet. He twisted the unresisting arm behind Skinner's back, and then put some upward pressure on it.

Skinner squealed. "Jesus Christ, man!"

"Let's go take a look in your strong room, Skinner. I want to check your collectibles against my property list."

"It's all there: Sergeant, every bit of it! You're breaking my goddamned arm!"

It was all there: the brown-tone cartoon; the tiny Corot, only twelve by fourteen inches, but with a gilded frame; and the Giacometti sculpture, an anorectic figure a foot high, mounted on a thick ebony base. The Klezmer turned out to be a painting of a tiny piece of yarn, about one inch in length, but the picture was in a two-by-two-foot black frame. A small magnifying glass was attached to the frame by a chain so a viewer could see all of the yarn's delicately painted hairs. The jewelry, and there was a good deal of it, including the elephant-hair bracelets, was all wrapped neatly in white tissue paper and packed in a cardboard box.

Skinner now sat in a leather chair. His face was a mixture of pink and gray. He was calmer now, but he covered his face with his hands. After Hoke checked off all the items on his list, he patted Skinner on the shoulder.

"Don't worry," he said, "you aren't going to jail. I wouldn't want something like this to get into the papers. It would be bad for the island and bad for the Supermare. My father's wife still has an apartment here, and it might make the value go down."

"I wasn't going to keep any of these things," Skinner said, looking up and wiping fresh tears from his eyes. "I'm not a thief—I don't even know how you knew I—"

"I didn't know. But I suspected you. I've got a good memory for details sometimes, Skinner. When Helen told me that Mr. Olsen and Mrs. Higdon were instrumental in getting you out of office, and then their names popped up on the list, I figured it had to be you. As the ex-president of the board, you still had a key to the office, so you probably found a way to get into any apartment you wanted to. Isn't that right?"

"I gave my master key back to Carstairs, but I had a duplicate made first in your father's hardware store. I thought that was how you found out."

"I never considered that. I suppose he still has a sales slip on file. But I just figured you went into the office at night, took the extra bolt-lock keys, and then swiped the stuff at your leisure. If I wasn't on the verge of quitting the police force, I wouldn't have hit you. I've been a cop for more than fourteen years, and you're the first suspect I've ever hit. I'd better get Figueras." Hoke put on his dark glasses and adjusted them.

"What'll he do? I mean—"

"By now, he'll need another beer. Put your slippers back on and open him another cold one."

Hoke went to the front door, opened it, and beckoned to Figueras. When Figueras came in, Skinner was behind the bar, opening a bottle of Michelob. "Would you like another beer, Officer Figueras?"

Figueras looked at the paintings and the cardboard box beside the leather chair. He looked sharply at Hoke. "What the fuck's going on?"

"Last night Mr. Skinner found all this stuff on the fire stairs. He didn't turn it over to the manager immediately, because he thought they might think he took it. That's why he wanted to talk to me alone. He was about to phone the police, in fact, when you and I showed up. So what we'll do, Figueras, we'll just say we found it on the stairs ourselves. Okay? Then we can turn it all over to Carstairs, and no one'll ever know the difference. Mr. Skinner's a rich man, with his own strong room full of collectibles. He doesn't need stuff like this. But he's got a few enemies in the building, he says, and this way it won't even make the newspapers."

"If that's the way you want to handle it," Figueras said.

Skinner came gingerly from behind the bar and handed the open bottle of beer to Figueras. Figueras took it and poured the beer over the two carved wooden fish on the lacquered table. He tossed the empty bottle behind the bar and listened appraisingly as it crashed. Then he picked up the cardboard box containing the jewelry. "I'll ring for the elevator, Sergeant. Want to give me a hand?"

"Sure," Hoke said. "But I get off at the twelfth floor. You can take everything down to Carstairs, and he can return the stuff to the owners. I'm going to take that swim in the pool."

Figueras went out the door with the cardboard box.

"What about me?" Skinner said, in a hoarse whisper. "What's going to happen to me?"

Hoke hit Skinner again with a hard right fist, and Skinner, clutching his stomach, fell to the floor. Hoke picked up the skinny sculpture and opened the door. Figueras came back in for the paintings, then rejoined Hoke at the elevator. If he was curious about Skinner, writhing and groaning on the parquet, he didn't say anything.

Hoke pulled out the red knob to release the elevator; then he pushed the button for twelve.

"One of these days," Figueras said, when Hoke got off the elevator at the twelfth floor, "I'd like to drop by and talk to you some about homicide work."

"Sure. I'm home every night. You ever play Monopoly?"

"Not since I was a kid."

"The short game is still fun. But if you come by, you'll have to bring your own six-pack. I'm trying to lose some more weight, so I don't keep any beer in the fridge to tempt me." Hoke patted his stomach and walked down the hallway to 12-C.

CHAPTER 14

Dale had most of the dinner on the table already by the time Troy Louden returned to the garage apartment. Stanley watched everyone's comings and goings from his chair beside the window. Troy came in carrying a large Naugahyde suitcase in his left hand and his cowboy boots in his right. He paused for a moment and, with his eyes closed, sniffed the aroma of the steaming food. Then he disappeared into the bedroom. He was wearing a dark gray *guayabera*, pleated khaki trousers, and a new pair of gray leather running shoes with slanted purple stripes on them.

A moment later, Troy reappeared in the bedroom doorway and crooked a finger at James. As James crossed the room, Dale whispered to him, "Tell him dinner's ready any old time."

James nodded, followed Troy into the bedroom, and closed the door.

Stanley got up from his chair and surveyed the table. "Everything sure does smell good."

"That's the pork chops," Dale said. Her face was flushed, and the hair at her temples was damp. "What I do, I pepper 'em real good and dip 'em in a simple egg-and-flour batter. Then I fry 'em in bacon grease. There's candied sweet potatoes, with little marshmallows on top, turnip greens in wine vinegar, spicy applesauce, and buttermilk biscuits. I'll finish up the milk gravy now, and that'll be dinner. I've got a Mrs. Smith's apple pie warming in the oven, and that'll be dessert. Mr. Louden does so much for all the rest of us, I want him to have a decent dinner."

The table was set for four, although there were not enough matching plates, cups, and saucers. There were only three silverware forks; Dale had put a plastic one at her setting, Stanley noted. A few minutes later, Troy and James came back from the bedroom, and they sat down to eat.

James was visibly nervous during dinner. He plucked at his ears, his lips, and his eyebrows, and he only ate one pork chop. Troy praised the meal, and Dale's puffy lips twisted into a grimace of pleasure.

"I had two brothers and two little sisters," Dale said, "and Momma taught all of us how to cook. She said us girls needed to know how to catch a husband, and the boys needed to know how so they could teach their wives when they got married."

"Let's not get into your family," Troy said. "We've got our own little family, right here. We're all starting out new, and the past is past. Why, James, are you picking your nose at the table?"

"I'm just nervous . . . it's . . . it's these greens, Troy," James said. "I don't like vinegar on my greens."

"Whether you like them or not you have to eat them. Otherwise you'll hurt Dale's feelings. And in America, you don't pick your nose at the table. Everyone, from time to time, has to pick his nose. That's a given, but it's a private thing, James, and should be done where people don't have to watch you. I remember once when I was in Whittier—that's the reform school in Orange County, California—a boy was picking his nose at the table and the guy sitting beside him jammed the boy's finger right into his nostril all the way up to the last knuckle. The kid's nose got all swollen, so fast that he couldn't pull his finger out. Finally, the matron led him out of the dining hall and took him to the clinic. It was funny to see, and we all laughed, of course, but it was a lesson in manners for us boys, too. No one after that ever picked his nose in the dining hall. Not only is it impolite, it's un-American. I realize that as a foreigner and as a black man, you'll find some of our customs strange, James, but you'll just have to abide by them."

"I'm sorry," James said. "I won't do it again."

"When you get up to New York, James," Troy continued, "you should rent a room with an American family instead of moving in with the other Bajans up there. Then you can learn our ways. Otherwise, when you have your first one-man show, and you're standing around in the gallery with two fingers up your nose, no one'll buy your paintings."

"I won't *do* it again, Troy."

"Good. Now eat your greens. At Whittier, if we didn't clean our plates, we didn't get any dessert. You could eat all you wanted, but once you put it on your plate you had to eat it."

"I didn't put the greens on my plate," James said. "Dale did."

"I'll eat your greens, James," Stanley offered. "I like the greens."

"If you want more greens, Pop," Troy said, "Dale will get them for you. James will have to eat his own greens."

James wrinkled his nose and ate.

"I'll get the pie," Dale said, rising from her chair.

"Put a scoop of ice cream on mine," Troy said.

"I don't have any ice cream," Dale said, hesitating in the doorway.

"Then cut a wedge of cheddar to go with it. I like cheese just as well."

"There isn't any cheese either." Dale put a hand over her mouth.

"In that case, skip me on the pie, and just bring me some coffee."

Dale cleared the table and served slices of pie to Stanley and James. She poured coffee for the three of them and retreated to the kitchen. James put three spoonfuls of sugar into his coffee and stirred it noisily. The spoon slipped from his fingers and fell to the floor.

"Maybe you shouldn't drink any coffee," Troy said, "if it makes you so nervous."

James glanced at Stanley, licked his lips, and looked back at Troy. "It ain't the coffee making me nervous. I'm afraid of what you want me to do."

"Do you want me to send Mr. Sinkiewicz instead? Send an old man to do a boy's job?" Troy shook his head and pulled back his lips in a lightning smile.

"I didn't say that, Troy. I *want* to do it. It's just that I've never done nothing like that before."

"What is it, James?" Stanley asked. "Maybe I can help you?"

"Please stay out of this, Pop." Troy held up a warning hand. "You've done enough already. I don't want you to be connected with this operation in any way. I told you that already. Dale, James, and I are the three who will benefit most, so we have to do the dirty work. And we each have to pull our own weight. As the head of the family and director of the operation, I've got to make the decisions on what each person has to do. You, of course, are retired, and although you are an important part of our little family—I hope you know that—you're also our honored guest. Here, before I forget, let me give back your cards." Troy took Stanley's Visa card, Social Security card, and a folded yellow receipt out of his wallet and pushed them across the table.

Stanley put the two cards away and examined the receipt. There was a letterhead that read: Overseas Supply Company, Inc. The address was a Miami post office box. At the bottom of the yellow sheet, in italics, *Se habla Español* was printed. The bill, for "used hunting supplies," was $1,565, but the supplies were not itemized. Stanley's Visa receipt was stapled to the bill.

"Where is this place?" Stanley asked. "The Overseas Supply Company?"

Troy laughed. "It isn't a place, Pop, it's an idea. Today it's a room in the Descanso Hotel. Tomorrow it's a house in San Juan, Puerto Rico. Everybody, nowadays, needs hunting supplies."

Stanley was unable to follow this line of thinking. He looked down, folded the bill and receipt, and tucked them into his wallet.

"But as you can see, Pop, I didn't need the full two thousand. And I still got everything I needed, including these new pants, goatskin gloves, the shirt, and the running shoes. Boots look good on a man, but for running, when you have to run, they aren't worth a damn."

Stanley cleared his throat. "I been thinking, Troy. And I think five hundred's too much to give me in interest. Now that you've only used fifteen hundred, let's cut it down to maybe a hundred and fifty."

Troy shook his head and smiled at James. "Look at this guy, James. Without Pop's help, we'd be sitting here without any tools, and we'd either have to borrow money on the street at leg-breaking vig, or hold up a half-dozen liquor stores. Nothing doing, Pop. You still get your five hundred, and you get it Saturday night. But James here, who stands to benefit more than you do, is getting cold feet on a little project I gave him."

"I'll *do* it, Troy," James said quickly. "I never said I

wouldn't do it. I just said I was afraid to do it because I've never done nothing like that before."

"I know you'll do it," Troy said, nodding, "because you have to. But I don't want you to be nervous. If you want me to, I'll go over everything with you again."

"Suppose I can't find one? What'll I do then?"

"All right, I will go over it again. First, I'll drive you to the Brickell Metrorail station. You ride it down to Dadeland North station, and then walk over to the Dadeland parking lot. This time of night, there'll be at least a thousand parked cars, probably a lot more. At least one in a hundred drivers leave their keys in the car, right in the ignition. It's one of those statistical truisms, I read about it in the paper. There was this Boy Scout troop that wanted to do a good deed on a Saturday morning, so they had little cards printed up, saying, 'Don't leave your keys in your car. It invites theft.' They found that almost a fifth of the cars they looked at in the Westchester Shopping Center had keys in the ignition. They then left the little card under the windshields, you see, so the owners would find them when they came back. So when you say you don't think you'll find at least *one* car out of a *thousand* with the keys in it at Dadeland, you're simply full of shit.

"I could do it myself, and I'd be back here within an hour with a nice big car for us to use, but I want you to do it as part of your on-the-job training. I've got other things to do. Dale can't go because her face is too conspicuous, even though she'll drive the car later on. Also, because of Dale, you have to get a car with an automatic transmission. She can't drive a stick shift. What else did I tell you?"

"You said dark blue or black."

"Right. But any dark color'll do. Just don't come back with some bright yellow or red car, or I'll send you right back. I don't want any Blazer, either, all shiny with chrome and those tires with big white raised letters. Understand?"

"I'm ready," James said, getting up from the table.

"What are you doing, Troy?" Stanley asked. "Are you sending James out to steal a car?"

"I'm trying to keep you out of this, Pop. You really should save your questions till it's all over. But the answer is no, James is not going to steal a car. He's going to *obtain* a car for our use in the operation, which we'll drive to the airport later, on Sunday morning. The owner will be notified by postcard where we parked his car at the airport, and I'll leave a generous rental fee for the use of his vehicle in the glove compartment. I guarantee that the person whose car we use'll benefit. Are you with me? You can see I'm explaining to you as we go along on a need-to-know basis."

Stanley nodded. "Sure, Troy. I just thought, from the way you were talking, that James was going to steal a car, that's all."

"Renting is a long way from stealing, Pop. While I run James over to the Brickell station, see if you can find some hacksaw blades down there in the garage. There's a vise on the workbench where James keeps his paints, and I remember seeing a box of tools under the bench. Then, when I come back, you can help me out."

Troy and James left in the Morris, and Stanley went into the kitchen. "That was a nice dinner, Dale, and I really enjoyed it. Want me to carry that bag of garbage down to the yard?"

"No, I'd better do it myself." Tears trickled down her cheeks. "You've got to look for the hacksaw blades like Troy said. When he tells you to do something, he means it. How was I to know he wanted ice cream on his pie? If he'd said, then I could've gotten ice cream and cheese, too. If you only knew how many rejections I've had in my life, Mr. Sinkiewicz, you'd feel sorry for me."

"I feel sorry for you already, Dale. That's why I loaned Troy the money he needed."

"Did I ever tell you about the lawyer I lived with once in Coconut Grove?" Dale wiped her eyes with her wet hands and then had to use the dry edge of a dish towel to get the soap out of her eyes. "I'd been living with him for two months in his apartment, you know, and I thought he really liked me. Jesus, I used to go down on him every morning before he went to the office, and I never had any complaints. Then one night, it was after midnight, he said, 'Get your coat.' I was wearing a nightgown, so I started to get dressed. Then he said, 'No, just your coat.' I had this fur coat he'd given me, but I'd never worn it. It was a good fur—dyed rabbit—but you never need a fur coat down here. Anyway, I put it on over my nightgown, and slipped on some sandals. I didn't have on panties or pantyhose or nothing else. Just the nightgown and the fur coat. We got into his Mercedes, and he drove to Biscayne Boulevard, downtown, and then he stopped the car and told me to get out. Nothing else. Not a word of appreciation or thanks or nothing. And after two months. I didn't have my purse, my clothes, my money, anything. Lucky for me, just after he drove away, another car picked me up—an insurance man from Hialeah. We went to a motel on Seventy-ninth Street, and I was back in business again. But my life's been one rejection after another like that, and sometimes I just don't think I can stand any more of it."

"You're lucky you have Troy now." Stanley patted her on the shoulder. "I'm sure he didn't mean to hurt your feelings about the ice cream. You saw the way he made James eat his greens. That shows how sensitive he is to your feelings. Next time, you'll know to get ice cream when you fix apple pie."

"I guess I should look on the bright side, huh?" Dale's twisted, toothless smile made Stanley turn his head away.

"I like you a lot, Mr. Sinkiewicz, and if you ever want a little action and Troy ain't around, you just let me know. Hear?" She reached amiably for Stanley's crotch, but he backed away before she could touch him.

"I'd better go down to the garage and look for those blades."

Stanley found a metal toolbox beneath the bench, but the box had been left open and the unused tools were rusty from long exposure to the humidity. There were a half-dozen hacksaw blades wrapped in waxed paper, and the rusty saw was usable. The garage was well-lighted with several overhead 150-watt bulbs. One of the shadeless bulbs was directly above James's easel so he could paint at night. Stanley looked at James's paintings until Troy returned, thinking that James was lucky that he didn't need subject matter to paint. The Bajan could paint day or night, or anytime he felt like it, and it wouldn't make any difference. He wondered if they would make James paint objects of some kind when he enrolled in the Art Students League up in New York. If they did, James was going to be in trouble . . .

Troy returned in the Morris and parked it beside Stanley's Honda. Stanley showed him the blades, and Troy went upstairs to get what he called his "new, but used" shotgun from his suitcase. He came down to the garage again, locked the shotgun in the vise, and sawed off the barrels as close as he could to the forestock. Then he turned the gun around in the vise and sawed off the rear stock. It took him a great deal longer to get through the wood than it had to shorten the metal barrels. When Troy finished it was an odd-looking weapon. He would have to hold it like a pistol to fire it. It looked unwieldy to Stanley.

"Won't that thing kick out of your hand when you shoot

it?" Stanley asked. "It won't be accurate, neither, if you go dove hunting."

"I'm not going to *fire* it, Pop. Jesus, there'll be double-aught shells in it. If I shot it, especially at close range, it would blow great big holes in a man's body. I just sawed off the barrels so it wouldn't look like some kind of sporting gun you see in the Sears catalog, but would look like a sawed-off shotgun, which it is now. It's a psychological ploy, Pop. A person associates long barrels with bird-shooting. But he associates a sawed-off shotgun with gangster movies, and he's afraid of it. This way, you don't have to shoot anyone, all you have to do is show the thing. If I do shoot it, I'll just shoot it up at the ceiling or something, and carry a few extra shells in my jacket pocket."

"It looks wicked that way, and you've sure ruint it for shooting birds."

"It was more accurate, or wicked as you say, with long barrels, Pop, and you just proved my point. But I'd never shoot birds with a shotgun. I think hunting for game of any kind stinks, and I'm against it. The only way to justify hunting is if you're lost in the woods or something, and you have to kill a bird or a rabbit to survive. Otherwise, hunting for sport is cruel. It ought to be outlawed. You don't think so?"

"I like quail, and there was a neighbor of mine up in Hamtramck who—"

"I don't want to hear about it, Pop. If you want to eat quail, Dale can get you some at the supermarket. All you want. They raise 'em for that purpose, and you can buy 'em fresh frozen. You don't hunt, do you?"

"No, not me, but I had this neighbor, and he used to—"

"I said I don't want to hear about it. Where's Dale?"

"After she finished the dishes I think she took a shower. I heard it running awhile ago."

"What do you think of Dale, Pop, now that you've met her and had a chance to talk with her?"

"She seems like a nice enough girl. A little forward, maybe."

"She come on to you while I was gone?"

"Oh, I don't know. A little bit, maybe. She felt bad about you not eating the apple pie."

"That's my fault, not Dale's. I'll have to make a list of the things I like and don't like, so she won't make mistakes like that again. I can't blame Dale for my own oversights. But she'll learn soon enough what I like and don't like. It's her face that makes her so sensitive, Pop. Dale's life's been one rejection after another, so if she offers you head, you'd better accommodate her. Otherwise, she'll think you don't like her."

"I like her fine, Troy, but I haven't done nothing like that in three or four years now, and I guess I don't have the desire anymore. But if there's any leftover pork chops, I wouldn't mind a cold pork chop sandwich before I go to bed."

"Good. I'll tell Dale how you feel, and I know she'll be happy to fix you a sandwich later on. Or, if you want, you can have my piece of apple pie and a glass of warm milk."

"I'd rather have the pork chop sandwich."

The doctored weapon was still in the vise. Troy used a file to smooth the ends of the jaggedly cut barrels, which were not cut off evenly, and then he filed off the splinters from the stock.

James drove a navy blue Chrysler New Yorker into the yard and parked beside the Honda and the Morris Minor. The big Chrysler dwarfed the two foreign cars. James honked the horn once and then jumped out of the vehicle as if it had been set on fire. He walked toward them, wringing his hands.

"Oh, a terrible thing happened, Troy! And I didn't know

what to do! I was chased, and if I hadn't cut off a pickup at the Miller exit they'd of caught me for sure!"

"You didn't lead anybody back here, did you?"

"No, I made sure of that. But I didn't mean to take the baby! I didn't see it back there when I got the car. There was this old lady with packages at the curb in Dadcland, and a younger woman was driving—" He was trying to catch his breath. "Then, when the woman got out to help the old lady with the packages, I jumped in and drove off. The keys were in the car and the motor was running. Both those ladies came running after me, and then a taxi chased me down Kendall Drive. I went through the red light and so did he, right on my back, all the way down the Palmetto to Miller—"

"What baby?" Troy said, going over to the New Yorker and opening the back door. "Oh, shit," he said as he looked at the baby strapped in its car-seat in the back.

"I never looked in the back, Troy. There wasn't time. I just took the car 'cause I only had a second or so to get into it and go. He didn't even start crying till I got onto Kendall Drive."

"This is a nice car, James, exactly what I wanted, but it's useless to us now. Everybody in town'll be on the lookout for this vehicle. I try to think of everything, but I didn't tell you not to steal a car with a baby in it. I thought you'd have more sense than that."

"I didn't *see* him," James said. "Then, when the cab started chasing me, I couldn't stop and get out. I had to lose him first."

"What is it," Stanley asked, "a boy or a girl? The way it's bundled up and all . . ."

"Boy or girl doesn't make a helluva lot of difference, Pop," Troy said. "Whatever it is, they'll want it back, and the cops'll be looking for this New Yorker all over the damned county. Are the keys still in the car, James?"

"Yes, sir."

"I told you before not to say that anymore, James. We're all equals here, so I don't want to hear any more of that no, sir, yes, sir crap. I just asked if the keys were in the car."

James nodded and gulped. The night was hot and humid, and James's shirt was soaked. Water ran down his flushed face as if he had just been doused with a hose.

"All right," Troy said. "I'll get rid of this car and come back with another. You two go on upstairs, but don't tell Dale about the baby. Women get upset over misunderstandings like that. I don't know when I'll be back, but when I do get back, James, I hope you realize that I'll have to punish you for this mistake."

James nodded and wiped his face with his fingers. "It ain't altogether my fault, Troy. These things happen."

"I understand. And I'll take under consideration that you're a foreigner here on a student visa. But if I don't punish you in some way, you might make more mistakes that are even more serious. So go on upstairs now, both of you. And ask Dale to fix your pork chop sandwich, Pop."

"I don't want it right now."

"When you do."

Troy took his shotgun out of the vise, loaded it, and put some extra shells into his *guayabera* pocket. He then got into the Chrysler New Yorker, backed and filled, and drove out of the yard.

James took a shower and put on a clean pair of jeans. His old jeans, which he had worn to Dadeland, were stained from when he had wet his pants during the chase by the taxicab. James rolled the soiled jeans into a ball and took them, together with the garbage bags, down to the trash can in the yard.

Stanley stripped to his underwear and went to bed on the porch. It was too warm to cover himself with a sheet, although a breeze from the bay made the porch a little cooler than the living room. The moon was up, and he could see everything in the yard from his window. The enormous two-story house was an ominous dark mass beyond the circle of light flooding from the bulbs inside the garage. James, apparently exhausted, slept on the couch in the living room, naked except for his jeans. Stanley couldn't sleep. He was worried about Troy driving around in the city with the baby in the back of the car. If they caught him in the car, he would be charged with kidnapping, as well as car theft. Troy should have made James take the car back to Dadeland. But that wasn't Troy's way; he was too responsible for that, despite all his other faults.

Dale, wearing her nightgown, came out to the porch and sat on the edge of the bed. "Do you mind if I lay down here with you, Mr. Sinkiewicz? Just till Troy gets back. I can't sleep all alone. It's scary in the big bedroom all by myself."

"I don't mind. But don't roll up against me. It's too hot for anything like that."

Dale curled into a ball, sighed once, and fell asleep. A moment later, she was snoring through her damaged septum.

It was well after two A.M. before Troy drove into the yard and parked a dark blue Lincoln town car beside the back porch of the two-story house. Stanley woke Dale up and told her to go back to the bedroom. Troy came upstairs, woke James, and whispered something to him that Stanley couldn't hear. The two of them went downstairs again. The garage lights were switched off. Without the lights, Stanley could barely see them in the yard as they walked to the Lincoln. He heard the trunk of the car being raised, and then heard it slam down again. For a few minutes, the lights in the big house were on, and then they were switched off again. It was about ten minutes or so before the two men came up the stairs quietly. Stanley pretended to be asleep. James went back to sleep on the couch, and

Troy went into the bedroom and closed the door.

Now that Troy was back safely, Stanley got so sleepy he could barely keep his eyes open. But then, why should he keep them open? He wondered, for a moment, what Troy and James had been doing in the big house, but he supposed that Troy had been bawling James out for taking the car with the baby in it. It didn't matter. As Troy said, if he needed to know, he would be told. After all, he was a guest here, and not part of the operation.

CHAPTER

15

Hoke was wearing his swimming trunks under his jumpsuit, but after he let himself in to Helen's apartment, he decided that he didn't want to swim in the pool. His right shoulder throbbed, and he rubbed it briskly. Massaging didn't help it any. He had a touch of bursitis, which came and went periodically and was back now because he had put too much shoulder into popping Skinner in the belly. Hoke had enjoyed hitting Skinner—both times—and he wouldn't mind going back up to the penthouse right now and hitting him again. But he would never hit the millionaire again, and he probably shouldn't have hit him the first time. Skinner was undoubtedly on the phone with his lawyer right now, getting some twenty-five-dollar-a-minute advice.

And what would his lawyer tell him? If Skinner had a good counselor, and there was no doubt that he did, he would be told to count his blessings. That would be the end of it. Hoke wasn't angry, although Skinner had apparently taken him for a fool. Otherwise, he wouldn't have asked Hoke so disingenuously if he had known about the so-called burglaries when he first met him on the beach.

Hoke looked incuriously around Helen's two-hundred-thousand-dollar apartment, taking in the beige leather furniture and the Dufy-blue carpet that picked up the tints in the Hockney painting of a swimming pool above the five-cushioned couch. He decided that Skinner was as bored with his life at the Supermare as Helen had been. Like John Maynard Keynes, who had purportedly picked up the phone every morning and made two or three hundred pounds before getting out of bed, Skinner led a dull existence. After checking the market each morning, and then selling and buying stocks, Skinner didn't know what else to do with his spare time. Helen hadn't known what to do with her time either, living in this designer-decorated apartment, so she had moved in with Frank. Helen still slept until noon, but at least now she had started to engage herself in a few social activities, and she and Frank could always discuss which channel to watch at night. The fact that they had never actually gotten around to getting married didn't really matter.

The spacious apartment had two bedrooms, two baths, and an enormous walk-in dressing room. Very few of Helen's clothes were in the closet. There was a layer of dust over everything, and an anthurium, leaning at a desperate forty-five-degree angle toward the window, had drooped and died from lack of sun and water.

Hoke poured himself two ounces of Booth's gin from an opened bottle at the bar beside the television-hi-fi console. The refrigerator door was propped open with a yellow kitchen stool, and the plug had been pulled from the wall, so he drank his gin without ice. Except for Helen's ocean view, and it was an excellent one, especially from her bedroom floor-to-ceiling windows, Hoke decided that her apartment wasn't worth two hundred thousand—in fact, *no* apartment was. After the residents of the Supermare looked at their view in the morning, what did they do with the rest of their day?

* * *

Frank was wise to go to the hardware store every day, Hoke concluded as he unlocked the chain from Aileen's bicycle down in the lobby. Of course, Frank had little or nothing to do with running the store any longer. Mrs. Renshaw now ran every aspect of the business. But Frank had his private office in the back, and he was on the telephone a great deal. There was big responsibility in handling a fortune. Occasionally, when Frank left his office, to go to the bank or to see his lawyer, he would wait on a customer—just to keep his hand in. But at least he had a place to go in the mornings.

What did he, Hoke, have now, now that he had decided to leave the police department? In Miami, except for his job and his two daughters, his life had turned to shit—a big *nada.* But when they began to overload him and crap on him in the department, too, his unconscious mind must have rebelled against the work as well. Now his two daughters were almost gone, too, or soon would be.

Hoke was feeling so sorry for himself that he was almost splattered across the pavement by a white Mercury convertible as he allowed his bike to wobble into the middle of the lane on Ocean Boulevard. Before reaching the mall parking lot, Hoke dismounted and pushed his bike for the rest of the way to the El Pelicano. He locked the bicycle in the small downstairs office, deciding to clean out the cluttered room some other time.

The door to Hoke's apartment was ajar. He knew that he had locked it when he left, so he stood to one side of the door and kicked it open with his foot. Major Willie Brownley, the M.P.D. Homicide Chief, Hoke's boss, was sitting at the dining table playing Klondike with Hoke's deck of cards. There was a steaming cup of coffee in front of him on the table, and he was smoking a cigar. He looked up at Hoke and tapped some ashes into the saucer that held the cup.

"I understand you're managing this apartment house now," Brownley said as he counted off three cards and looked at a three of hearts. The chief was wearing a Miami Dolphins No. 12 T-shirt, with "Free Mercury Morris" in white cutout letters across the chest. Hoke had rarely seen the major out of uniform, and it looked strange to see this relaxed black man sitting at his dining table.

"I—I'm trying to, Willie," Hoke said, at last. "How'd you get in here?"

"With my passkey. I hung around downstairs for a while, waiting for you, but people kept looking at me funny, as if they'd never seen a black man before. So I decided to wait up here in your apartment. If I were you, Hoke, I'd put a bolt lock on the door—especially if you're going to be fucking off somewhere instead of staying here to rent out your apartments."

"I had some other business to attend to."

"You know, the ten of diamonds and the four of clubs are missing from this deck, and I don't think you're playing with a full deck either. I lost two games before I found out." The major gathered the cards together and shuffled them. Willie Brownley's face was the color of an eggplant, and the corners of his mouth dropped sharply. His gray kinky hair was clipped short, with a razor-blade part on the left side. The yellowish whites of his eyes made him look jaundiced.

"Sit down," Brownley said, putting the cards down and indicating a chair with his left hand. "Don't make me look up at you, you sneaky bastard."

"Who's sneaky?" Hoke sat across from the chief. "You broke into my apartment."

"You and Bill Henderson aren't half as smart as you think you are, Hoke. I signed your emergency leave without pay because I believed him when he told me your father was dying. But just because I believed him at the time didn't mean that I wouldn't check it out later. And I did. Your daddy told me on the phone that he was fine, that you seemed to be your old self again, and that it was nice to have you home.

"Then I asked my secretary to call Ellita. Ellita, of course, gave Rosalie a full report and told her that you were under a doctor's care up here in Singer Island. Then I braced Bill Henderson, and he told me what really happened. As a reward for Bill's disloyalty I gave him all of your unprocessed homicide cases to work on—in addition to his other duties, of course. That should keep him so busy for a while that he won't be able to cover up anything else on me for a few weeks. While I pondered various disciplinary measures, if any, I wondered why you hadn't come to me with your problems, even if they were imaginary problems. Surely, by now, I thought, Hoke trusts me to do the right thing. Hoke"—Brownley shook his head and tapped his chest with his right palm—"it hurts me right here to have my trust in you violated."

Hoke cleared his throat. "I can't explain myself, Willie. But I wasn't trying to bypass you, or anything like that. I was suddenly overwhelmed, that's all, and sort of blacked out. What I needed, I guess, was a rest. I'd been pushing hard, and I—"

"Spare me the bullshit, Hoke. I had a call from Mike Sheldon."

"Who?"

"Mike Sheldon. The Riviera Beach police chief. Are you going to pretend you haven't talked with him?"

"Oh, sure, Chief Sheldon. I met him at my father's house. He seems like a nice guy. Used to be a homicide detective up in New Jersey. What's wrong with that?"

"He called me and asked for a written recommendation, that's what. It appears that you applied for a lieutenancy in his department, and he wanted a letter so he could start on the paperwork."

"He made a tentative offer, but I turned him down, Willie. I didn't *ask* him for—"

"Bullshit! What hurts me, Hoke, you went behind my back. Why didn't you tell me you wanted to be a lieutenant? How many times, in the last three years, have I suggested that you take the exam?"

"Several. But I told you I don't want to be a lieutenant."

"What you mean is you don't want to be a lieutenant in Miami, working for me, but you'd like to be a lieutenant up here at half the salary you already make as a sergeant. That doesn't make any sense."

"No, I don't want to be a lieutenant here, either. I do plan on taking an early retirement, but I'm not joining the Riviera force, Willie. The job's too much for me—at least I think it is. I don't really know any longer."

"If you wanted an easier job, why didn't you come in and see me? My door's open at all times."

"I *have* seen you! I've bitched about my overload plenty of times, for Christ's sake."

"Everybody has a lot to do, Hoke. Didn't I give you Speedy Gonzalez as an assistant?"

"He spends half his time in gas stations, asking for directions—"

"He's getting to know the city, Hoke, and you just proved my point. It takes a long time to train a man for homicide work, and that's why I can't afford to lose you to some jerkwater little town like Riviera Beach. Hell, you'd die of boredom here. And you've already proven you can't run this little apartment house."

"How's that?"

"There was no note on your door saying when you'd be back. And some old redneck from Alabama, who thought

I was the janitor, asked me to fix his toilet for him. He said no matter how much he jiggles the handle, the toilet still keeps running. You'd better do something about things like that."

"Fuck him."

"See what I mean? Here, I've got something for you." Brownley opened his briefcase, which was on an adjacent chair, and took out a large brown envelope. He put it on the table. "You don't have to open this now, Hoke, but when you come to your senses again, it'll come in handy. I put your name down for the lieutenant's exam next month. You'll have to write your own essays, on Part Two of the exam, but here are all one hundred and fifty answers to the multiple-choice questions in Part One. With these answers memorized, you should be at the top of the list when the results are posted. Only minority applicants will have any priority on you on the next vacancy. That's because of Affirmative Action, and there's nothing I can do about that. But otherwise you should head the list."

Using his thumbnail, Hoke opened the envelope and took out the Xeroxed answer sheets.

"I said you didn't have to open it now," Brownley said. "Memorizing all of those answer sheets'll take several hours of uninterrupted study."

Hoke laughed. "Hell, these aren't the answers, Willie, they're just letters. Without the questions that go with 'em, they don't make any sense."

"They don't have to make sense, and you don't need to know the questions. Besides, I couldn't get a copy of the questionnaire. The right answers have all been blacked in, so all you have to do is memorize them in order. See? Number one is C. Number two is A. Number three is C again. You go over them again and again until you've got 'em in your head, like reading them off a blackboard. Hell, you've got a month. I give you a beer, and now you want an egg in it, for Christ's sake."

Hoke returned the sheets to the envelope. "Why are you doing this, Willie?"

"I want to keep you in the division, and I like you, Hoke. It also occurred to me that I might've been working you too hard. But that's the way it always is, Hoke. People who can do more than other people always get more to do. I'll tell you right now, though—when your leave is over, I'll see that you get a lighter load."

"I don't want the answer sheets, Willie. When I decide to go for a promotion, which I doubt, I'll study for it just like everyone else. Besides, I haven't made any decisions. Let me finish my leave, and I promise I won't make up my mind till I've talked to you first."

"Fair enough. But keep the answer sheets anyway, in case you have a change of heart."

"No." Hoke shook his head. He put the envelope back into the major's open briefcase and shut the lid. "I wouldn't feel right about it. Besides, I have a hunch I'd be pretty high on the list even if I didn't study for the exam. You may not remember, but I was first in my class at the FBI course."

"I remember. How many years have you got left to go? Exactly?"

"For regular retirement? About seven and a half years."

"That isn't too long, Hoke. And if you weren't a cop in Miami, you'd still have to be a cop somewhere. You don't know how to do anything else."

"You might be right. But I can learn."

"I know I'm right."

There was a knock on the door. Hoke got up from the table. It was Professor Hurt, and Hoke introduced him to Major Brownley.

"I came up to invite you to dinner, Mr. Moseley, but

there's plenty, so you're included in the invitation, Major Brownley." Hurt shook hands with Brownley.

"I've got to drive back to Miami."

"No use going back on an empty stomach. Besides, I've got four liters of Riunite on ice."

"I guess I could have a glass or two with you, but I really have to get back to Miami."

"Let the traffic thin out a little, Willie," Hoke suggested. "Eat dinner with us."

"Beefy Winters is coming, too," the professor said. "He's an elephant trainer with Ringling Brothers, Major."

"He was," Hoke amended. "But that'll make four of us, and then maybe we can play some Monopoly?"

"I should go back—" Brownley said. "But I guess I can stay for one game. If we play the short game. The regular game takes way too long."

"I like the short game myself," Hoke said.

"Okay," Hurt said, rubbing his hands together. "I've got a dozen Swanson Hungry Man dinners. What'll you have? There's fried chicken, macaroni and cheese, spaghetti and meatballs, you name it. What I've found out with Swanson's is that one isn't quite enough, but two of them are too much. So what I usually end up doing is heating up two different kinds, and I eat what I want from both of them at the same time. I suggest that you do the same. I'll pop 'em in the oven, and they'll all be ready in a half-hour or so. Meanwhile, we can start on the Riunite and the game."

"You two go ahead," Hoke said. "I'll dig out the Monopoly set."

Major Brownley picked up his briefcase and went with the professor, telling him he liked the kind of dinner with the little square of apple pie better than he did the kind with the little square piece of cake. Otherwise, he said, he didn't much care whether he ate macaroni and cheese or the ham with the sweet potatoes.

Before joining them downstairs, Hoke took the Monopoly game out of the cardboard box and arranged the property cards so that when he dealt them around for the short game he would end up with Boardwalk and Park Place. Hoke knew that if he played Monopoly against Major Brownley, he would need an edge.

CHAPTER 16

It was 10:29 exactly when Stanley Sinkiewicz parked his Honda in the asphalt lot outside the supermarket in the Green Lakes Shopping Center. There were seven cars in the lot, not counting his own—more than he had expected—but some of them, he concluded, belonged to store employees. The uneven façade of unfinished buildings, dark and unoccupied, stretched for almost three hundred yards down the lot before the two-story windowless department store blocked and anchored the northern end. Only the supermarket was lighted. There were dozens of tall street lamps scattered at intervals throughout the lot, but none of the sodium-vapor light clusters was turned on. A few four- and five-foot palm trees, propped up by two-by-fours, had been planted recently in some of the concrete islands in the lot.

Stanley locked his car, and then remembered his cane. Troy had told him to take it with him. The cane gave him a distinguished look, he said—meaning, Stanley supposed, that he'd look like a harmless retiree whom nobody would notice. Stanley unlocked his car, retrieved his cane, buttoned his suit jacket, and walked purposefully toward the glass doors of the supermarket, reviewing Troy's instructions. Once more he marveled at how Troy had managed to make him a part of the operation, yet had allowed him to remain aloof from anything untoward and not become a part of the robbery itself. The store closed at eleven, but as a general rule one of the bag boys, or the assistant manager, would then stand by the doors to let late shoppers out, but he wouldn't admit anyone. Stanley's assignment was to walk into the store at ten-thirty and to shop for small items. He was to keep shopping until ten-fifty, or a little later than that, before getting into the line at the checkout counter.

"If possible," Troy had told him, "and it is possible, you should be the last shopper in the line. See that you are before you get into the line. By ten-thirty they'll be down to only one lane anyway. The other checkers will turn in their trays and leave by ten-fifteen, James says. So all you have to do, Pop, is dawdle. If you overlooked someone, and they get behind you, let them go ahead of you in the line and say you forgot something."

"Like what?"

"It doesn't matter. Bread, toilet paper, anything. You leave your cart in place, and you don't come back until you're positive you're the only one left. With only small items to check off, and your cart loaded, it'll take the checker a long time to ring up all your stuff. When you're the last customer in the store, I'll bang on the door. The boy won't let me in, of course, and that's when you say to the checker, 'That's my son. I forgot my wallet at home, and he's brought it.' I'll wave the wallet at the boy. They'll see the mountain of groceries in your cart, with some of 'em rung up already, and the boy'll let me in."

"What do I do then?"

"When I tell 'em it's a stickup, you just hold up your arms like any other smart customer, and you're in the clear."

"Suppose they ask me later why I said you were my son?"

"You don't have to worry about that. But if they do, just

say you're old, which is obvious, and that you were confused for a moment when you couldn't find your wallet. So you *thought* I was your son. The point is, Pop, I don't want you involved in this in any way. That's why I've come up with this foolproof method of letting you help us, but one that'll keep you out of it at the same time. But if you think it's too much for you to handle, let me know now, and I'll work out another way of doing it."

"No, no, Troy, I'm sure that I can handle it. It's just that . . . well, after the robbery, what?"

"You can't leave with us, naturally. So you just stay there, and when the police come you act a little dazed and scared. If you can avoid it, don't say anything at all. Just pretend that you were overwhelmed by the whole thing, and you don't remember what any of us looked like. Finally, after they've let you rest for a while, tell the cops we were wearing masks and plastic gloves, but you think we were black men from the way we talked. They'll jump on that idea. Just don't change your story. Then they'll let you go."

"Suppose, just suppose, they ask me why I've driven all the way down to the Green Lakes mall in Miami to buy groceries, when I live seventy miles away in Riviera Beach?"

"That's easy. They won't ask you that, but if they do, tell 'em you were down here in Miami to see the sights, and you stocked up at this new Green Lakes market because the prices were cheaper down here."

"They aren't, Troy. Things are a lot cheaper up in Riviera than they are down here."

"Christ, Pop, the cops don't know that! They aren't going to give you any third degree. You're wearing a suit and tie, you're a property owner, and you own your own car. You're above suspicion. Can't you see how this all works?"

"I guess so, Troy. But these questions just come to me, and I want to do everything right, that's all."

"You'll do fine. Take off your shoes now, and let James give 'em a good shine. Also, clean out your pockets and give everything to me. I already collected James's stuff, so he can't be identified. If you don't have your wallet on you, your story'll hold up. Put your traveler's checks in Dale's purse, over there on the table. She'll keep things safe for you, just in case."

"In case of what?"

"Unforeseen eventualities. Sometimes there are unforeseen eventualities that no one can predict. At any rate, when they let you go—which won't take long—drive back here to the house. Then we'll get ready to leave in the morning for Haiti."

"Maybe it would be best, Troy, if I didn't go with you. To Haiti. Right away, I mean."

"Hell, I've already got your ticket."

"You can turn it back in when you leave. I can buy another one later. I'd better go back up to Ocean Pines Terraces first, then I can join you later on. Maya might have some second thoughts, and if I'm missing and she calls the police, they might be out looking for me and then they'll find you and Dale. But I can go back home for a few days, call my son, and then a few days later I can call him again and tell him I'm going to the islands on a vacation. You know, I can sort of set things up. If I leave my car in the carport, and tell my neighbors I'm going on a vacation, too, nobody'll look for me."

"Okay, Pop, if that's the way you want to do it. Dale and I will be in Haiti waiting for you. By the time you get there, I'll have a house rented and a room for you. When you get to Port-au-Prince, go to the American embassy; I'll leave the address there for you. Either that, or I can call you from Port-au-Prince and tell you where we are."

"Can you phone from there?"

"Sure."

"I've already had my phone disconnected. Maybe you'd better just leave the address at the embassy. How do I find it?"

"Take a cab from the airport to the embassy. Then you hang on to the cab, get our address, and join us. If we don't have a house yet, we'll be at the Gran Hotel Olofsson. The hotel doesn't take reservations, but all of the hotels have empty rooms down there because of the troubles they've had. So we'll be easy enough to find. People have a tendency to remember Dale's face. You'll find us all right."

They had left it at that.

During the last few days, there had been a great deal of tension in the apartment. James was so apprehensive, he jumped at the slightest sound, and Troy had given him money to buy rum at the liquor store. James picked at his food, and instead of sleeping at night he sat on the lumpy couch smoking one cigarette after another. He drank Mount Gay rum from the bottle, without even a water chaser. He would finally fall asleep well after midnight. Once James fell asleep with a cigarette still burning between his fingers, and Stanley had seen it just in time. As a consequence, Stanley was afraid to go to sleep until after James had passed out on the couch.

During the daytime, James, because of his trembling fingers, was unable to paint. He spent the day looking at his pictures, wondering what to do with them. After James received his share of the money, five thousand dollars, he figured on driving directly to New York, but there was no room in his little Morris Minor for all of his paintings. He had already packed his paints and clothing in the car, and his plan was to keep driving until he got to Valdosta, Georgia, before stopping at a motel. Finally he asked Stanley for advice.

"What I'd do, James, I'd just leave the old paintings here and forget about them. Let the Shapiros have them. You owe them something for not taking care of the grass and the yard. You'll be going to school, and starting over again anyway. After you've had some instructions, you won't want to be reminded of your old work. That's what I think."

"They're a part of me," James said. "I hate to just leave them."

"I know how you feel. I used to feel the same way after I striped a new car. It was a part of me, I guess you could say, and now it was leaving the line for the whole world to see. But you'll be painting new pictures in New York, and these old paintings'll just clutter up your new studio."

"I won't have a studio. I'll just rent a little room somewhere. I'll have to use the studio at the school to paint."

"So leave the pictures and forget 'em."

James nodded grimly and stacked all of his paintings in a corner of the garage. Even so, he would return to the pile from time to time, examining the compositions as if he were trying to memorize them.

Dale kept busy. She washed and scrubbed and cooked plain but ample meals, as well as baking cakes and pies. For breakfast she served them not only fried eggs, but bacon, sausages, and pancakes. She scrubbed and waxed the hardwood floors of the apartment, then washed all of the windows. She polished the furniture, using Lemon Pledge, and the apartment smelled like a lime grove. She used Bon-Ami and elbow grease and managed to get almost all of the mildew off the tiles in the bathroom.

Troy taught James and Dale how to hold and aim their pistols. There was a .38 Smith and Wesson for James, and a small .25 caliber pearl-handled semi-automatic pistol for Dale. James refused to load his pistol. He remained firm that he would just take an empty pistol to hold during the robbery, but Troy still made him aim and practice dry-firing at a target he drew on the garage door.

"Even if you don't intend to shoot it," Troy said, "you have to look like you know what you're doing. It's like with the shotgun. People have to think that you'll shoot. Now Dale, on the other hand, has to keep her pistol loaded because she might have to fire it from the car to warn us when I come out of the market. That way, if someone tries to follow me out, her firing into the air will make 'em stay inside."

Troy oiled and loaded his shotgun. He bought a khaki windbreaker at Sears, one like James had, and crammed double-aught shells into the pockets.

Sometimes Troy was silent for hours at a time. He would sit in the back yard with his shirt off, brooding, not moving, soaking up the sun.

In the evenings, after dinner, and after Dale had finished cleaning up the kitchen, Troy made her dance for them. She needed to keep in practice, he said, to be ready for her night club debut in Haiti.

Dale was not, in Stanley's estimation, a very good dancer, but he kept his opinion to himself. Troy tuned to a rock station on the radio, and Dale would gyrate in her G-string, and her bare breasts would bounce up and down; but she was awkward; she stumbled frequently; and she seemed to be out of synchronization with the music, Stanley thought. But Stanley figured that night-club patrons in Haiti wouldn't be so critical. After all, Dale had a spectacular figure, and as Troy said, she would be wearing a voodoo mask to hide her face.

James, drinking his rum neat, watched Dale gloomily and without comment. One evening, joyous on rum, he showed them all how to limbo. With Stanley and Dale holding a broom, and with salsa blaring on the radio, James kept saying, "Lower, lower, limbo like me!" Finally, he writhed under the broom without touching it while it was held less than a foot above the floor. Troy and Stanley both tried it, but they couldn't get below three feet. Dale, bottom-heavy, couldn't limbo as low as Stanley and Troy. Stanley had enjoyed watching James limbo, but he hurt his stiff back after his third try and had to lie down.

After the heavy meals and the dancing, everybody except James went to bed early. Stanley missed his color TV set. He still took afternoon naps, and he couldn't go to sleep so early. He would lie there on his bed on the porch, listening to Troy and Dale make love in the bedroom. Afterwards, Troy always sent Dale out to sleep with Stanley, because Troy didn't rest well if there was another person in the bed with him. Dale, exhausted from her long day of housework, dancing, and love-making, and wearing her shorty nightgown, would fall asleep immediately. Sometimes, in her sleep, she would snuggle up against Stanley, and her body was so hot she reminded him of an overloaded heating pad. By this time, James would be quite drunk, muttering to himself and dropping ashes on Dale's clean floor. It would be better, Stanley thought, when the job was all over and James was up in New York, and they were down in Haiti. He was looking forward to the trip. After Dale got her operation, and was recuperating, he and Troy could bum around town together, just the two of them, taking in the sights, and they could eat some of that Creole food Troy had talked about. But he really couldn't go with them right after the job, not with all of his responsibilities. In Detroit, if a man left his car at the airport for a week or so, when he came back the car—or at least the battery—would be missing. It was undoubtedly the same way at the Miami airport. Besides, he did have the house to worry about; he would have to arrange with the bank to have his mortgage payments made while he was away. And there was Stanley Junior. If Junior couldn't get ahold of him, he would report him missing to the police. The best thing to do was to go home first, call Junior, and tell him and the neighbors that he would be away on a vacation. That way, he could leave his car in his own carport, take the bus to the West Palm Beach airport, fly to Haiti from there, and save ten dollars a day in airport parking fees. He could get a plane to Haiti just as easily from West Palm as he could from Miami. Besides, he didn't know how long he would be away. This way, if he didn't like it down there, he could use his return ticket to fly back to West Palm whenever he felt like it.

Troy hadn't liked it much when he told him he would join them later in Haiti. He could tell, by the way Troy squinted his eyes. He should have worked it around so that Troy could have been the one to make that suggestion, the way Maya had got around him when she wanted to do something. But Troy would get over being mad about it, once he had joined them down there . . .

Stanley pushed his cart to the back of the store, passing a pimpled teenage employee who was mopping the floor with a wet mop and whistling tunelessly. The boy wore a black bow tie, a white short-sleeved shirt, and blue jeans. A red plastic tag, with white letters spelling RANDY, was pinned to the pocket of his shirt. Stanley stopped at the meat counters, but the meat had all been collected and put away for the night. The refrigerated bins were bare, and the butchers had left. He went to the gourmet section and began to drop small items into his cart, taking them at random from the shelves—a can of anchovies, a bottle of capers, a flat can of smoked oysters, a jar of cocktail onions, an oval tin of pâté. He felt in his pocket for his car keys; for a panicky moment he thought he had left them in the Honda. But the keys were there . . .

Stanley looked at his watch. Ten fifty-five. His cart was filled to the brim; it was so full of canned goods it was hard to push. On the shelf below the basket, he had placed an orange, an apple, a sweet potato, one tomato, one head of cabbage, and a six-pack of Stroh's light beer. Stanley headed for the front of the store. Randy, the boy who had been mopping the floor, now stood beside the locked front doors. The key was in the lock. The night manager, a middle-aged man with a long-sleeved white shirt and a loosened maroon wool tie, was in the open-topped cage behind the service counter with a gray-haired woman employee in a blue-and-white uniform. There was a woman checker at the second checkout counter, and she was ringing up sales for a plump, very pregnant Latin woman who had driven three blocks from home to buy a loaf of Cuban bread, a dozen eggs, a quart of skim milk, and a box of Fruitful Bran. The checker, a young woman with tight yellow curls, purple lipstick and eyeliner, and with too much blusher on her cheeks, was asking the pregnant woman how much longer she had to go when Stanley stopped behind the woman's cart. The checker glanced over at Stanley's overloaded basket and groaned good-naturedly at the sight of all his groceries.

"At least another week, maybe ten days," the Cuban woman said, with a little laugh, "but it might be sooner" —she picked up her bag of groceries—"if he feels like it."

Stanley took his cane out of his cart and tucked it under his left armpit. With his right hand he began to take out the items, one at a time, and place them on the counter.

" 'Evening, sir," the girl said cheerfully. "Looks to me like you're starting your own store."

"Just stocking up a little," Stanley said, not looking up from the cart.

At the door, Randy tried to take the pregnant woman's bag of groceries from her, but she smiled and shook her head. "I can manage it all right—Randy," she said, glancing at his name plate. "Are you?"

"Am I what, ma'am?"

"Randy?"

"Yes, ma'am," he said, letting her out of the store. He relocked the door.

"Maybe," Stanley said, "I'd better get this stuff off the bottom first." He bent over and got the six-pack. As he straightened up, he saw Troy at the door. Troy waved the wallet in his hand and grinned wolfishly at Randy through the glass.

As he had been instructed to do, Stanley patted his empty pockets. His heart was fibrillating slightly, and he found it difficult to breathe. He clutched the handle of the cart for support, and his cane clattered to the floor.

"That's my son at the door," Stanley said to the checker. "I forgot my wallet at home, and it's got all my money in it."

The checker, by this time, had run up $28 worth of groceries, and the cart was still two-thirds loaded.

"For God's sake, Randy," she called to the bag boy, "let him in."

Randy unlocked the door and let Troy in. Before he could relock the door, Troy kneed the boy in the crotch.

Randy dropped to the floor, keening and clutching his genitals with both hands. James slipped through the unlocked door, carrying a black, doubled-up Hefty garbage bag in his left hand and his .38 pistol in his right. James had pulled one leg of a pair of Dale's pantyhose over his head and face, and both legs trailed down his back in foxtails. The pistol danced in his gloved hand, and it looked, for a moment, as if he was going to drop it.

"This is a holdup!" Troy announced, taking the sawed-off shotgun from beneath his jacket. He lifted the hinged top at the service counter to enter the cage.

James stood midway between Randy, who was still on the floor, and the second checkout counter. First, he would point the pistol at the checker, then he would wheel and point it at Randy. In his fear and excitement James kept pulling the trigger, and the empty pistol clicked away like a cheap alarm clock.

The safe was open, as James had said it would be. The night manager and his assistant had their arms high above their heads as Troy entered the crowded cage. The manager kicked back with his left foot and hit a buzzer on the wall. Bells clanged all over the store, and a red light began to flash outside, above the entrance door.

Troy shot the manager in the stomach, and a dark red splotch the size of a grapefruit appeared instantly on his white shirt. The dark blood was a much deeper shade than his maroon tie. As the heavy pellets came out of his back and the blood splattered the woman beside him, the pattern got larger. The gray-haired woman yelped once as the shotgun fired, and her slightly popped eyes rolled back in her head. Her legs gave way, and she fell over sideways in a faint on the manager's dead body. Troy stuck the short barrel against the back of her neck and fired the second round, half severing her head from her body.

Troy reloaded his shotgun and left the cage, pocketing the used shells. James managed to slip his pistol into his own pocket and came through the opened counter into the cage. He knelt by the two bodies, shuddered, and began to transfer the money from the safe into his Hefty bag.

At the sound of the first shotgun blast, Stanley had dropped to the floor and crawled over to the next checkout counter. He stretched out on the floor and covered his head with both hands. Something, he thought, has gone wrong. Troy had told them there would be no shooting at all. The manager must have tried to pull a pistol on Troy.

The checker, except for quivering, hadn't moved from the moment Troy announced the holdup. Her face had a greenish pallor beneath her heavy makeup, and there was a thin ring of white encircling her purple lips. She began to urinate, couldn't stop, and a large puddle formed around her feet. Her lips quivered, but she couldn't make any sound come out of her dry throat as Troy walked toward her with the shotgun extended in his right hand. When he was about two feet away, Troy shot her in the face, and blood and brains erupted from her blonde head. She fell backward and slid to the floor. With his left hand, Troy scooped the bills from her register and jammed them into the pocket of his windbreaker. As he turned back toward the cage, Randy, crouched low, was on his feet again, hobbling as fast as he could toward the dairy section at the back of the store.

Running lightly in his Nikes, Troy overtook the boy and shot him in the back of the head. The boy's body fell forward and slid across the clean floor into a six-foot pyramid of canned peaches. The stack toppled, and the heavy cans bounced and gurgled on the brown linoleum.

Stanley lifted his head above the counter, high enough to see Troy shoot Randy. As the pyramid collapsed, Stanley dropped to his hands and knees and crept as rapidly as he could to the square U that made up the produce section. There was no place to hide, but he wedged his body as close as he could against a large bin of White Rose potatoes.

"Be sure you get the change, too, James!" Troy called out above the clanging bells as he reloaded his shotgun.

"I got it! I got it *all*, man!" James shouted. He came out of the cage and slipped sideways through the passway at the service counter. There were stacks of banded bills in the bag, but the rolls of halves, quarters, dimes, and nickels made the bag heavier than he had expected it to be. Troy raised the shotgun, put the muzzle against James's chest, and fired. Troy picked up the bag and jumped up on the nearest counter, surveying the store.

"A change in plans, Pop!" he shouted. "Instead of staying

here, you'd better come with me now. I mean it, Pop! Those bells are ringing in the police station, too, and I can't hang around here while you make up your mind!"

There was no movement anywhere.

"Pop, let's shake it. Come *on!*" Troy jumped down and took a step toward the closest aisle, cereals, but then he stopped. There were altogether at least a dozen aisles in the store. In the back, there were two open service doors leading to the stockrooms. "Shit," he said under his breath.

Troy turned around and walked to the door, carrying the bag slung over his left shoulder.

"Okay, Pop, see you in Haiti, and thanks for the help!"

Awkwardly, with his shotgun hand, Troy unlocked the door. He pushed it open and stepped into the humid night.

Ellita Sanchez had reached her car and unlocked the door when the first shotgun round was fired. She dumped her groceries behind the seat as the second round was fired, and took her .38 Chief's Special out of her purse. She did it all automatically, without thinking about it, but now, with her pistol in her hand, she hesitated and stared at the brightly lighted supermarket and the flashing red light. She was on a maternity leave, so technically she was not even an off-duty cop. She had no radio. Perhaps she should drive away, find a pay phone, and call 911? No one could blame her for that. On the other hand, if someone was shooting a shotgun inside the store—and the sound was unmistakably that of a shotgun—there was no way after nine years on the force that she could just jump in her car and drive away without investigating what was going on. The clanging bells were insistent. She could at least try to get a look inside.

Ellita took her badge out of her purse. She held the badge in her left hand and the pistol in her right as she lumbered heavily toward the lighted glass doors of the store. As two more shotgun rounds were fired, she gripped her pistol tighter. She hesitated, looking around for suitable cover as the shotgun went off for the fifth time. She knelt behind a newly planted palm tree, a few yards away from a brown Honda with a roof rack on it, where she could watch the door. A tallish man, carrying a Hefty bag and a sawed-off shotgun, came bursting out of the store. He was silhouetted against the lights inside, his features in such dark shadow that Ellita couldn't see what he looked like. The flashing red light made his movements seem jerky.

"Freeze! Police!" Ellita yelled, trying to keep her large body behind the tree. She fired a warning shot into the sign above the doors.

The robber fired once in her general direction and dropped into a crouching position. Then he fired again. The double-aught pellets scattered all over the lot at this distance, but one of them hit Ellita in the face, and another tore into her right shoulder. She could hear some of the buckshot hitting and ricocheting off the Honda. Ellita dropped to the asphalt and tried to wedge her pregnant body under the Honda, without success. Her face and shoulder seemed to be on fire. Her right arm was numb, so she fired the rest of her rounds blindly toward the store, trying to steady the pistol with her left hand.

Dale Forrest, who had been parked around the corner of the building with the engine running, pulled up in front of the double doorway and stopped while Ellita was still firing. One of Ellita's bullets hit the right front fender of the Lincoln town car. Troy threw the Hefty into the back seat through the open window and told Dale to move over so he could get in and drive. Dale shot him in the face with her .25, and Troy fell sideways onto the pavement, dropping his shotgun and clutching his face with both hands.

Dale drove away, flooring the gas pedal so hard she almost killed the engine. She made a wide circle in the parking lot and exited onto State Road 836, heading west.

Ellita felt the first strong contraction of what she feared was early labor. She rolled over on her back and bit her lower lip as two matching pains gripped her unexpectedly, beginning at the small of her back, encircling her waist, and then meeting in front to interlock. The pain didn't last long, and when it subsided she got onto her knees. She watched an old man come out of the store, leaning heavily on his cane. She crawled backward into the darkness as she realized that the old man was coming toward the brown Honda, but she kept behind his car and he didn't see her. She ducked her head. Her pistol was empty, useless. Where the hell was her purse?

The old man got into his car without seeing Ellita. He drove up beside the wounded man who was still holding his face and kneeling on the sidewalk. The old guy got out, helped the groaning man get into the car, and then drove away. When he reached the State Road 836 exit, he turned east and disappeared into the traffic.

Ellita walked unsteadily into the store, surveyed the dead bodies, and leaned against a pay phone while she called Commander Bill Henderson at home. As she explained what happened, another contraction gripped her hard, and her water broke with a rush of fluid down her legs.

"Everyone's dead, Bill. Everyone. But you'd better have an ambulance sent anyway. I'm slightly wounded, but the pains are getting closer together, and oh Jesus I'm going to have this baby any minute!"

But Ellita's baby, a nine-and-a-half-pound boy, wasn't born until ten the next morning at Jackson Memorial Hospital. A nerve in Ellita's right shoulder was half-severed, and there was an ugly hole in her face. Her right cheekbone was chipped off cleanly, right below the eye, and there was a jagged two-inch tear in her right cheek.

The pantyhose robber with the empty gun had died instantly. His partner with the sawed-off shotgun had wounded Ellita Sanchez and murdered four store employees for what was estimated to be less than twenty thousand dollars.

CHAPTER 17

The supermarket robbery-massacre got considerable play in the Miami press and on the radio and television stations. Very little information was released to the media by the Homicide Division, but pictures were printed in the papers, and the headline, SUPER-MASSACRE AT SUPERMARKET, frightened everyone who read it, especially old-line Miamians. The story revealed that all of the victims were white, Protestants, and native-born Americans. There had been mini-massacres in Miami before, with four or five men and their women and children killed all at once, but those victims had been Colombians, or other Latins, or blacks; and usually they had been connected in some way with the drug industry or with organized crime. These innocent victims, on the other hand, were not only white, they were respectable middle-class people, and all of them were residents of the predominantly native-born Green Lakes subdivision.

The night manager, Victor Persons, forty-five, was married, the father of three children, and a paid soloist on Sunday evenings at the Green Lakes Methodist Church.

His assistant, Ms. Julia Riordan, fifty-eight, was a former schoolteacher who had taught fourth grade in Dade County, at various schools, for twenty-two years. According to one of her Green Lakes neighbors, she had retired under the old Florida Retirement System, before Social Security had been withheld from teachers' pay, and she had taken the night-shift job at the supermarket so she could build up enough credits to obtain a second retirement from the Social Security system when she reached sixty-two. The gruesome photographs of Mr. Persons and Ms. Riordan beside the open safe, which appeared in both Miami papers, though not on television, brought dozens of angry letters to the editors of both papers, protesting their publication.

Sally Metcalf, twenty-three, the blonde checker, or "scanner-assistant," as her position was called by the supermarket chain (her job, apparently, was to assist the electronic scanner in its task), had been a member of the Miami-Dade Community College's South Campus volleyball team before she graduated, and she was engaged to be married to her high school sweetheart as soon as he finished his first hitch at Fort Benning, Georgia.

Randolph Perkins, seventeen, the bag boy, a high school student at Miami-Norland, was remembered by his fellow students as "a real good guy who was always ready with a joke, and liked to kid around alot *(sic).*" His principal also told the same reporter that Randy had already passed Florida's 11th Grade Achievement Test, and that he had a "very high C average" in all of his classes. There was a black-and-white photograph of four of Randy's buddies and two crying girls in the paper, all of them wearing black ribbons pinned to their T-shirts, in mourning for their classmate.

Fred Pickering, twenty-eight, the produce manager, who had rushed through his closing work at the store so he could leave early to watch a tape of *Ghostbusters* his wife had rented that afternoon, credited his Sony VCR with saving his life. "God," he told the TV reporter, "evidently has other plans for me!" He broke down, then, on camera, and cried. "Here I was," he sobbed, "laughing my head off at home at *Ghostbusters*, while Ms. Riordan was getting her head blown off down to the store! It could've been me. It could've been me!"

Letters were written to the Cuban-born mayor and to the multi-ethnic members of the city commission. The tone of the letters varied, but the essential message was the same, reminding the commissioners that when they ran for their six-thousand-dollar-a-year seats that they had all claimed that they would serve *all* of the people in Miami if elected, not just their ethnic groups. They were also reminded that WASPs, although they only numbered approximately eight percent of Miami's population, still had a lot of money to spend in future elections.

The mayor and the other members of the commission put considerable pressure on the city manager. The city manager, who had the authority to hire and fire police chiefs, applied even more pressure on the chief of police to find the killers. He, in turn, appointed a Special Task Force to solve this crime, to be headed by Major Willie Brownley. Major Brownley, in turn, made Commander Bill Henderson his operations officer, to coordinate activities, and Bill Henderson, in turn, canceled Hoke Moseley's leave without pay and called him back to do the actual work on the investigation with the help of Detective Speedy Gonzalez.

Hoke and Gonzalez had lots of help from within the division and the department. Ellita, not only because she was a wounded cop, but because of her cheerful disposition and willingness to lend small sums of money, was popular with all of the detectives in the Homicide Division. They volunteered their off-duty time to Hoke the moment their shifts ended. Hoke gave them things to do, like the routine roundup of tall, black holdup men with previous convictions, who were then interrogated about their whereabouts at the time of the robbery-massacre. These interrogations didn't get any concrete results, but were considered necessary to eliminate possible suspects and on the off-chance that some information would turn up.

Gonzalez and Sergeant Armando Quevedo interviewed the day-shift employees at the supermarket, and the day manager quickly identified the dead mulatto's photograph as that of a bag boy he had fired for stealing a couple of months back. The man's name, according to the three-by-five employment card, was John Smith, but the rooming-house address on the card did not exist, and the Social Security number on the card belonged to a forty-seven-year-old John Smith in Portland, Oregon.

"We don't run background checks on bag boys," the manager said. "They don't handle money, and they come and go too fast. Smith had a Caribbean accent, so maybe he gave us a phony name and Social Security number because he was here in Florida illegally. That sometimes happens with foreigners on student visas, who ain't supposed to work either. All I know about Smith is, he was a thief, and as soon's I spotted him stealing I canned him."

Quevedo then checked the dead man's clothes in the lab with the head technician. Here their luck changed, and they got a valid lead.

Hoke, of course, had to read and cross-check every supplementary report with the others, and the pile of paper mounted hourly on his desk. Hoke's phones, as well as Bill Henderson's, were busy night and day, after the numbers were listed in the newspapers. But Hoke welcomed the activity, knowing, from experience, that it was the kind of things they were doing now that eventually provided a breakthrough in any investigation.

Hoke would have returned to Miami anyway, whether his leave had been canceled or not. He considered himself partly responsible for his partner's injuries. If he had been home instead of trying to "find himself again" up in Singer Island, he would have been the one to go to the store instead of Ellita, and she wouldn't have been wounded. Her face, the surgeon told him, when Hoke talked to him at some length in the hospital, would be okay when the surgery healed. The hole could be filled in with a piece of plastic, and the skin would stretch over it. Except for a small dent, and a fine line across her cheek, which could be camouflaged easily with pancake makeup, no one, unless he looked very closely indeed, would notice the repair work. The arm, unhappily, was a more serious injury, because of the nerve damage. In time, Ellita would regain partial use of her arm, eighty to eighty-five percent perhaps, with a lot of therapy, but the disability meant the end of her career insofar as full-time police work was concerned.

The surgeon would recommend a thirty-percent disability pension for Ellita Sanchez, and because disability pensions paid a higher sum than regular police pensions, Ellita would make almost as much money as she would have made if she had stayed on the force for twenty years. In fact, in the long run, she would make a little more, because she still had eleven years to go for normal retirement, and she would be drawing the disability pension for those eleven years without working. Moreover, the disability payments would continue for the rest of her life, with a three percent COLA every year. She also received a Heroism medal from the Chief of Police, and considerable space in the newspapers.

On the even brighter side, she would be able to stay home and raise her son, and the boy, Pepé Roberto St. Xavier Armando Goya y Goya Sanchez, was a healthy, beautiful blue-eyed baby. And, the surgeon added, he wished that Hoke, if he had any influence with Ellita at all, would ask her to reconsider and let him circumcise the boy before she took him home from the hospital.

Hoke told him that he would think about it, although he didn't intend to say anything about it.

Mr. and Mrs. Sanchez, Ellita's parents, were in Ellita's hospital room when Hoke and Sue Ellen visited her. One or the other had been there every minute since the time she had been brought back to a private room from Recovery. They sat quietly on metal folding chairs beside the bed. Mr. Sanchez, who had disowned his daughter when he had discovered that she was pregnant, still didn't speak to her, but the fact that he was there, and smiled in spite of himself when the baby was brought in for nursing, was a sign that there might be, eventually, some kind of a reconciliation. Hoke shook hands with the tight-lipped Mr. Sanchez, and smiled at Mrs. Sanchez, who merely pursed her lips and shook her head. Hoke kissed Ellita lightly on the forehead.

"Have you seen the baby?" Ellita asked, smiling.

"I sure did. He's a monster with black hair and blue eyes."

"Didn't I tell you he would be a boy?"

"I never doubted it. They wouldn't let Sue Ellen go up there, though, and she's dying to see him."

"She can see him in here, when they bring him back to nurse. But you'll have to leave then."

"I've quit my job, Ellita," Sue Ellen said. "So I'll be there to help you with the baby when you come home."

"You didn't have to do that—"

"It was my idea," Hoke said. "Aileen's coming back from L.A. next Saturday, and she's going to spend the rest of the summer with my dad in Singer Island. Those sisters at the convent straightened her out in a hurry. But she'll be back home when school starts, and the manager at the car wash said Sue Ellen could have her job back anytime she wanted it."

"How's the investigation going?"

Hoke turned to Sue Ellen. "Wait in the waiting room, honey. You can come back when they bring in the baby. Could you ask your parents to leave while we discuss this, Ellita?"

Ellita said something to her parents in Spanish. They didn't reply, but they didn't move, either.

"They won't leave, Hoke." Ellita shrugged. "But they won't repeat anything you say, don't worry."

Sue Ellen went out, closing the door softly behind her.

"The dead guy with the stocking cap was identified," Hoke said. "There was a numbered yellow cleaning tag stapled on his jacket, and I gave it to Sergeant Quevedo to track down. He was on the phone for four hours, tracing it to Bayside Cleaners. He went down there, but they didn't have any slip for the cleaning on file. The woman in the shop, though, a woman from Eleuthera, recognized his picture, because of his little car. He had an old Morris Minor, and when he came in she told him she hadn't seen a car like that since she left Nassau fifteen years ago. They had talked some about the islands, and she remembered that he told her he brought the car from Barbados with him. So Quevedo did some legwork in Bayside, found the mail carrier on the route, and the mailman knew him because he delivered his mail from Barbados. He was living in a garage apartment that belonged to Sidney Shapiro, watching their house while they were up in Maine. His name was James Frietas-Smith, and the little Morris was parked in the yard, all packed up with his stuff, and there were some weird paintings stacked up in the garage. Quevedo called Smith's father in Barbados, and he's going to make some kind of arrangements with a shipping firm to take the body back to the island."

"That was good police work on Quevedo's part."

Hoke grinned. "That's why Quevedo's a sergeant, and also why I'm thinking about sending Gonzalez back to duty in Liberty City. Gonzalez ain't gonna make it as a detective, and he should be back in uniform."

"Give him time, Hoke."

Hoke shrugged. "Anyway, that garage apartment was incredibly clean. The furniture was polished, and you wouldn't believe how neat it was. Not a dirty dish. But there was no evidence of anyone else living there. But that wasn't the main discovery. Quevedo asked Shapiro to come down to see if anything valuable was missing from the big house in front of the garage. Shapiro flew down, and when he and Quevedo went through the house, they found a dead guy and a dead baby rolled up in a carpet in one of the guest bedrooms on the second floor."

"A dead baby? I don't under—"

"The baby, about eighteen months old, had been strangled, but the dead man, a guy named James C. Davis, had been shotgunned. The baby had been kidnapped at Dadeland, and we got an ID from the mother already. They took the car and the baby, and then dumped the car and kept the baby to kill it. Davis was a detail man—"

"A detail man?"

"From a pharmaceutical firm. Lee-Fromach Pharmaceuticals, in New Jersey. A detail man is a guy who goes around and talks to doctors about his products. These guys work alone, you see, and Dade County was Davis's territory. That's why no one reported him missing. He was a bachelor with a pad in the Grove. We found his car, a blue Lincoln town car, parked at a Denny's on Biscayne Boulevard."

"I still don't understand why they would kill a baby, Hoke." She brushed her eyes with the back of her hand.

"An eighteen-month-old baby couldn't identify anybody. He'd hardly know his mother!"

"It was a little girl. I know, it was totally senseless. But what we're dealing with, Ellita, is a crazy double-donged sonofabitch. The same guy who shot you probably killed the baby, and they must've shot Davis when they took his car for the robbery. This killer's a scary guy."

"What about prints on the car?"

"Nothing, except for smudges and Davis's prints. You said the person driving could've been either a man or a woman, probably a woman because there was the scarf over her head, but we can't verify that. You can't describe the guy with the shotgun because he was in silhouette, so we don't know if he was black or white."

"That red light, flashing off and on, was like a strobe, Hoke. I couldn't tell anything for sure."

"Well, we know the Bajan was a high yellow, so we've been figuring the guy with the shotgun's probably black, too. But that still doesn't explain the old white man. You say he was a shopper in the store, but he must be a member of the gang if he left with the one who was shot. The collection of groceries in his cart was such a weird mixture, he was obviously killing time in there for some reason or another.

"Anyway, we circulated the Identikit picture of the old man you described, and now I've asked the TV stations to run it in the 'Crime Stoppers' series. At first, we thought the way you did, that the old man was a customer, just somebody doing a good-Samaritan act and driving the wounded man to the hospital. But none of the hospitals have reported any gunshot men who haven't been accounted for in some other way. If the gunshot killer was hurt as badly as you say, he needed medical attention. We've been checking clinics and hospitals by phone from Key West to West Palm Beach, but so far, nothing. There were no prints on the two weapons found either, so the guy must've been wearing gloves."

"How much did they get in the robbery?"

"About eighteen thousand. There should've been more, but because of those armored car robberies last month, Wells-Fargo's been varying their pickup schedules. They picked up at noon on Saturday instead of waiting for Monday. The chain had insurance for the money, but they may have to close the supermarket. People are scared shitless. It's not open at night anymore now, and a few of the businesses that had signed leases to move into the new mall have just canceled them. Willie Brownley asked the chain to increase the reward from ten to twenty-five thousand, and they probably will. If we don't catch the killer, nobody'll visit that mall when it finally opens—not at night, anyway."

"I should've been more alert, Hoke. I was crouched right behind the Honda and I didn't get the license number. It didn't even occur to me. I noticed the roof rack, however, and those aren't standard."

Hoke patted her arm. "If I'd been shot in the face and was going into labor, I wouldn't have thought of the license either. The Identikit drawing's a good one, you say, but do you realize how many old men there are who've retired to Florida and look like that? Every pensioner in Dade County owns at least one wash-and-wear seersucker suit."

"What about the cane, Hoke? There was a brass dog's head on the cane, I think. Not every old man carries a cane. So why not run a picture of that along with the Identikit photo?"

"What kind of dog was it?"

"I don't know. But it was a shiny brass dog's head, not a duck or a snake, I'm almost positive."

"Were the ears up or down?"

"Down, like flaps, and the nose was a little pointed, I

think, but it wasn't any special breed. I didn't pay that much attention, but I did notice the cane when he put it under his arm at the checkout counter."

"Okay. We'll get 'em to run a picture of the cane, too. A cocker spaniel, maybe."

"I wish there was something else, Hoke." Tears formed in Ellita's eyes again. "When I think about that dead baby . . ."

"Don't think about it. I'll leave Sue Ellen here so she can see your baby, and I'll pick her up tonight on my way home. Do you need anything?"

"Well, if you can, smuggle me in a can of Stroh's." Ellita wiped her eyes with the corner of the sheet. "My mother says that an occasional beer makes your milk richer. Because of the hops, and all. And the doctor said I couldn't have any."

"Sure, I'll sneak you in a couple of beers, kid. Do you need anything for pain? I can bring you some codeine tablets if you want some."

"No, I'm okay there. It's a steady kind of pain, in my shoulder, and it shoots down my arm once in a while, but I can stand it. They've been giving me Darvon every four hours, and that helps."

"I know how these bastards are, Ellita. Doctors call pain 'discomfort,' and they don't give a shit whether you're suffering or not. If it gets too bad, you tell me, and I'll get you some codeine."

Hoke patted Ellita on her good shoulder, nodded goodbye to the Sanchezes, and left to drive back to the police station. The Sanchezes, to Hoke's amusement, suspected that he was the father of Ellita's baby, and hated him for not acknowledging it, and for not marrying their daughter after getting her pregnant. Ellita had told them that Hoke wasn't the father, but they had never believed her. Hoke, of course, didn't care what the Sanchezes thought about him, or what they had thought his reasons were for telling them, in his halting Spanish while Ellita was in surgery, that he'd find the son of a whore who shot at her and her baby if it took him twenty-five hours a day.

The next break in the case came when a black man giving his name only as Marvin telephoned Commander Bill Henderson and said he had some information on the robbery. But he wanted to make a deal, he said, before he would pass it on. Marvin also said he wanted the reward money, and a statement, in writing, that he was entitled to it, before he gave Henderson any information.

"We get a lot of strange calls, Marvin," Henderson told him. "What've you got?"

"Do I get my deal first?"

"That depends on your information, and the deal you want."

"I'm out on bond," Marvin said, "for soliciting a minor for prostitution, and I want the charges dropped."

"That's a serious charge. How old was the girl?"

"It wasn't no girl, it was a boy. He's fourteen, but he was already hustling when I recruit him. It's a bum rap, but they don't like me over here on the Beach and they set me up."

"You realize that Miami and Miami Beach are two different jurisdictions?"

"I knows that, but I also knows that deals can be made, 'specially on something like this massacre."

"I'll see what I can do, Marvin. But you'll have to come to the station to talk to me."

"I can't do that. I done been told by a Miami vice cop never to come over to Miami again, or he'd shoot me on sight."

"Who told you that? What's his name?"

"A Miami vice cop. I don't know his name, but he knows

mine and he knows me. I'll meet you this afternoon at four-thirty at Watson Island. In the Japanese garden, at the gate. I'll show you some proofs of what I'm saying, and then we can dicker."

"Okay, Marvin. See you at four-thirty."

Bill Henderson passed this intelligence on to Hoke, and then returned to making up duty schedules for the following week. He also had a supplementary payroll for the division to get out.

That afternoon, Hoke and Gonzalez drove to Watson Island, only an eight-minute drive from the police station, and parked in the lot outside the Japanese garden. The garden, donated to Miami by a Tokyo millionaire in 1961, hadn't been maintained, but it was still open to the public every day until five.

There was no one at the gate. Gonzalez looked at the jungly growth in the garden and shook his head. "This place was really something a few years ago, Sergeant. I remember bringing my girl friend over here on Sundays, just to walk around and look. There used to be a beautiful stone lantern over there, right by the bridge."

"Somebody probably stole it. The city can't afford to have twenty-four-hour security on a place like this."

"Maybe not, but it's a shame to let it run down this way. You think this Marvin guy'll show up?"

"You never can tell, Gonzalez. Usually, anonymous callers don't show the first time, but if they really have something, they'll call again. That's the usual pattern. If this guy's got anything at all, he'll meet us eventually. Reward money brings them out, and it was in the paper this morning, about the reward being increased to twenty-five thousand."

At four-thirty, Marvin Grizzard left his hiding place behind the Japanese teahouse with the sagging roof, ambled over the arching bridge, and introduced himself. He was a tall black man, wearing pleated gray gabardine slacks, a long-sleeved flowered sport shirt, and shiny white Gucci shoes. The left sleeve had been rolled back one turn to show a gold Rolex watch on his wrist. He handed Hoke a square piece of black plastic, approximately six by six inches.

"Here's part of it," Marvin said.

"Part of what?" Hoke said.

"Evidence, man. I cut that out of the Hefty bag."

"What Hefty bag?"

"The bag that held the money taken in the robbery."

"Shit," Gonzalez said. "A piece of plastic cut out of a Hefty don't mean anything."

"It does," Marvin said, raising his chin, "when you got the rest of the Hefty, which is complete 'cept for this piece I cut out. In fact, it's two Hefty bags, one inside the other. And I've got all the money, too."

Marvin unbuttoned his shirt and took out a stack of banded twenty-dollar bills. The paper band was green, and the initials "V.P." in black ink were scrawled on the band. Hoke riffled the bills and studied the initials for a moment.

" 'Cuff him," Hoke said to Gonzalez. Hoke then moved to a stone bench, sat down, and carefully counted the money. It was a thousand dollars even. It was almost too much to hope for, but the initials should be those of Victor Persons, the murdered night manager of the Green Lakes Supermarket.

CHAPTER 18

Marvin protested about being handcuffed, but to no avail. Hoke told him to sit on the bench and explain how he obtained the banded one thousand dollars.

"What about my deal and the reward?"

"Don't worry about the reward. That money's paid only if an arrest leads to a conviction. But if you're a perp in this case, you can't collect it."

"I'm not! I didn't have nothin' to do with it, and I got an alibi for the robbery. I was at the Dania fronton till it closed, and I got friends who was with me."

"You aren't charged with anything yet," Gonzalez reminded him. "And you don't have to tell us anything. We can take you in on what we have, and anything you say can be held against you."

"You can have a lawyer present, too, if you want one," Hoke added. "And if you can't afford one, we'll get one for you. D'you understand that?"

"I don't need no lawyer. I ain't even no 'cessory after the fact. I'm a good citizen doing his public duty for the reward money, and a registered voter."

"You're a convicted felon," Gonzalez said. "How can you be a registered voter?"

"Who told you 'bout that? Besides, I registered once, and

I thought it was still good. My card's right there in my wallet."

"Just tell us where the money came from, Marvin," Hoke said. "We'll check out everything you tell us, and if you're in the clear, getting the reward money won't be a problem."

"What about the soliciting charges?"

"That'll be up to the State Attorney. But she's a reasonable woman, and if you help us, I'm sure she'll do something for you. We can't speak for the State Attorney, but we can make a recommendation. And that's it. We won't promise you doodly squat."

A middle-aged Latin man drove up to the gate, got out of his car, closed the gate, unlocked the padlock on the dangling chain, and then relocked the padlock on the chain.

"Hey!" Hoke called out. "Don't lock the fucking gate! Can't you see us over here?"

"*¡Cerrado!*" The man tapped his wristwatch, got back into his Escort, backed up, and drove down the gravel road to the causeway.

"Jesus," Hoke said, "the assholes we've got working for this city—"

"That includes us, Sergeant," Gonzalez said, "for arguing overtime with this funky bastard. I've got some leg-irons in the trunk. Why don't we put 'em on Marvin here, and put him under the bridge overnight and come back tomorrow morning some time. If it's five o'clock, it's our quitting time, too, and I could stand a beer."

"We don't have to do that," Hoke said. "Marvin wants to tell us all about it. Don't you, Marvin?"

Marvin did, and he did.

His story took them back to the night of the robbery. Dale Forrest, who had parked around the corner of the supermarket, with the nose of the Lincoln extended out far enough so she could watch the glass doors, had been instructed to wait for three minutes before driving up to the doors to pick up Troy and James. Troy had estimated that the job would only take three minutes, four at the most. When Dale heard the first two shots and the clanging bells, however, she had panicked and almost driven away without them. It was an instinctual feeling, but she didn't leave because she knew, an instant later, that if she did drive away Troy would find her, no matter where she went, and kill her. Besides, Dale had never acted that independently. A man had always told her what to do, for as long as she could remember, beginning with her father, and her Uncle Bob, who had lived with the family and seduced her when she was eleven, and all of her brothers, and the men she had lived with, off and on, since she had left home. So she had gripped the wheel hard with both hands and kept her eyes on the luminous dashboard clock. She twitched and bit her lip when the shotgun fired again, but she waited till the three minutes were up before she left the concealed parking spot. She looked through the window just in time to see Troy deliberately kill James. She knew then that Troy was probably going to kill her as well, that Troy did not intend to take her with him to Haiti, and that there wasn't any plastic surgeon in Haiti to fix her face, either. The pearl-handled .25 semi-automatic pistol was in her lap. When Troy threw the Hefty bag into the back seat and told her to move over so he could drive (that wasn't the original plan; *she* was supposed to drive), she knew damned well that he would kill her, and she panicked, and with a swift motion she picked up the little weapon, fired, took her foot off the brake, and pushed the gas pedal to the floor. The heavy car, already in drive, sprang forward with the tires squealing as Troy dropped to the sidewalk. Dale heard him scream, so she knew as she turned onto State Road 836 that he wasn't dead. She hadn't seen Mr. Sinkiewicz either, so she suspected that Troy had killed him, too.

At first, Dale was going to follow the original plan and drive back to the garage apartment, but she quickly changed her mind. Her packed suitcase was already in the back of the Lincoln, and so were Troy's things. And with Mr. Sinkiewicz's Honda still in the parking lot, Troy would undoubtedly follow her back to the apartment in the old man's car. At the next exit, Dale got off the overpass and drove through unfamiliar neighborhoods until she reached Biscayne Boulevard. She stopped at a Denny's, parked and locked the car in the back lot, and went inside, taking a booth in the corner. She ordered a ham sandwich she didn't want, to go with the coffee she did, and tried to figure out what to do next. She couldn't think very well at all, and she had to hold the cup of coffee, which was only lukewarm, with both hands to drink it. Dale was truly afraid for her life. Everything Troy had told her about going to Haiti and getting plastic surgery for her face and buying a nice home on the island where she could lie on the beach and recuperate, everything, including her dancing career, had been destroyed when she shot him in the face. Now that she had a little time to think it over, she decided that maybe he wouldn't have hurt her. In all probability he had just killed James and Mr. Sinkiewicz so he wouldn't have to share the money with them. After all, Troy had loved her, and told her so, lots of times, especially when they were doing it in bed. For the first time in her life she had met a man who loved her, who appreciated her for herself instead of just for her body, and she had spoiled it all by panicking and shooting him. But if Troy found her now, he would *surely* kill her, and she could hardly blame him. Troy would believe—and how else could he think?—that she had intended all along to shoot him and keep the money for herself. She didn't know what to do, she didn't know where to go, and she couldn't think of anywhere to hide where Troy couldn't find her. With her face, her badly disfigured face, she could be tracked down no matter where she went.

Not only that, but the car she was driving was stolen. Troy and James had hidden the owner's body in the big Shapiro house. Mr. Sinkiewicz hadn't been told about that because, as Troy had said, it might upset the old man, but the man and his car had been missing for three days now, and the chances were that the police were looking for the car. And if they found her driving it, and then found the owner's body, she would be blamed for his murder and then it would all come out about the supermarket robbery plus the death of James and Mr. Sinkiewicz and she would be charged with those murders, too. Troy, of course, was way too smart to be discovered or caught, so she would be blamed for everything! And that could mean the electric chair.

She ordered another cup of coffee.

"Anything wrong with the sandwich?" the waitress asked as she refilled Dale's cup.

"It's fine. But I think I'll take it home and eat it. Have you got a doggie bag?"

"No problem." The waitress left with the sandwich.

Doggie bag, Dale thought. She had all the money in that sack in the back seat of the Lincoln. She needed some advice and a place to hide and she needed it right away. That's when Dale remembered Marvin Grizzard, the pimp she had hustled for when she had first moved down to Miami Beach from Daytona. Because of the way she looked she had been lucky to get as much as ten dollars a trick hustling Mariel Cuban refugees on the Beach. She hadn't brought in enough income for Marvin, so after two weeks he had driven her across the causeway, dropped her off on Biscayne Boulevard, and told her she was on her own. He had been nice enough to give her a twenty-dollar bill, so she could rent a motel room, but he said that with her face she simply didn't bring in enough money for him to take care of her. What little she did bring in each night wasn't enough to pay the lawyer he had on retainer to get his girls out of jail when they were picked up by the vice cops. Dale hadn't blamed Marvin. In his own way, Marvin had been decent to her, but business was business to Marvin, and he had a lot of expenses.

But now she had a lot of money in the car.

If she gave the money to Marvin, he would help her get out of town, or he'd come up with some way to hide her from Troy. She was sure she had never told Troy anything about Marvin. In fact, she had almost forgotten about Marvin until now. He was the only man she could think of who would know what to do.

Dale paid for her sandwich and coffee at the cashier's, then threw the foil-wrapped sandwich and Mr. Sinkiewicz's signed traveler's checks into the dumpster on her way to the car. She retrieved her suitcase and the Hefty bag from the car, wiped the steering wheel and door handle with a paper napkin from the restaurant, walked to the taxi stand at the Omni Hotel, and took a cab to Miami Beach. She checked into Murgatroyd Manor, a pink and green art deco hotel on Ocean Boulevard, paid a week's rent in advance, and got a room overlooking the sea. She looked up Marvin's telephone number, called his apartment, and spoke into his answering machine after the little ding.

"Marvin, this is Dale Forrest. I've got the money I owe you. Five thousand dollars. If you're interested, I'm in room 314, at the Murgatroyd Manor." She hung up the phone, waited for a minute, and then called the desk and asked the clerk to send up a bottle of Early Times and a bowl of ice.

An hour later, after she had had three drinks and had calmed down some, and decided not to drink any more, there was a knock on the door.

Marvin, worried about some kind of a trick, but keenly interested in the sum of five thousand dollars, although Dale Forrest didn't owe him any money—no one ever owed Marvin any money for very long—had sent Hortensia, one of his girls, to check on the situation while he waited in his Cadillac a block away. Dale handed Hortensia two hundred dollars in twenty-dollar bills.

"Tell Marvin this is a sample, but tell him I want to talk to him in person."

Hortensia walked back to the car, gave Marvin the money, and told him that Dale was alone in her hotel room. She hadn't seen anyone else lurking around, either. There was no one in the lobby, and the desk clerk was half-asleep behind the desk.

Marvin went down the alley, climbed the fire escape to the third floor, walked down the corridor, and knocked on Dale's door.

The money, almost nineteen thousand dollars, had been counted and stacked on the double bed. The rolls of coins were beside the rows of stacked bills, and the Hefty bags, folded neatly into squares, were side by side on top of the pillows.

Dale poured Marvin a drink over ice cubes in a plastic glass and told him about the robbery. She also told him that she had shot Troy, but that Troy, though he was wounded, was undoubtedly looking for her and the money, and that he was, in all probability, driving a brown Honda Civic. Marvin had nodded, asking a few questions but looking at the money instead of Dale. When she finished talking, he took another drink from her bottle of Early Times, this time drinking from the bottle instead of pouring a shot into his glass.

All of this had taken considerable time. Dawn arrived before they finished discussing the situation. What he would do, Marvin told Dale, he would get her out of the country. He would get her a ticket to Puerto Rico, and a passport so she could enter that country, but he would drive up to West Palm Beach and buy a ticket to the island from the Palm Beach airport, instead of Miami's, because it would be unlikely that Troy Louden would think she would leave from Palm Beach. Troy might have the Miami airport covered, but he wouldn't cover the Palm Beach airport.

It would cost, Marvin told her, three thousand dollars to get her a false passport. The remainder of the money, except for a thousand dollars, which she would need to get started on in San Juan, would be his fee for these services. It might take a couple of days to get the passport, but she would be safe here in the hotel if she didn't leave the room; meanwhile, he would drive up to West Palm and buy the ticket. He realized that his fee was high, but this Troy she told him about was a dangerous bastard, and he, Marvin, was putting his ass on the line—

At this point, Gonzalez broke in: "You asshole. You don't need a passport to go to Puerto Rico. It's part of the United States!"

"Since when? I thought it was like El Salvador—"

"Never mind," Hoke said. "Tell us the rest of it, Marvin."

"I reckon Dale don't know that about Puerto Rico, either," Marvin said, shrugging. "Anyway, that's the plan I came up with. I took three thousand for the passport, and two hundred more to get the ticket, but I left the rest of the money in the room—to show my good faith and all. Then I left. I ate breakfast back in my apartment and watched TV. There was something about the robbery and massacre, but not too much details. I went down for the *Miami Herald*, you know, but there was nothing in the paper about it. The story had happened too late at night to get in. But at ten, when the *Miami News* came out, the first street edition, with the pictures and all, I realized that this situation was too heavy for me. I was gonna help Dale get away. I was gonna have a fake passport made up, and drive her up to Palm Beach myself, just like I said. But this was a big Murder One thing, so I put off doing anything, you see, trying to figure out what was best for me. If there's one thing I don't need, it's a 'cessory rap to a Murder One rap, and on top of that, whenever I thought about this Troy dude my balls turned to ice cubes.

"I went back to Dale's room late that afternoon and told her it would take more time than I thought to get the passport. I also took a Polaroid snapshot of her, which I said the passport man needed. I been stalling for three days now."

"What's the passport man's name?" Gonzalez asked.

"There ain't no passport man. I was just gonna paste Dale's picture on Hortensia's passport. Hortensia's here on a student visa from the Dominican Republic. But the more I thought about it, the more worried I got. Then when they come out in the papers this morning with the new reward, which is more than the nineteen thousand, I got this new idea—to turn Dale in."

"Where's Dale now?" Hoke asked.

"Like I said, 314, Murgatroyd Manor."

"Okay, Gonzalez," Hoke said, "let's go over to the Beach and get her."

"Shouldn't we notify the Beach cops we're picking her up?"

"We should, but we won't. This is an emergency, and the massacre was in Miami, not in Miami Beach. In the state she's in, she's liable to take off any second. Would you trust an asshole like Marvin?"

"Not for a minute," Gonzalez said.

"I resent that," Marvin said. "I done told you everything, like a good citizen. Besides, she's quiet because I been giving her Percodans. Hortensia's outside watching the building, and if Dale leaves she'll follow her."

They left the handcuffs on Marvin and boosted him over the gate before climbing over it themselves. Marvin, because his wrists were handcuffed behind his back, fell on his face, and some flinty pieces of gravel got embedded in his right cheek. They put Marvin in the back seat of their unmarked Fairlane and took the MacArthur Causeway to Miami Beach.

When Hoke rapped on Dale's door at the hotel, there was no answer. The television was on in the room, however, so Gonzalez went downstairs and got the extra key to the room from the desk clerk. When he came back, Hoke unlocked the door and pushed Marvin in ahead of him, in case Dale decided to take a shot at them. Gonzalez covered Hoke and Marvin with his pistol.

Dale was on her back, snoring, and a half-eaten Domino pizza was on the bed beside her with the stacks of bills and rolls of coins. She had finished the first bottle of Early Times, and she had made sizable inroads into a second bottle. Two grinning Channel Ten newscasters were making kidding remarks to the weatherman on the TV set. Gonzalez turned off the television and picked up Dale's purse from the bedside table. The little .25 pistol was inside. Gonzalez reclasped the purse without touching the weapon and tucked the leather purse under his arm. Hoke was unable to rouse Dale from her drug-and-alcohol slumbers. Hoke unfolded the Hefty bags and put the money inside without counting it.

"Where's the place on the Hefty where you cut out that little square?" he asked Marvin.

"I didn't cut it outa that bag 'cause I couldn't give Dale no reason for doing it. I cut it out of another Hefty I had in my apartment."

"Jesus Christ, Maria," Gonzalez said, shaking his head.

Before they left, Hoke and Gonzalez shook down the room, found nothing of interest in Dale's suitcase, and then drove back to Miami to book Marvin and Dale. Hoke had carried Dale downstairs over his shoulder, and Gonzalez had brought the bag of money, Dale's suitcase and purse, and a small sack of toilet articles that belonged to Troy Louden.

Marvin was isolated in Interrogation Room Two. The story he told and retold several times to Major Brownley and Bill Henderson was substantially the same as the one he had told Hoke and Gonzalez.

By the time Dale sobered up enough in the female annex of the city jail to realize that she was going to be charged with murder and robbery, she had decided not to say anything else to anyone. In jail, she knew she would be fairly safe from Troy Louden, and the prospect of spending a few years on Death Row, or with good luck, twenty-five years in prison, seemed for the moment like a reasonable exchange for her life.

Dale regretted telling everything to Marvin, but they couldn't use most of what she had told him against her in court. And she certainly wasn't going to tell the police anything she knew about Mr. Sinkiewicz and Troy. Troy was mad enough at her already, and even the women's prison wouldn't be safe enough distance from him if he knew she blew the whistle on him to the cops.

For the next two days, Hoke and Gonzalez spent hours at their desks writing up their reports and supps, supps, supps.

CHAPTER 19

On Saturday morning, Hoke picked up Aileen at the Miami International Airport and drove her up to Singer Island. Aileen—if there had been anything seriously wrong in the first place—seemed to have made a prompt recovery. She had gained eleven pounds, and she wore a pair of black velvet toreador pants and a matching bolero jacket her mother had bought her for the trip. Curly Peterson, elated to see her departing his home and life, had put two crisp fifty-dollar bills into her purse as a going-away present. Aileen was happy to be back, although the trip and all of the excitement had been an adventure to remember and she had met this boy who lived three doors down from her mother's house in Glendale. His name was Alfie, and his father was a composer who scored music for movies. She had a snapshot of Alfie, which she had shown Hoke, and she told her father that she and Alfie were going to be pen pals.

Hoke looked at the photo—a grinning teenage boy with unkempt hair and a cotton string for a backbone—and told her that he was a handsome boy indeed. The boy, in Hoke's private opinion, looked like a congenital idiot, but he took it as a favorable sign that Aileen was taking an interest in boys. After all, Aileen was his daughter, so she was certainly smart enough to know by now that boys were not interested in skinny, bony girls who looked more like boys than they did girls.

Still, Hoke would be watching her and Sue Ellen both a lot more carefully now. And maybe that wasn't so bad, either.

After they got on the Sunshine Parkway, Hoke told her in more detail than he had on the phone about the supermarket murder-robbery, and the progress they had made on the case, so far. Aileen, however, was more concerned about Ellita than she was about the manhunt. She was also disappointed that she hadn't had a chance to see Ellita and the new baby.

"Instead of staying with Granddad, wouldn't it be better for me to stay home? I can help Sue Ellen with the housework and the baby while Ellita's going through her therapy."

"I thought about that, honey. But Mrs. Sanchez's going to live with us for a month or so when Ellita comes home, and the house would be too damned crowded. Besides, I want you fattened up a little, and Inocencia's going to keep you on a separate diet the doctor gave us. I've been worried more about you than Ellita. I should've paid more attention to you instead of being so damned wrapped up in my own problems. I probably shouldn't've sent you out to L.A. in the first place."

"No." Aileen shook her curls and laid a hand on Hoke's arm. "It was my fault, Daddy. I know now I was only trying to get more attention from you than I deserved, and it worked too well. That's why I always vomited by the professor's window. I guess I knew he'd tell you about it sooner or later."

"From now on, baby, no matter what's bothering you, come to me and we'll talk about it, okay? Lately I've been busier than a cat covering shit on a marble floor, and sometimes I might forget to be a father."

Aileen started to cry, but stopped just as abruptly. She wiped her cheeks with the back of her hand, leaned over, and kissed Hoke's right hand, which was holding the steering wheel.

"What's that thing on the chain around your neck?"

"It's a Saint Joseph's medal," Aileen said, holding it up for him to see. "Mother Superior gave it to me. She said I was a pretty girl, and when I gained more weight, boys would want to kiss me. Instead of letting them kiss me, she said I should tell them to kiss the Saint Joseph's medal."

"That's good advice if you ever date Cuban boys in Miami, but it won't work with WASP boys. By this time next year you'll be beating off boys with a stick."

"Maybe next summer Alfie can come and visit us from California? He's never been to Florida, but his father's got lots of money."

"Why not? But a year's a long time. Ask me again next summer, and if you still want him to visit, then I'll write and ask his father—or phone him."

"Would you?" Aileen sat back and looked at Hoke with new regard.

"Sure. Why not?"

Hoke stopped at the El Pelicano to collect his belongings, Aileen's boxes, and her bicycle, before driving to Frank's house. Once the car was packed, he told Aileen to ride her bike to the house while he took a last look around the apartment and said good-bye to Professor Hurt.

Hoke's small apartment needed cleaning, but it still looked good to him, and he knew that he would miss living in it. He hadn't forgotten anything. For a long moment, he looked out the window, across the crowded beach to the water. As an experiment, it hadn't worked out, but it had still been worthwhile, despite the negative results. Scientists always considered negatives as positives because they didn't have to try the failed experiment again. They could go on to something else. Hoke had learned that there was no way a man could simplify his life. In managing the apartment house, as simple as that had seemed to be, he would have had just as many problems as he had as a detective-sergeant. They would all be petty problems, however; little annoying things that would have to be done, but would occupy his time without producing any sense of satisfaction or accomplishment. Right now, he was stymied in his manhunt for the killer, but he knew in his heart that he would find him eventually.

He didn't like the idea of the grim-faced Mrs. Sanchez moving in with them, but at least Mr. Sanchez wasn't coming with her. That meant the move would be temporary. Without his wife to look after him, old man Sanchez would be almost helpless, so she wouldn't stay any longer than necessary. By the time school started again, everything would be back to normal, except that he would never have Ellita back again as his partner at work. The girls would have to take more responsibility for their lives, but they were maturing fast, and Sue Ellen, in spite of her green hair, was as stable as a stone house. Hoke shrugged, picked up the three volumes on horseflies, and went downstairs to Dr. Hurt's apartment to return the books.

Itai was glad to see him.

"How about some wine?" Itai said, grinning. "I got a case of last year's Beaujolais Nouveau at Crown on a special sale."

"I haven't got the time, Itai. I'm going to have lunch with my father, and then I've got to get back to Miami."

"We're going to miss you around here, Hoke, but I've decided to go back up to Gainesville in September myself.

In the last two days I've only written eighteen words. So I've decided to abandon my novel for a while—the way Valéry said you should abandon a poem. I miss teaching and my lab, and I'm vacationed out."

"What'll your chairman say, if you don't come up with a complete manuscript?"

"He'll be glad to have me back, and I've already written to tell him I'm cutting my leave short. Now he won't have to hire a substitute. Besides, I may finish the book back at school. I've got enough down on paper to still plug away at it. But there're too many novels already, and not nearly enough books on horseflies. I'm going to save my dough and take a leave without pay in another year or so and go to Ethiopia. The flies will still be there, waiting for me."

Hoke gave him his card. "Keep my card, Itai, and drop me a line. Or if you ever come down to Miami, call me and we'll have a few beers. I really enjoyed our little dinner party."

"I did, too, even though Major Brownley won every damned game. A game with dice should be a game of chance, but his luck was uncanny, I thought. He never landed on anyone else's property but his own."

"He plays Monopoly with his kids all the time, that's why he's so good. But at least I didn't let him talk you into playing for real money."

"Sure you won't have a glass of wine?"

"No, I've got to go."

"I'll walk you to your car. By the way, Hoke, that Riviera Beach detective was here this morning looking for you."

"Detective Figueras?"

"Yeah, that's his name."

"Did he say what he wanted?"

"No, just that you should get in touch with him. I guess he heard you were leaving, and wanted to say good-bye. Everybody on the island's following this case, you know.

Your name's been in all the papers, although most of the people around the mall call you 'the man in the yellow jumpsuit.' "

Hoke laughed. "I still wear 'em around the house." They shook hands. "Anyway, if Figueras comes around again, tell him I'll call him."

Aileen was given the large guest bedroom at the back of the house, the same room where Hoke had spent three happy days in quiet contemplation. With this room she could open the sliding doors to the patio and swim in the pool anytime she wanted. Hoke and Frank carried her boxes into the bedroom, and Helen stayed with her to help put her things away. Frank and Hoke had a glass of iced gin apiece while they waited for lunch.

"I'm not very hungry, Frank," Hoke said. "And I really ought to get back to Miami. You should see my goddamned desk. It's piled up to here with autopsy reports, folders, and paper. You wouldn't believe how much paper a case like this generates. Everything has to be written down, checked, rewritten, distributed—"

"It'll all wait another hour or so, son. Detective Figueras called me earlier, and I told him you'd be here for lunch. He said he'd come by at noon."

Hoke looked at his Timex. "It's eleven-thirty now. I'll call him at the station and save him the trip."

Hoke used the phone in the kitchen to call the Riviera Beach police station. "What's up, Jaime?" he said, when he got Figueras on the line. "This is Hoke Moseley."

"I think I've got a tentative lead on your supermarket massacre, Hoke. It may turn out to be nothing, but it looks pretty good, and I was going out this afternoon to check it out. But when your father told me you were going to be here today, I thought maybe you'd like to go with me. Like I say, it may be nothing, but I got what looks like a positive

ID on the old man's picture. It's not him so much as it is the cane. The woman says that the old man was carrying a cane like that—the one with the dog's head handle."

"What woman?"

"Mrs. Henry Collins. Her story was weird enough to have some truth to it, so I checked it out. What happened, she said, was that this old man told her to tell her husband to drop charges against a guy named Robert Smith, or her husband would be killed. This guy was a hitchhiker Collins had picked up, who then pulled a gun on him. Collins wrecked his car at a bridge outside Riviera, and then the hitchhiker was booked in the Palm Beach County Jail. At any rate, Collins believed this threat and dropped the charges. No weapon was found in the case, so Smith was released. I took a gander at the jail records, and this old man, Stanley Sinkiewicz, Senior, was Smith's cellmate for a few hours. He was arrested for molesting a child, but wasn't booked because the father of the little girl said it had all been a mistake. Interesting parallel, you know? Charges dropped by the complainant in both cases. The old man was released, and the father of the girl, a guy named Sneider, drove him home."

"And Mrs. Collins gave you a positive ID from the picture in the paper?"

"That's right. Her husband was up in Jacksonville when she called me, and I went out to talk to him yesterday when he came home. He's a truck driver, and he didn't get back home till yesterday. He was really pissed off at his wife for calling me and didn't want to get involved. Being away from home three, sometimes four days a week, he was afraid that this Smith guy would do something to his wife and kid while he was on the road. Anyway, I checked back, and the fingerprint report, when it finally came in from the FBI, was just filed away because Smith had already walked, and nobody did anything about it. But this Smith is a career criminal named Troy Louden. He's wanted in L.A. for killing a liquor store owner and his wife in a robbery. When I got the printout of his rap sheet, it was two fucking feet long. He's a dangerous sonofabitch, and Collins was smart to drop the charges."

"D'you have the old man's address?"

"Sure. You want to go with me and see if he's home? I doubt if he'll be there, but maybe we can find something there that'll lead to something else."

"Where should I meet you?"

"I'll meet you in the parking lot behind the Double X Theater at Dixie and Blue Heron Road."

Hoke hung up and told his father that he couldn't stay for lunch. He might be back a little later to say good-bye, but right now he had to go check on something with Jaime Figueras.

"I understand," Frank said. "But I'll have Inocencia fix you some sandwiches before you drive back to Miami."

"That'll be fine."

Figueras drove, and it took only a few minutes to drive out to Ocean Pines Terraces.

"When I left Riviera," Hoke told him, "this was all dairy farm land."

Figueras cruised slowly down the curving streets, taking the speed bumps at an angle and looking for Sinkiewicz's house.

"It's a mixed subdivision now, Hoke. About half retired people, and half working people with kids. I don't think Riviera'll get any more subdivisions like this one. Most white people are building north of North Palm Beach now. In another ten years, this'll probably be an all-black subdivision if the interest rates come down a few points."

There was a brown Honda parked in Stanley Sinkiewicz's carport. Figueras pulled in and stopped at the curb, two houses down. "There's a car. Somebody home, after all."

"And the Honda's got a roof rack. You go to the front door, Jaime, and I'll slip on around to the back. Nobody locks Florida rooms, and I'll come in the back way."

"Don't you think we should get some backup first?"

"If no one's there, we won't need any backup. And if someone's home and resists, I want to take a shot at the bastard. What do you want to do?"

"I'm with you, Sergeant. Why don't we see what happens?"

Hoke took out his pistol. He circled behind the house to cut through the two back yards. Figueras waited, to give Hoke enough time to reach Stanley's yard, then walked up the concrete path to the door. He rapped on it with the barrel of his pistol.

Stanley Sinkiewicz opened the door, left it open, and walked back to his dining room table. Stanley didn't say a word, but sat at the table and began to spoon tomato soup into his mouth. Figueras followed him inside and closed the door with his foot, covering the old man with his weapon. Hoke entered the dining room from the screened porch, also holding his pistol on Stanley. He looked at the old man's lined, pigeon-gray face, and shook his head. Hoke knew an old lag when he saw one, and he could tell, just by looking at this old con, that the man had spent most of his life in prison. When they finally got his record, it would probably be three feet long.

"Sinkiewicz?" Hoke asked. "We're both police officers."

"I been waiting." Stanley nodded. "But I ain't ate nothing for two days now. I just fixed this soup, not really wanting it, but knew I had to eat something pretty soon. Maya—that's my wife—when she fixed it for me, used to put a little whipped cream in it. The milk in the icebox went sour on me, and I had to fix it with water instead of milk. But it still tastes pretty good, once I got started on it."

"Are you alone, Sinkiewicz?" Figueras asked.

Stanley nodded and crumpled two soda crackers into his soup.

"Do you know Troy Louden?" Hoke said.

Stanley nodded.

"D'you know where he is?"

Stanley pointed down the hall with his spoon. "In the bedroom."

"I thought you said you were alone." Hoke had reholstered his pistol, but he quickly withdrew it again. " 'Cuff him, Jaime."

Hoke started down the hall. Figueras handcuffed Stanley's wrists behind his back. Hoke hesitated outside the closed bedroom door, waiting for Figueras to cover him. Figueras, holding his pistol with both hands, stayed ten feet behind Hoke. Hoke twisted the knob, threw open the door, and jumped inside with his gun in front of him.

There was no one else in the room. Figueras joined him. The bed was piled high with a half-dozen sheets, a comforter, a bedspread, and was topped by a woman's red plastic raincoat. There was a discernible mound beneath all of these coverings. Hoke peeled them back from the head of the bed, one at a time, and uncovered Troy Louden as far as his waist. The corpse was ripe, and the washcloth over Troy's face had dried. Hoke picked it gingerly away and thought he could detect the odor of burning almonds, but later he was never sure whether he had or not. Dale Forrest's little .25 caliber slug, a crisscrossed lead dumdum, had hit Troy's left cheek, penetrating the bone, and then fragments had been deflected upward, exploding the left eye and skating through the eye socket. Troy had suffered a good deal of pain before he died. Hoke covered the dead man's face back up with the dry washcloth, then drew the bottom sheet over the upper body and head. He and Figueras went back into the dining room.

Stanley, with his thin arms handcuffed behind his back, was staring at his cooling soup, but he had apparently lost interest in it.

"How long's he been dead?" Figueras asked the old man.

"Three days. I didn't know what else to do. He was suffering, but he wouldn't let me call no doctor or let me take him to the hospital. I brought him home, and when I thought he couldn't stand it no more I gave him two cyanide pills. I didn't know what else to do for him."

"Cyanide?" Hoke said. "Where in hell did you get cyanide?"

"Inside my cane. Sometimes people keep vicious dogs that bite strangers and little kids. They won't bite their owners because they feed them, you know, but you can walk down any sidewalk and they'll come right at you before you know it. So I always kept some pills to poison a bad dog once in a while, when I got the chance. Troy was a good boy, good to me, anyway, maybe because I fed him, too, I guess. But he was a lot like a bad dog. I didn't want to do it, but I didn't know what else to do. I even thought about taking some pills myself. But then I thought, Why should I? I ain't done nothing wrong. Troy managed to keep me out of everything so I wouldn't get involved, so all I'm responsible for is putting to sleep the only person who ever really loved me. Anyone who ever heard Troy cry and carry on that way would've done the same. You just can't imagine."

"Why did he kill all those people?" Hoke said. "Did he say?"

Stanley shook his head. "He never said, but I think I know why. It was the responsibility. Me and Dale and James. We was all too much for him, and he couldn't stand the responsibility. That's what it was . . ."

Stanley began to cry then, and Hoke didn't try to stop him. He realized that the old man had been holding it in for a long time, and that it would be best to let him get it all out. There would be time for more questions later.

"I'll Mirandize him, Jaime, while you call Chief Sheldon. This is going to be a jurisdictional ordeal, but no matter what you people up here in Palm Beach County think you want to do, I'm taking this old fart back to Miami with me to be tried first for the supermarket murders."

"What difference does it make, Hoke," Jaime said, "whether he's tried down there first, or for the guy?" Figueras pointed down the hall.

"There're lots of reasons, but I'll give you one you can understand. Before the old man and the whore are tried to fry in Raiford, I'm going to make lieutenant out of this case. When the next promotion list is posted, I'm going to be at the head of it."

Hoke was so pleased with the way it sounded that he left off the part about the answer sheets Major Willie Brownley still had in his briefcase.

It was well after nine P.M. that night before Hoke got onto the Sunshine Parkway and headed south for Miami. Stanley, handcuffed to the D-ring Hoke had welded onto the passenger door, sat quietly beside him in the dark. Stanley had promised not to try and run, so Hoke hadn't put leg-irons on him. Ordinarily, the drive to Miami would have been a six- or maybe a seven-cigarette ride, and for the first time, Hoke truly missed his Kools. But he was over the habit, and he wouldn't smoke again. Not smoking, and counting the weight he had lost, his blood pressure was almost normal again for a man his age.

To get around the heavy, crazy traffic at the Golden Glades exchange, which every wise Floridian avoided, if possible, Hoke left the Sunshine Parkway at the Hollywood exit and picked up I-95 for the rest of the way into the city. As the thousands of lighted windows in the tall Miami buildings came into view, Stanley spoke for the first time on the trip.

"What's going to happen to me, Sergeant?"

"Hell, Pop," Hoke said, not unkindly, "except for the paperwork, it already has."